Also by Edward Mathis
Published by Ballantine Books:

FROM A HIGH PLACE

DARK STREAKS AND EMPTY PLACES

Edward Mathis

BALLANTINE BOOKS • NEW YORK

Library of Congress Catalog Card Number: 86-15454

ISBN 0-345-34305-0

This edition published by arrangement with Charles Scribner's Sons, a
division of The Scribner Book Companies, Inc.

Manufactured in the United States of America

First Ballantine Books Edition: February 1988

To my parents, Mary and Matt

ACKNOWLEDGMENTS

I would like to thank my fellow members of the Dallas/ Fort Worth Writers Workshop for their faith, critical assistance, and their unstinting hard work in my behalf.

And, once again, I want to thank my wife Bonnie for her unswerving loyalty and encouragement—with love and gratitude.

1

PAIN WAS THE PREDOMINANT THEME. NEXT CAME LOSING, followed by unrequited love. Lonely nights and weeping women, cheating men. Wasted years. Lamentations and breast beating, self-pity so thick you could serve it with a fork.

Country western music; sometimes it made you want to throw up. Other times it made you want to cry, left a warm dry lump in your throat, a tight knot behind your heart.

Today, it left me cold and searching the dial for just one golden oldie—Sinatra or Martin, Tony Bennett, Lawrence or Gorme, Connie Francis or Doris Day. But they were hard to come by, good singers having gone the way of real ice cream, corn-fed beef, and Zane Grey westerns.

So I twirled the knob and punched the buttons. All to no avail. Orgiastic cacophony ruled the airways, unintelligible lyrics and frantic music without recognizable form.

My own damn fault, I thought, a misguided bit of parsimony having kept me from adding a tape deck to the staggering bottomline total of my new Ramcharger pickup, a gut-swooping figure only a few hundred dollars less than I had paid for my home fifteen years before. Writing the check had been a traumatic experience; it left me dazed for days.

Defeated, I punched the off button and lit a cigarette, realizing as I did so that my feeling of malaise sprang not so much from distaste for today's prevailing music as from the knowledge that I was going back to work.

I was on my way to see a man named Macomber Beechum, *the* Macomber Beechum, a name only slightly less notable than Hunt, or Bass, or Perot. This, despite the fact that Beechum was something of a recluse, shunned with an almost religious fanaticism the high-society shindigs that old Texas money finds so irresistible, egregious displays of affluence and pampered elegance designed to dazzle, to shrivel with envy those less fortunate mortals who wash their own clothes, clean their own toilets, and line their bird cages with society pages.

If the stories could be believed, Macomber Beechum was *nouveau riche*, having sprung full-blown on the big-league Texas scene shortly after World War II. He had been born and raised in the piney woods of East Texas, and it was easy to believe the rumor that his first five million had come from his own backyard, millions of board feet of lumber to feed the insatiable hunger for housing in the fifties.

Money begets money, as they say, and here in the mid-eighties the Beechum logo, MCB, graced company mastheads all across Texas.

I lit another cigarette as the outskirts of Dallas fell away behind me, anonymous clusters of condos, low-rise apartment buildings, and strip shopping centers giving way to the first hint of country, gently rolling terrain, wide fields black with recently turned earth, others yellow-green with winter oats, speckled with grazing cattle.

It took longer each year to reach the country, more time on the aggravating freeways that crisscrossed Dallas like a tangled wad of Siamese tapeworms. But the country was always there, clearly etched where rolling land collided with the sky, impervious to man's puny efforts to alter its silhouette for very long.

The pickup hummed across a Corp of Engineers bridge, slipped past a clump of trees clustered protectively around an old abandoned farmhouse like a cadre of loyal soldier bees guarding a decaying queen. Something had ended, somebody's dream. And there had been no fanfare or cotton candy, only the rattle of the auctioneer's gavel, sharp and decisive and final, the dismal sound of foreclosed farm equipment being hauled away.

Thirty minutes southeast of Dallas I turned west. I checked my mileage and lit another cigarette.

"Two miles from the interstate," the voice had said, Macomber Beechum's voice, authoritative and harsh, too strong for a man in his eighties. "Pay no attention to the signs," he had said. "And don't worry about the dogs. They're mostly for show, anyhow. I'll try to have them sedated when you get here."

Dogs? Show? Sedated? Vague assurances that were anything but.

I saw the first of the signs a quarter of a mile from the lane—POSTED, STAY OUT. They were repeated at regular intervals thereafter, different versions, dire warnings that the rolling land beyond the white, welded pipe fence was inviolate, to be invaded at your own risk.

The Ramcharger clattered across a cattle guard and I saw one last sign, an unexpected touch of humor: LAST WARNING! TRESPASSERS WILL BE VIOLATED.

The crushed-rock lane shot straight as an arrow across a small grassy valley and was flanked on either side by naked pecan trees too evenly spaced and meticulously trimmed to be a part of nature's original random plan. Empty nut casings still festooned the spidery leafless

3

limbs, and I suspected that part of the crunching beneath my tires came from the residue of last year's crop, paper-shell pecans and their fragile desiccated cocoons.

At the end of the valley I topped a small rise. Another grassy meadow lay before me, fenced and cross-fenced, this landscape dominated by grazing cattle and clumps of live oak left to guard the herd against the relentless summer sun. To my left I saw the glistening oval of a stock tank and a long metal-roofed building enclosed only on three sides, tractors and plows and planters crouched within.

The pickup rumbled across another cattle guard, followed the dusty curving road into a gentle incline. Through a copse of trees ahead I caught a flash of white, a fleeting glimpse of red. Rock dust swirled behind me in a billowing whirlwind of white, and the pickup's motor hummed a higher note as the angle of ascent increased.

Seconds later, I broke free of the trees, careened through yet another cattle guard into the hardpan front yard of Macomber Beechum's country estate. Estate was what they called it in the infrequent articles in the Dallas newspapers, but as far as I could see it was just another old ramshackle ranch house. Larger than most, two stories along the edge of the hill, surrounded by longleaf, slash, and loblolly pines. It needed paint and a new post at the end of the sagging front porch. The steeply pitched asphalt-tile roof showed recent signs of repair, and a broken dormer window had been patched with a piece of cloudy plastic and black electrical tape; a TV antenna drooped drunkenly along the crown of the roof, a headless rooster weather vane trapped firmly within its spiny clutch. Off to one side of the driveway an old red-and-white Scout sat propped up on blocks, hood up, wheels gone. In the semicircle formed by the drive, a gleaming white satellite dish pointed its huge concave eye into the southern sky.

Not exactly an opulent retreat. Not in a state where wealthy people spend an inordinate amount of time dreaming up ways to out-lavish their megabuck friends—and enemies. Not among people whose idea of understated elegance is designer undies and barbecued lobster on a hamburger bun, where mixing with the common folk equates with a Republican fund-raiser at the Dallas Hyatt Regency or an afternoon chatting with the clerks at Neiman's.

I saw no dogs, heard none as I crunched to a stop a dozen yards from the house and rolled down my window. I sat there for a moment wondering if the dogs could have been the ratchet-voiced old man's idea of a joke, a figment of a shaky imagination, paranoia.

He had not sounded too tightly wrapped on the phone, had even called me boy a couple of times, and had it not been for the call I received a few minutes earlier from Senator Lucas Drumright, I probably would have graciously declined his offer of employment.

I didn't want a job, didn't need one. I had just come off a case that had swept me across eight states in thirty-five days, into God only knows how many bars and motel rooms, plastic sandwich factories and stinking service-station toilets.

I needed peace, solitude, quiet introspection, a good woman, time to let the keening in my head subside. I needed non-movement and sloth; I didn't need a crabbed old man's "matter of extreme importance." But debts need to be repaid and I owed Senator Lucas Drumright more than a dozen favors could repay.

"Are you Dan Roman?" The voice was quiet and flat. It came from behind me, off to my left, just beyond my peripheral vision. I swiveled my head a quarter turn, hoping the movement would hide my guilty start.

"Mr. Roman?" he asked again.

5

"That's right," I said, hiding my annoyance at being startled behind a friendly smile. "I was looking for dogs. He said there might be dogs."

"I had them penned." He took a couple of steps toward me, boots crunching in the gravel. I wondered how he had managed to be so quiet before. "He's waiting for you."

I nodded and opened the door, climbed out onto the crushed rock. It slithered and grated noisily.

He stepped forward again, holding out a long slender hand. "I'm Victor Starling."

"Nice to meet you," I said agreeably and gripped the cold sinewy fingers, wringing them once and letting go before the unpleasant sensation could begin. It was a re-action to shaking hands—men's hands—that I had never fully understood, a vaguely disquieting feeling that began the instant our hands touched, accelerating exponentially with pressure and time.

"This way, Mr. Roman." Starling turned and headed for the house, a tall lean man in well-worn Levi's and run-over boots. Straight black hair hung to his shirt collar, framing a long narrow face with high cheekbones and deep-set black eyes, eyebrows as thick and bushy as a small mustache.

He looked friendly enough if you discounted the col-orless voice, the vaguely disconcerting shine to his eyes. But he didn't fool me for a minute. I had met him before. Or men just like him. Ten years of being a cop had taught me to read the signs, the potential for violence that some men exude like fever sweat. It had something to do with pride, honor, a sense of self so deeply ingrained it showed in the way they walked, talked, in the tilt of their head, their watchful eyes. You didn't kid around with men like that, goose them, or pull their chest hair. Not unless you were looking to fight, to maybe kill or be killed; dignity was a most serious matter.

Starling held the door for me, then preceded me down a dim hallway to the third door on our right. He went in without knocking. I followed him.

The room was as dim as the hallway, large, penumbral, crowded with dark ancient furnishings: hump-backed couches with brass studs, tiger-claw legs and scratchy-looking fabric, mismatched overstuffed chairs, fringed lampshades, and a chifforobe that might well have been my grandmother's. Oval-shaped portraits dotted the walls and milky white glass figurines gleamed dully on a knick-knack shelf in one corner. A Confederate flag covered the wall above a rock fireplace, crisscrossed with two gleaming military swords. A number of model airplanes, WW II vintage, hung suspended from the ceiling.

"Mac, Mr. Roman is here." Starling had crossed to a high-backed chair in front of the smoldering fireplace, stood with his hand on the shoulder of a man with his head slumped forward on his chest, a head without hair, heavily veined at the temples, a ragged sunken spot high on the crown. The rest of him was hidden within the confines of the chair and a thick white shawl wound round his shoulders.

I crossed the room as the head moved, bobbed, jerked upright. I caught a glimpse of pale blue eyes, unfocused, uncertain.

"Yes . . . yes, what is it, Vic?"

"Mr. Roman, Mac. The private detective. He's here."

"Oh." He stared up at me, his right hand, liver-spotted and bony, coming through the folds of the shawl. "Mr. Roman. Of course."

"Mr. Beechum," I said, collecting the limp hand in mine, squeezing once, and letting go. "It's nice to meet you, sir."

Macomber Beechum stirred, straightened, the pale blue

7

eyes acquiring light, the slack face tightening, achieving form and substance, strength.

"Have a seat, Mr. Roman. Vic, kick up that fire, will you? Too damn dark in here. Mr. Roman, what would you like to drink?"

I wet my dusty lips, hesitated, then resolutely put the thought out of my mind. "A Coke will be fine. Or a glass of water. That road in is pretty dusty."

Beechum tilted his head, eyes twinkling. "Did I detect a note of hesitation? Good. I like a man with willpower. Vic, did you hear what he said? I'll have my usual."

Starling turned away from pecking at the fire. He pointed the poker at Beechum. "I heard him and it's way too early for your usual. You can have a Coke—half a Coke." The flatness had gone out of his voice, replaced by a tone of amused affection, the kind of tone a mother might use with a pouting child. Smiling, he left the room.

Beechum made a face, then gave me a toothy grin. "He's worse than an old-maid nurse. Hell, I'm gonna die. It's only a matter of time. I know that. He knows it. Everybody knows it. So what the hell's one more brandy more or less?" He squirmed and leaned forward. "You smoke?"

I nodded.

"Light us up a couple, will you? It'll take him a while to go to the kitchen for them Cokes. Bastards won't let me smoke, either." He snorted balefully. "Hell, ain't nothing wrong with my lungs. It's my damn liver that's doing me in."

I hesitated, slowly reached inside my jacket. "I don't know. You sure?"

"Oh, hell yes. I'm allowed a pack a day. One more sure ain't gonna hurt. Hurry."

I lit two, gave him one. He sucked on it like a pacifier, closing his eyes, dragging smoke deep into his lungs, a blissful look on his lined face. He expelled the smoke lustily and began to cough. I began to have misgivings.

"You sure they let you smoke?"

Beechum nodded earnestly, sucking on the slim white tube again. "Hell yes," he gasped. "Anyhow we can hear him when he starts coming down the hall."

He took one last deep drag, bright eyes beaming at me over the dribbles of smoke. He tossed the butt toward the fireplace just as footsteps sounded somewhere outside the door. It hit the edge of a log and bounced back onto the hardwood floor.

"Oh, shit!" He threw up his hands and struggled forward in the chair. I beat him to it, scooping up the butt and dropping it and mine into the fire before he could get unwound from the shawl. He gave me a grateful look as I sauntered back to my seat. I sat down as Starling came in the door, a small bottle of Coke in each hand.

He gave one to me without speaking, then turned toward Beechum. He stopped, looked back at me, his thin nostrils flaring, a single deep line etched across his bony forehead.

"Do you smoke, Mr. Roman?"

I nodded guiltily. "Yeah, sometimes."

He nodded as if relieved, handed Beechum the half-filled bottle. Beechum accepted it graciously, his face a study in innocence. "Thank you, Vic."

Starling turned to me. "I don't mean to be inhospitable, Mr. Roman, or hard-nosed, but Mr. Beechum suffers from a chronic lung disease. Even residual smoke can sometimes bring on an attack."

"I'm sorry," I said. "He didn't tell me." I looked at Beechum. He stared into the fire, absorbed, pensive.

Starling's hand dropped to the frail shoulder again. "That's always been one of his biggest problems—he's too damn selfless." His voice rang with genuine admiration, and I tried once again to catch Beechum's eye. Without success. He sighed and drank the four ounces of Coke in one long draught, ran a thin coated tongue across his lips, and abruptly got down to business.

"It's my granddaughter, Mr. Roman. I've been told that you're a whiz at finding people, and my granddaughter's missing. I want her found. Can you do that for me?"

"That depends, sir. On a lot of things. How long she's been gone, how old she is, the circumstances of her leaving . . . and one thing I have to make clear, Mr. Beechum, even if I find your granddaughter, I won't bring her home unless she wants to come. I find people. I don't take them anywhere they aren't willing to go."

"That's no problem," Victor Starling said. "You find her and we'll take it from there." He leaned against the mantel and crossed his booted legs at the ankles.

"How old is she?"

"Thirty-two," Beechum said. "Just a baby."

"She's an adult," I said. "Adults generally leave home because they want to. How long has she been gone?"

"A week," Beechum said.

"Have you filed a missing persons report?"

Beechum looked up at Starling. Starling nodded. "Yes."

"Where?"

"In your city, Midway City. That's one of the reasons we want you to handle it. She lives in your city." Beechum rubbed his cheek briskly with one fleshless hand. "Her and that nogood sonuvabitch she's married to."

"I doubt that I'll find her there," I said dryly. "There's not all that many places to hide in Midway City."

"Conrad," Beechum said as if I hadn't spoken. "Peter Conrad is his name. Bastard only married her for the money. Since she's been gone I've been hearing how he treated her. Like dirt, they say. Goddammit! Somebody oughta told me. I'da sent Vic here to straighten the bastard out. Any damn man who'd abuse a woman ain't worth killing!" He lurched forward, knobby fisted hands waving, a bubble of foam at the edge of his lips. He bunched one end of the shawl against his mouth and coughed.

"Take it easy, Mac," Starling said. "You don't know that for sure. You know how the twins are. They exaggerate things." He turned to look at me. "They also like to agitate." A fleeting look of amusement crossed his face. "The twins are Mercy and Hope, Mr. Beechum's other granddaughters. He has a grandson named Claudell. They all live in the Mid Cities area. Claudell is a . . . writer, a poet. The twins . . . well, they . . . socialize."

"Shit," Beechum muttered, wiping his lips on the shawl, grimacing at a streak of red. "They ain't got a brain between the three of them. Sandy's the only one left in my whole damn family that's got sense enough to pour piss out of a boot."

"Have you contacted the twins and Claudell?"

Starling nodded. "The twins saw her about ten days ago. She came by their apartment to visit. Claudell said he hadn't seen her for a couple of months or longer. He and Sandra aren't very close. He resents the fact that she controls the purse strings for all of them. His allowance doesn't seem to cover all of his . . . pursuits." He made no attempt to hide the contempt that edged his voice.

"How did you find out she was missing? A week isn't a long time. Maybe she just decided to get away for a while."

"Naw." Beechum waved a gnarled hand. "She always calls me once or twice a week, and anyhow last Friday was my birthday. She ain't missed one of my birthdays since she was eight. If she'd seen she couldn't make it, she would have called. Anyway, I called her three or four times Friday. No answer. Saturday, Vic here went down

11

there and found the house locked up tight. Even that Mexican cook of theirs wasn't there.''

Starling shook his head. "She wouldn't have been. She doesn't work weekends unless they're giving a party or something. But I did get to talk to their yardman. He usually works Tuesdays and Thursdays, but he was there doing some extra work on their fruit trees. He said he saw Sandy and Peter on Tuesday, said they were talking to a man and woman out in front of the house. He said the man and woman were dressed in funny-looking clothing, like Daniel Boone he used to see on TV. He said the man's hair was longer than the woman's, and that they all seemed to be angry about something, especially Mr. Conrad.'' He stopped and shrugged. ''Yardman's Vietnamese and doesn't speak good English, but that's the gist of what he told me.''

"He didn't know what they were arguing about?"

"No. He was too far away, he said."

"Have you talked to Conrad? You or the police?"

"I did," Beechum put in harshly. "The sonuvabitch said he didn't know where she was and, what's more, didn't give a damn. Then he hung up on me. All I got since then is that damn answering machine of his." He pressed a quivering hand against his chest. "You just wait. Something has happened to that girl, and I'm gonna kick that bastard out of that house and that cushy job she gave him so damn fast he'll think his ass stripped gears." He choked and coughed, then went on, his voice strained and weak. "And Jonas'll go along with it, I know he will. Jonas loves that girl like a daughter."

I looked at Starling.

"Jonas is his son," he said shortly, and pushed away from the fireplace. He crossed behind the old man and took a seat off to my right. "Sandy's uncle," he continued, crossing his legs, his dark face unreadable again, the

12

flat tone back in his voice. "But I don't think we need to go into that."

I looked back at Beechum. He appeared to be nodding off, the large veined head too heavy for the scrawny neck. But his eyes were open, and in a few moments he lifted them to mine.

"Well, Mr. Roman." It was Starling who spoke, and I turned to face him.

"I'll need more information, a recent picture, a list of family, friends, addresses. Some of that I can get from the missing persons file in Midway City, but—"

Starling stood up abruptly. "I have a copy of what I gave them and I can answer any other questions you may have. Mr. Beechum needs to rest, so if you'll just follow me . . ." He let it drift away.

I nodded and stood up. Beechum appeared to be asleep again. I followed Starling to the door, then stopped as the old man's voice caught up with me, reedy and weak. "Find her, Mr. Roman. Find her, please."

"I'll do my best, sir," I said, and watched his head fall back to his chest, not sure he had heard me.

I waited at the front door while Starling went to get the information. I lit a cigarette and thought about the case so far. Not exactly routine. Heads of multimillion-dollar corporations rarely vanished without a proverbial trace. A bored housewife, perhaps, seeking a better way, a new love, peace. But not the top lady executive/owner of a company like MCB. Not unless something had happened.

"Here you are." Starling materialized as silently as he had at the truck. He handed me a single folded sheet of paper and a photograph. I nodded and slipped it into my coat pocket. "Thanks." I turned and opened the door.

"Mr. Roman." Starling brushed a long-fingered hand down across his narrow face. "I didn't want to say anything in front of Mac—he's upset enough the way it is—

but Sandy's a pretty dependable woman. She never forgets his birthday—any holiday, for that matter. She takes a lot of vacations, but she's always careful about letting him know in advance. She's real considerate that way." He hesitated, looked toward the rear of the house. "Maybe he's right, maybe something is real bad wrong."

"That's where I come in, Mr. Starling. I'll see if I can find out."

"I hope so," he said, his long face troubled.

"I'll be in touch." We shook hands again and I crunched through the gravel to my truck. He was still standing there when I went over the dusty rise, leaning ramrod straight against the doorjamb, like a weary, but undefeated old soldier home from his final war.

2

It was dark when I reached my house in Midway City. I trundled the Ramcharger into the driveway, shut off the engine, and sat for a moment, winding down from the freeway madness.

I lit a cigarette, listened to the tocking of the pickup's motor, and thought about loneliness. Loneliness and space, the eighteen hundred square feet of emptiness behind the Old English brick that encased my home. Dark blank windows and rooms that rang with silence. I thought about fate, about whimsical malevolent nature, about loving hearts and good times that seemed too long ago and gone for good.

Most of all I thought about whiskey and drinking, wondered if I would make one more day, then found myself wondering if it really mattered. I was the only one keeping count.

"One day at a time, boy," is what the old-timers would tell you, smacking their lips, wiping a runny nose on a ragged sleeve. "Hell, boy, it's easy to quit. I've done it dozens of times."

But they, of course, were alcoholics, boozers, drunks.

Derelicts who hunkered in dark doorways, slept in alleys in cardboard boxes. They'd lie and cheat and beg to get their daily alcohol fix, kill sometimes for a cheap bottle of wine.

On the other hand, I didn't crave it, went for days at a time without a drop, weeks sometime, so it wasn't as if I were an alcoholic.

I could take it or leave it; I had it roped, tied, and branded. I drank for recreation, relaxation, from simple force of habit. I could drink Coke, beer, Pepsi, orange juice, milk, Shirley Temples.

Okay. So what was my problem?

"No problem," I said aloud.

I went inside wondering why I thought about it so damn much. But maybe that was simply because I liked the nasty stuff.

Around nine o'clock the next morning I went to the Midway City police station. Sergeant Al Dreyfuss, Missing Persons, could tell me little beyond what I had learned from Victor Starling. The file was marked Pending Further Information instead of Active, and when I questioned Dreyfuss he gave me a weary look, a shrug, and a wintry smile.

"Husband says she ain't missing. Says she's down in East Texas with some old friends. Don't know where exactly. Seems this feller and gal she went off with are part of some kooky survivor group that's got themselves some land down there around Beaumont, somewhere in there. You know the type. Bunch of nuts running around playing Daniel Boone, living off the land, building fallout shelters so's they'll be ready when the Big One comes. Gonna rise out of the ashes and rule the world." He snorted and rapped the file with a thick knuckle. "Ain't no way I know of to contact them, so until we find out different, she's taking a vacation."

"I don't suppose you gave Conrad a polygraph test."

He gave me a pitying look. "You know better than that, Dan. A senile old man gets all hot and bothered because his favorite granddaughter don't come to his birthday party? Come on. By rights I shouldn't even have this file set up. I only did it . . . well, because he's who he is." His broad face wrinkled in a shamefaced grimace.

I grinned and nodded. "I remember. It's called covering your ass."

Dreyfuss laughed and slapped the desk with a pudgy hand, berry brown eyes almost disappearing behind puffy lids. "I always said you was quick, best damn lieutenant I ever worked for. You ever think about coming back?"

I shook my head and stood up. "Not very often. Besides, I wouldn't know how to deal with this new breed of cop coming up. Long hair and .44 Magnums. Designer uniforms. Whatever happened to the .38 Special?"

He snorted again. "Hotshots. It's the Clint Eastwood syndrome. They can't wait to pull them cannons and yell 'make my day'." He got up and followed me to the door. "Everybody has to be a Racehorse Haynes. Ain't like the old days. Nobody can do their damn job no more." His voice sagged with nostalgia for the good old days.

I shook his hand briefly and punched him on the arm. "Stay with it, Al. Remember the pension."

"You bet," he called down the corridor after me. "Six years, man. Six years and I'm turning this mother loose."

I lifted a hand and turned the corner, headed for Homer Sellers's office. I couldn't spare the time, but for a change I had reason to gloat over our last poker game. It didn't happen often, not often enough, and I wanted to get some mileage out of it.

But he was gone, of course, polishing a chair in the

witness room of Superior Court #3 in Fort Worth, according to his secretary, Mitsi.

Short and stocky, fiftyish, she had a head of iron gray
hair, lovely gray eyes to match, and the disposition of a
friendly pup. Fast, efficient, Mitsi knew everything that
went on in Homer's life, including a lot of things she
shouldn't. A longtime widow, she had managed to put
three girls through college on a secretary's salary, not a
mean feat considering Midway City's employee pay scale.
She had a soft melodious speaking voice and a terrible
whinnying laugh she used often.

"What's the bear doing testifying in a case? He working
his own cases now, or what?"

"It's that Nelson McAfee killing, Danny. You know.
That old man who killed his wife because she had cancer,
then tried to shoot himself and messed it up. He knew
Homer from that Club .45 you all go to, and he wouldn't
talk to anybody else. Homer took his confession."

"That oughta brighten his day."

"His week, you mean. This is his second day already.
Did you know Mr. McAfee, Danny?"

"No, but I don't spend as much time in Club .45 as
Homer does."

She sighed. "I know. He drinks too much." She
paused. "He's eating too much, too. Junk food. He's putting on weight. That's hard on his heart. Maybe you ought
to talk to him, Danny."

I hooted. "That isn't the way it works. He lectures me."

"I know," she said, her round face disconsolate, "but
he would listen to you. He sure won't listen to anybody
else."

I lit a cigarette, studying her downcast face, thinking of
all the years they had been together—twenty at least—and
wondering for the very first time if there could be something between big hulking Homer Sellers and this little

round woman with the merry eyes and the scratchy laugh—
no, not possible, I couldn't make the image jell.

"See you later, Mitsi." I leaned for a moment on the
doorjamb. "Tell him I really appreciate his donation the
other night and I'm ready for a rematch, same place, same
time, same stakes."

She smiled politely, poised over her Selectric. "I'll tell
him, Danny."

Outside, I sat for a time in the Ramcharger, reassessing
the possibilities. Homer and Mitsi, Mitsi and Homer. The
very idea brought a chuckle to my throat, an unexpected
feeling of warmth.

Naw . . . it couldn't be.

Or could it? Stranger things had happened under the
sun.

Peter Conrad lived in the Sunnyvale development, Midway City's answer to Highland Park in Dallas. Impressive
homes on quiet tree-lined streets, each with its own small
spread of well-tended greenery, no plot less than three
acres, none larger than ten, five the average. Each house
was radically different from its neighbor, from sprawling
Spanish haciendas to barnlike Dutch colonials, each one
a pocket estate, a graphic expression of the original owner's individuality and taste—and bank balance.

Number 704 appeared to be larger than most, a stately
Victorian with gleaming new paint, cupolas, towers, and
balustrades with only a modest amount of gingerbread. A
mix of towering elm and blackjack oak flanked the concrete driveway, and thick banks of blue-green Armstrong
pfitzers lined the front of the house and front porch.

There were no cars parked in the driveway and the garage was out of sight somewhere around in back, so I had
no idea if anyone would answer as I lifted the heavy brass
knocker and let it drop. Three times seemed about right,

three dull metallic clacks that came back as amplified echoes.

While I waited, I stepped to the edge of the porch and field-stripped my cigarette, tossing the balled-up remnants into one of the pfitzers. Up close the house looked even more impressive, and I couldn't help contrasting it with the seedy country estate of Macomber Beechum. I had read somewhere that Beechum had another estate north of Dallas, a Southfork kind of place, a modern mansion with all the amenities, rolling acres with gleaming white fences and white-faced cattle strung out across the hills like picture-postcard silhouettes. But, somehow, it was difficult to picture the Macomber Beechum I had met in that kind of ostentatious setting. He had seemed perfectly at ease, at home, in the rambling old ranch house with its air of sad decrepitude, its faintly shabby atmosphere that spoke of real people and hard work and no-nonsense living.

A quiet clatter of bolts came from behind me, the soft squeak of protesting hinges. I turned and stepped the few feet to the double doors, peering into the gloom, into a pair of liquid black eyes watching me steadily out of a pretty, tawny face.

"Yes sir, may I help you?" Obviously of Mexican descent, she spoke with a soft inflectionless voice, displaying, suddenly, a white-toothed radiant smile that almost made me forget to wonder why a cook would wear her hair in a disarrayed bouffant on a working day, why she would wear a knee-length sheath with a plunging neckline, wear eye shadow and smeared lipstick, and blush so prettily over such a mundane task as answering the door.

But maybe I was only being picky. How many cooks had I hired lately?

"My name is Dan Roman. Mr. Conrad is expecting me."

She bobbed her head and stepped back, swinging the

door wide. "You may come in," she said formally, articulating each word precisely, a bit stiffly, as if aware of the possibility of error and determined to avoid it at all cost.

She closed the door. The gloom deepened, the only light in the small foyer coming from a stained glass fanlight above the double doors and a dimly glowing open doorway to our right. Sounds came through the doorway, muted music and the clink of glass, a human throat clearing itself.

"Please come," she said softly and passed in front of me, high heels snapping firmly on terrazzo tile, lithe buttocks working beneath the silky sheen of the dress. I was almost positive I could hear the slither of fabric against living flesh, a sound that once heard could never be forgotten. I followed blindly.

She led me through the lighted doorway, into spaciousness and pomp and overstated opulence.

The predominant theme was silver and white, intercalated here and there with startling bursts of black, or kelly green, throw pillows and antimacassars, tidbits of color to catch the eye, to draw it irresistibly along the white velvet sofas and chairs, the stunning expanse of silver carpet, to the white rock fireplace that covered one entire wall, the shantung silk that draped the large windows. The room rocked the senses, seemed to exude its own pale light. It made my eyes hurt, made me wonder if I had wiped my feet.

"Mr. Roman to see you, sir," my escort said, a subtle change in her voice, a certain pneumatic sibilance on the word "sir," a lilting warmth that hinted fellowship, that spoke—if not volumes—then at least paragraphs into my already suspicious ear.

I felt a glow of pleasure of my own; I hadn't seen him yet and already I knew he had been dallying with the lass, either at the time I arrived or shortly before.

21

"Mr. Roman." A slab of white broke away from the fireplace, rushed across the room toward me, hand outstretched; a wide slab, a thick body beneath a white bathrobe and matching pajamas, fuzzy silver house shoes that hadn't come from a man's shop, a broad pale face squeezed unconvincingly into a welcoming smile. He had thin blond hair and big ears, and couldn't seem to wait to get at my hand. I disliked him on sight.

"Mr. Conrad," I said.

He had a truck driver's grip, hard, fast, and away. I took back my hand liking him a little better.

"I've been expecting you," he said, looking at the drink in his left hand as if he had just discovered it was there. "That . . . uh, Victor Starling called me last evening. He said the old man had hired you to find my wife." His voice had turned bitter toward the end, and his right arm swept outward in a short violent gesture. "Goddammit! I told that bastard the same thing I told the cops. She ain't missing, dammit! She knows where she's at. I don't know exactly, but she damn sure does. She went of her own sweet will, even after I told her—" He broke off abruptly, made the violent gesture again, then whirled and fell into a chair. He upended the glass and drained it. He held it up. The woman came and took it out of his hand, then turned and swivel-hipped out of the room.

I found a chair of my own, sank gingerly into pristine white. "After you told her what?"

He shrugged. "After I told her I didn't want her to go," he said dully.

"Go where, exactly?"

"I don't know where exactly. Somewhere in East Texas. Down around Irondale, around in there. I heard him tell her east of Irondale. I don't know how far."

"Who?"

"Twill. She said his name was Jacob Twill. I never saw him before."

"Who was he? I mean, what was he to your wife?"

"An old friend. Boyfriend, I guess. From back in college."

"What was the argument about?"

His head jerked around. "How—what argument?"

"The one you had out front."

He shrugged and settled back. "I didn't want her to go. We argued about it a little."

"Why would she go against your wishes? She ever do anything like this before?"

"No," he said quietly. "Never."

"Then why?"

"I don't know why. Look, this is all a bunch of bullshit. I told you she left with them of her own free will. She's all grown up. She likes it out there crawling around in the woods; she can stay as far as I'm concerned. You want to waste your time looking for her, well, go right ahead. But I'm telling you, this is all a crock of shit. That old man sits up there in his ivory tower messing around in everybody's lives like he's God or something. He can't stand to think he don't control his business anymore. It's eating him worse than the cancer."

"Who controls it? You?"

He started a chuckle, then broke into uproarious laughter. "Me? That'll be the day! No, hell no. Sandy. She's been running it ever since her Pa died three—no four years ago now. Been doing a hell of a job, too."

"You mean she runs MCB? All of it?"

He grinned and nodded. "Yep. The whole shebang. Sandy don't act much like it some of the time, but she's smart as they come. Her daddy knew it. That's why he set it up the way he did. Nobody else in that family's got sense enough to run pigs out of the corn."

"Doesn't she have an uncle named Jonas?"

"Yeah, Miles's brother, twin brother. Aw, Jonas's smart enough, I guess, but he's a dreamer, a coon and hound-dog man. No education to speak of. He still lives in East Texas, down around Crater. Don't want nothing mor'n he's got. Two thousand acres of timber, a little old house, and a bunch of dogs. Wife Myna's just like him. Big cities scare the hell out of them."

"Miles was your wife's father?"

"That's right. Looked a lot like Jonas, but they were as different as daylight and dark. Miles was a hustler like the old man, not as much of a pirate, but almost. He was hard, ruthless. That's why it surprised the hell out of everybody when he pulled the plug."

"Pulled—suicide?" I felt a faint tingling chill of surprise.

His lips curled sardonically. He nodded. "Come into work one Monday morning. Sent his secretary down to fetch the head of security. While she was gone, he took a brand new Smith and Wesson .38 out of his briefcase and let fly. Nobody knows why. Never left a note or anything. My guess is the old man being on his case all the time drove him to it. I don't know. All the Beechums got a dark streak in them, even Sandy. A cold, empty place that never gets warm. That asshole Claudell is something else."

I stirred restlessly in the soft confines of the chair. I was learning more about the Beechum clan than I wanted to know. What I really wanted was a cigarette, but there were no ashtrays in evidence and, like beleaguered smokers everywhere, I was getting wary about lighting up without prior approval—and I wasn't about to ask.

"She's been gone eight days now. How do you account for the fact that you haven't heard from her?"

He shrugged and scowled in my direction without meeting my eyes. "I ain't trying to account for it. She's headstrong as a mule, knows her own mind. She wants to call me, she'll call me. She don't, she won't."

"What were your fights about?"

He scowled again, then let it dissolve into a mocking smile. "You fishing again, Mr. Roman? I don't recall saying anything about any other fights."

I imitated his elaborate shrug. "Married people fight, that's no secret. But most women don't run off with ex-boyfriends. Not with their husband standing around watching."

"I wasn't watching," he said, his tone surly. "I left." He pushed abruptly to his feet. "That's it. Even though I think this is all a bunch of crap, I've been cooperating—"

"Why wouldn't you cooperate? She's your wife. I assume you want her back."

"Of course I want her back! Look, all I'm saying is she won't come back until she's damn good and ready. No matter—"

"How do you know that if she's never done this before?"

"I know her, dammit! She's all upset—" He broke off, looking like a man who had just bitten into something soft and slimy and wriggling.

"Upset about what?" I stood up, watching his face close down, flood with color.

He took a step forward, beefy hands clubbed into fists. "None of your damn business! Okay, goddammit! That's it! I invited you in here, now I'm inviting you out." He took another step forward, bringing those knobby fists within easy range, his broad face churning with emotion, eyes slitted, shiny and bright with hostility, a transformation so rapid and so complete it caught me totally off guard.

Time slowed, rocked to a halt. I could see his fists in my peripheral vision, but I watched his eyes. Hot and raging, the eyes of a man who understood violence, liked it, hard bone on yielding flesh, blood, pain, the thrill of victory.

"Think about it," I said softly. "Maybe you can take me, maybe you can't. Either way we trash this room." My throat was dry, adrenaline pumping in my veins, a stillness inside, a vigilant part of me tensed and watching for movement, for a flicker in the menacing eyes.

Air rushed out of him in a gusty sound meant to be a laugh. His breath smelled rancid and sour. The thick body relaxed, hands unfolding, raising in the time-honored signal for peace.

"Hey," he said shakily. "You tense, or what?" He worked at making a smile, only partially succeeding. "You're a guest in my house. I don't hassle guests, man, it ain't polite."

"It ain't safe, either," I said, imitating his drawl, letting my jacket drift open far enough for him to see the gun.

He blinked slowly, twice, then shrugged and turned toward the door. "This way out."

I followed him out of the room and through the short foyer. He chuckled as I went past him at the entrance door, let it escalate into a low rumbling laugh.

I walked out to my truck feeling slightly foolish, a little disgruntled. Whatever else I had or hadn't done, I hadn't scared him much.

He waited until I was getting into the truck before bellowing across the immaculate lawn, "You going to Irondale, look up a man named Teesdale!"

"Who is he?"

He threw up his arms, turned, and went back inside the house.

3

IT WAS MIDAFTERNOON WHEN I DROVE THE RENTED CAMARO into Irondale, Texas, from the southwest. Less than an hour's flight by shuttle jet from DFW Airport to Houston, it had taken two hours to shake clear of the nightmare Houston traffic and make the fifty-odd-mile drive to Irondale.

The weather was warm and sticky for March, the air heavy, unpleasant to smell, even more unsavory to breathe. The pallid sky hovered like an empty promise, dingy clouds threatening oily rain, a grim reminder of progress from the refineries on the Gulf Coast some fifty miles away.

Teesdale turned out to be the owner of a combination grocery and army/navy store that sold everything from ice cream bars to cheap leather saddles. An ancient building, barnlike, with a new false front of native quarry stone and lurid neon, it blended well with its surroundings, more than a mile of garish highway haunts, honky-tonks and fast-food restaurants, gas stations and rinky-dink motels geared to the card-carrying Mexican nationals who worked the lumber camps and smaller plants in Houston and Baytown, the sludge jobs that nobody wanted.

The state highway along the strip was a minefield of

potholes filled with grimy brackish water. Dusty battered pickups careened the obstacle course with ease and nonchalance, seemingly oblivious to snapping tires and clacking shocks, fans of dirty water spraying opposing traffic and their own gummy windshields. Cowboy-hatted heads peered through side windows, wide grins under Mr. Magoo mustaches.

The Camaro bucked and hopped on its truncated wheelbase, jarring coccyx and brainpan alike. I buckled up in self-defense, slipped on the flat-crowned businessman's Stetson I had dug out of the closet for camouflage purposes in the hinterlands. I gave up trying to smoke.

I negotiated the turn into Teesdale's parking lot just as a Southern Pacific train thundered along the far side of the highway, bearing car after car of pine logs. The cars rocked and weaved on the unsteady tracks, and the ancient engine shrilled a useless warning halfway through a cross-street intersection. Pickup horns blasted angry defiance—tick birds challenging a runaway rhino.

I left my jacket in the car, folded my shirt sleeves a couple of turns. I was wearing faded jeans and an old scuffed pair of boots, a frayed western shirt I wore only to rodeos. I had raised a few eyebrows on the plane, but here I felt right at home, one of the good old boys, a cowpoke or a truck driver, a wildcatter fallen on hard times. Not exactly my old stomping ground, but close enough that I knew how to act.

I found Moon Teesdale leaning against his cash register, tall and thin, gimpy bowlegs in too-tight Levi's, a John Deere gimme cap perched precariously on a tangled nest of tightly curled gray hair. He was blue-eyed and long-jawed, and had an easy affable grin that was only lip-deep and slowly faded when I told him who I was and asked about Jacob Twill.

"Jacob Twill? Never heard of him," he said, the blue

eyes leaving mine, squinting as he looked out over his jumbled store. His voice was high and thin, and carried. I saw heads turn among the aisles, a blur of faces from a group of hangers-on watching a domino game.

"Dresses funny," I said. "Buckskins, maybe. Long hair, longer'n most women, I hear."

He snorted. "Lots of folks got long hair nowadays. Them hippie fellers, cowboys, Injuns, and about all them country western singers got it. Nope, can't say as how I know your man."

"Funny," I said, propping a hip against the counter and trying to capture his roving gaze. "He said he had business with you. He's a survivalist. Coulda had something to do with outfitting, maybe. I see you handle dried foods, camping equipment, hiking, fishing, all things a guy needs living with nature."

"That I do," he said gently, studying a table display of slickers and rubber boots, a pained expression on his weathered face as if it had been far too long between rains. "I'd sell you any of that stuff you might want. I wouldn't ask your name, either."

"He's got a place east of here. Men, women, kids. Probably had two women with him. Might not, though. Tall man, blond hair, probably thirty-two, -three, along in there, muscular, brown as a nut." I was improvising, embellishing the scanty information the yardman had provided Victor Starling.

He screwed up his Gary Cooper face while he thought about it. He closed one eye and shook his head.

"Nope. Like I said before, I don't recollect him off-hand. Don't mean much, though. Lots of people come through here going in the Big Thicket. Big tourist attraction."

"Twill's not a tourist. He's a Texas boy and he lives in

the Big Thicket, or close to it. I don't think you'd have mistaken him for a tourist.''

He brought back the grin. "I don't know. You don't much look like a big city private eye, either. Looks can be deceiving.''

I nodded and lit a cigarette, feeling defeated. He knew Jacob Twill. I had seen too many good liars to be deceived by a poor one. But it was obvious he wasn't going to admit to it, and short of catching him alone and shoving a .38 up the end of his aristocratic nose, I couldn't think of any handy way to change his mind.

I thanked him politely and stepped away from the counter. I fed quarters into a nearby Pepsi machine, popped the tab on a multicolored can, and made a show of drinking thirstily while I casually searched the big room for other employees. The only one I spotted was a tow-headed teenager in a white apron who had been standing close enough to overhear our conversation. No good. He wouldn't go against the boss. At least not here, not now.

I left, dropping the half-empty can in a trash barrel near the front door. I sauntered around to the side lot where I had parked, propped my elbows on the Camaro's roof, lit another cigarette, and thought about it.

It wasn't an insurmountable problem, mostly a vexing one. There were other ways to find Jacob Twill, other people who knew him. All I had to do was find one of them. In all probability he would have electricity. That would mean records, a geographical location listed at the local co-op. A little finesse, a couple of twenty-dollar bills. Failing that, I could try the county treasurer's office. Taxes. A pretty sure bet if he owned the land in his own name. A little more money, probably. Government employees, even county government employees, generally had an inflated idea of their own worth.

There were ways, all right, but they were tedious and

sometimes uncertain, certainly dishonest to a degree. That didn't bother me a lot, but it went against the grain to pay to find out something that maybe everybody else knew, and I was back to thinking about a gun barrel up Moon Teesdale's thin nose when I became aware that a runty, red-faced man leaning against the side of Teesdale's store was trying to attract my attention. Trying hard. Actually, he was waving, apparently reluctant to come out into view of the domino players near the store's side window.

I slouched around the front of the car, made my way across the thirty-odd feet of macadam that separated us. I pulled up a few feet away, leaned against the building, nodded pleasantly.

"How much for Jacob Twill?" he said, going to the core of it, his voice thick with whiskey hoarseness, a noticeable English accent beneath an overlay of acquired Texanese. A man after my own heart. No vacillation. How much?

"Twenty," I said, then added five for no shilly-shallying. "Twenty-five."

"Shit," he snarled, digging his hands in an ankle-length tan coat that looked as if it had recently been used to wipe down freight cars. He cocked his unkempt head and closed his eyes, face screwed up as if engaged in some arcane permutation.

His bloodshot eyes snapped open. "I need thirty-two," he said hopefully, giving me a brown-stained grin, his red pug nose tilting rakishly.

"Thirty-five," I said. "And that's my last offer."

He blinked, started a scowl that faded slowly to a sheepish grin. "You're all right, mate," he said.

"Maybe," I said, "but don't trust me with your daughter."

His head bobbed eagerly, his right hand coming out of the coat pocket with a crumpled wad of paper. He smoothed it against his palm, held it out, then drew it back and extracted several folded sheets of paper.

"A letter from me dear old mum," he said proudly. "I'm a remittance man." He stuffed the sheets in his pocket. "I drew you a map right to their door. Just follow the arrows."

I studied the map drawn shakily on the back of the envelope. Tiny one-barbed arrows followed a heavy line that moved northeast out of Irondale. Thirty miles, perhaps, then a complicated intersection of state and county roads, the arrows heading due east from there to a heavy black dash marked 'gate, J. Twill prop.' It looked simple enough, maybe a little too simple. I slipped it into my shirt pocket and took out my wallet.

"I don't suppose it would occur to you to run a number on me?" I extracted thirty-five dollars and put the wallet away, watching his features reshape to wide-eyed innocence.

He straightened to his fullest height, trying his best to look indignant. "Absolutely not! Just because I am a drunk, sir, doesn't mean I am dishonest. I'll have you know I have noble blood in my veins. I am twenty-seventh in line to be a king!"

I gave him the money, watched it disappear. "If you're lying to me, noble-blooded or not, you'll be first in line to be a queen. Not that you'd probably miss them much."

But he wasn't listening, already edging away, a drunkard's flush giving his face an almost healthy glow, eyes alight with the secret knowledge of whatever pleasure thirty-two dollars would bring.

I watched him scuttle around the corner and out of sight.

Feeling an empathetic twinge, I lit another cigarette and went back to my car.

4

THE BIG THICKET. APPROXIMATELY FIFTEEN HUNDRED square miles of densely packed hardwoods and soft pine. A scratchy tangle on the chest of Big Daddy East Texas, a sometimes Gothic wood that stretches from Galveston Bay all the way to Paris, Texas, and maybe beyond. East Texas is oftentimes a state of mind as much as a territory, synonymous with southern hospitality and genteel living to some, considered a breeding ground of individualistic, hardheaded conservatism by others. It is probably both, and more.

Jacob Twill lived at the back door to the Big Thicket. I drove straight to his gate using the map the little drunk had sold me. Without a bobble. Through a sea of pines: loblolly, longleaf, shortleaf, slash—others that looked familiar but I couldn't name.

It was a sturdy gate, welded pipe, painted white, a big sign that said: PRIVATE, NO TRESPASSING, JACOB TWILL OWNER, ENFORCER. Simple, direct.

After the well-made gate and the classy sign, the small pine building set fifteen yards up the grade at the edge of the woods was something of an anticlimax. As was the

33

man who sat outside its door and watched me make the turnout and nose up to the gate, expecting, no doubt, that I would turn around and go back the way I had come.

When I didn't, when I shut off the engine and opened the car door, he came alive, reaching inside the raw pine hut as if he had all the time in the world, his left hand lazily scratching his stomach while the right came back bearing a rifle.

I thought about the .38 under the front seat of the car and shrugged. I wasn't trespassing. Not yet.

I folded my arms on the top rail of the gate and watched him trudge down the slope toward me. A big man, mostly belly. Long arms and a bushy beard, a sweat-stained cowboy hat tilted low over a Roman nose. Run-over boots and patched jeans, a faded flannel shirt with longjohns visible at his neck. He swung the rifle easily, like a toy. Every third step he whistled as if walking hurt.

He was still ten paces away when I heard his rumbling laugh.

"Lost, right? Well, don't feel bad. Fellers get lost up here all the time. Them county roads are real bitch-kitties. Took me six months 'fore I knew how to get to Burlwood and back without a guide. Irondale took a year. Reckon I'd never find my way back to Houston." He ended with another laugh, bumping the gate with his belly as he switched arms with the rifle and offered a skillet-size hand. "Name's Ralston, just like the feed company. Front name is General. My dad had dee-lusions of grandeur." He guffawed and mangled my hand, then turned it loose and spat an amber stream at the cedar gatepost. "Folks call me Genny mostly, when they don't call me somethin' worse. What's your name?" He had large eyes for a fat man, the dark liquid brown of a Mexican saint.

"Roman. First name Daniel. Folks call me Dan. I'm not lost, at least I don't think I am. I'm looking for a man named Jacob Twill. If that sign ain't lying I guess he's somewhere on the other side of this gate." I tried out a friendly, nonthreatening smile.

He smiled back, small yellow teeth barely visible between beard and mustache. "This is his place right enough. You sellin' somethin'?"

I shook my head. "I'd just like a minute of his time, if it's possible."

He frowned and turned to look at the ill-defined road that disappeared into the trees beyond the hut. He turned back and pushed the hat high on his broad forehead.

"Thing is, I don't think you can make it to the main camp in that little city car of yours. We got four-wheelers up here." He dug thick fingers into the beard and scratched his chin. "What I could do is, I could call in on that little squawk box in the hut there. Maybe I could raise old Jake and he could come on down here." He looked at me, the brown eyes anxious. "Would that be okay?"

"That would be fine," I said. "But I don't want to be a bother."

"Hey, cowboy, ain't no bother a'tall. Fact is, I'm out here too danged early the way it is. Had to get Cletus to drop me off 'fore he went to work on the pump. Them reds ain't likely to be stirring 'fore three, four o'clock nohow. Plenty of time." He grinned his yellowish grin and propped the rifle against the cedar post. "Be right back." He lumbered off up the grade, whistling every third step.

I reached over the gate and picked up the rifle. Marlin semiautomatic, .22 caliber, a slender two-power scope attached to the barrel. Reds?

Realization prickled like a tweaked nose. Red squirrels, fox squirrels. He was a squirrel hunter and I had taken him for a guard. A natural assumption, I told myself; nevertheless, I felt a little foolish. I put the gun back

35

against the post and lit a cigarette. I could hear faintly his rumbling voice, an occasional electronic squawk. Somewhere a squirrel chattered; a blue jay shrilled an angry reply. A sudden gust of wind soughed through the pines; the sullen sky hovered.

He was back in less than five minutes. I crushed the butt carefully under a heel as he approached. Beaming.

"Gott'em, by golly. Jake'll be on out here in a few minutes. Said he'd hurry."

"Great. I really appreciate this." I resumed my stance at the gate and decided to check out my deduction. "Lots of squirrels around here?"

"You bet." He pointed across the road behind my car. "See that line of hickory there along the creek. They're just beginning to bud out good. Them little critters love them new buds 'most as well as they like the nuts, I reckon. I bring my chair down here to the gate where I got a good rest, and couple of hours later I got me enough squirrels to feed the whole shebang. Young squirrels, juicy." He smacked his lips.

"How many is that?"

He looked off, squinting his eyes. "Let's see . . . About twenty-seven or -eight, I reckon. Hard to keep track what with all the new babies and all. Getting kinda crowded. Gonna have to put up some new cabins 'fore next winter." He tilted his head, stared at me thoughtfully. "Why, you thinking about joining?"

"I'm a city boy. Don't think I could stand all this space."

"You get used to it. I usta be a truck driver. Too long. Messed up my kidneys."

"How do you live? Even up here it must take a lot of money for that many people."

"This and that. We eat game, make gardens. Grow corn, make our own flour, like that. Then some of the fellers work the lumber camps, oil patches, a couple of the ranches during branding time. Everything goes in the pot. We do all right.'' He turned and glanced up the slope as the sound of a distant motor reached our ears. ''That's him coming.''

''Get many visitors up here?''

''Not many. Sometimes somebody's relative coming up to check us out. Nosy folks wanting to see what them sinful kooks are up to now. They figger we gotta be a little touched, some kinda cult, free sex, orgies, devil worshipers, something. They can't believe we're just ordinary folks trying to get along best way we know how.''

''Any visitors right now? A lady, maybe, thirtyish, slender, good-looking, with shoulder-length black hair.''

He frowned and turned again as the sound of a vehicle backfiring came from just beyond the tree line. ''None that I know about. But I been down on Crooked Creek the last eight or nine days tending—'' He broke off, looking sheepish. ''Working on the new fence,'' he amended. ''I only got back last night.'' He made a big-eyed, evil face. ''Me and the old lady was kinda busy. We didn't talk much.'' He loosed another guffaw as an open Jeep broke out of the pines and slowed, backfiring again. A man and a woman inside.

I laughed with him, wondering what it was he had been tending. A moonshine still was the only thing that came to mind. Nobody tended a fence. Maybe moonshine was the business Twill had had with Moon Teesdale. It could easily explain Teesdale's reluctance to discuss Twill with anyone remotely connected to authority, even a quasi cop like me.

Jacob Twill was at least two inches taller than my six feet, wider of shoulder, leaner of hip, long legs tightly encased in new-looking jeans, his upper torso adorned with a splendid creation of tawny deerskin, fringes, and beads, a deep V throat with leather lacing. He moved with the lazy grace of a natural athlete, smiled with a dashing charm. On the surface, an easy man to like. I watched him come to greet me and thought of big cats, caged, pacing.

"Mr. Roman. I'm Jake Twill. A pleasure to meet you." A quick firm grasp and he dropped my hand and stepped back, smothering a cough. "I won't come too near. I think I've picked up a flu bug somewhere." Up close he appeared older, a fine cross-hatching of lines at his eyes, at the edges of his lips. His eyes were bloodshot.

He turned to the unsmiling woman now standing by the Jeep. "Joline Coldwater."

As dark as Twill, she was tall and slender, high cheekbones and big black eyes. She inclined her head, a sleek cap of black hair descending out of sight behind her back, bound at her temples with a red-and-black headband. She wore faded jeans and a long-sleeved checkered blouse.

"I appreciate your courtesy," I said.

"Not at all. We seldom get visitors. Particularly back here. It would be interesting to know how you came to our back door, by the way."

"Just someone I ran into in Irondale. I didn't catch his name."

He nodded. "Well, you're here, that's the important thing. Would you care to go back to our camp or . . ." He let it drift, smiling easily, the dark eyes as friendly as a Sunday preacher's.

"Thanks. I appreciate the invitation, but I only need a few moments of your time. A couple of questions, if you don't mind. I'm a private investigator and I'm looking for a lady named Sandra Conrad. I understand from her husband that she left her home with you and . . . a lady last Tuesday." I looked past him at the woman. She nodded, her expression serene. She smiled encouragingly.

Twill flashed a smile and chuckled. "I wish all our

problems were so easily solved. Yes, of course, she did. She was with us for a week, I believe." He looked at Joline for confirmation. She nodded again.

"Tuesday, yesterday, Joline and I took her to her uncle's place over near Crater. Left her there. We were sorry to see her go."

"She's an old friend of yours, I understand."

"An old friend. A good friend. From our college days. From mine, that is. Joline's younger." He coughed into his fist, squinting his eyes as if it hurt.

I smiled at Joline. She smiled back. All this niceness was beginning to make me a little ill.

"Could you tell me where exactly . . . around Crater?"

"Absolutely," Twill said. "Take FM 92 north out of Crater . . . about ten miles, wouldn't you say, Joline?"

Joline nodded. Twill turned back to me.

"Little house, gray siding, sets back about fifty yards off the road. Huge live oak in the front yard. Eight or ten white beehives down near a new red barn. You can see all this from the highway. You can't miss it."

"Her uncle, you said?"

"Jonas Beechum. Yes. Sorta odd old geezer. Wears an old .44. All the time, I hear, except when he's in town. Then he carries it in a paper bag. Understand there's some bad blood between him and one of the lumber companies. He lives on original Beechum property, according to Sandy. Two thousand or so acres the old man gave Jonas when he split with the rest of the family. He's lived there, or right close by, all his life. He won't let the cutters come within a mile of his place. I've heard estimates of eight to ten million dollars worth of timber."

"Good for him," Ralston said, swinging the rifle like a baton.

"Was Mrs. Conrad feeling all right? I understand her

39

husband didn't want her to leave with you, that they argued about it."

Twill looked uncomfortable. "As a matter of fact she was pretty depressed. Not about the argument so much, I think. She just seemed drawn down, exhausted. She perked up some the last couple of days, though. I guess the rest did her some good. She spent a lot of time by herself, sitting on the bluff above the Neches. We let her alone, let her work out whatever was bothering her. She seemed in better spirits when she left. Joline made her a buckskin blouse like mine and that seemed to please her."

"She was sick," Joline said quietly, crossing the short distance from the Jeep. "A sickness of the spirit, I think. My grandfather was a shaman, a medicine man. I've heard him talk of such sickness. It attacks the soul and shrivels the spirit. There is no cure short of death."

Twill looked uncomfortable again. He put his arm around her shoulders and smiled. "Hogwash. You don't believe that any more than I do. An old man's ramblings. Indian voodoo. Superstitious mumbo jumbo. She was simply tired and depressed."

Joline shrugged free of his arm, turned, and walked back to the Jeep.

I took out a cigarette, then put it back as a fat raindrop spattered on the back of my hand. Other drops pinged on the hood of the Camaro.

"Uh-oh," Ralston said. "She's finally decided to cut loose. There goes my squirrel breakfast, dang it." A gust of wind stirred the pines; the raindrops quickened. He turned and legged it up the slope toward the shack. He threw up his arm. "Nice meeting you, Dan."

"Same here, General." I looked at Twill, still slouched lazily against the gate, smiling. "Sorry about getting you out in this."

"Won't melt," he said. "But you might ought to hurry

on out of here. Some low places between here and the highway that get downright nasty with a good rain. They'd eat that little car of yours.''

"Right. And thanks again." I gave him a half-salute and climbed into the Camaro. He joined Joline in the open Jeep, the buckskin jacket already smeared and splotched with rain. They sat erect, uncowed, apparently impervious to the pelting drops that turned the Camaro into a booming drum.

I backed the car out of the turnout, spun the wheels a little in loose gravel, righted, and got the hell out of there.

5

I SPENT THE NIGHT IN A MOTEL AT THE EDGE OF CRATER, another small Texas town with its very own garnish strip of roadhouse America, grimy and depressing in the daylight, glitter and glitz at night, soggy and sordid after the soaking rain.

I shelled out thirty dollars and laid claim to a small square cell, thin walls and a cracked tile shower, a lumpy bed and uneven drapes, linoleum floors. But it wasn't all bad. The TV worked, the toilet was sanitized, and it was dry.

Jonas Beechum's house was right where Twill and Joline said it would be, on a hill ten and two-tenths miles north of Crater. I made the short drive after a midmorning breakfast of bacon, sausage, three eggs, and flapjacks, something called a Waddy Special. It took me a while to remember what a waddy was.

Loblolly pine lined Beechum's driveway, tracked around the giant live oak tree in front, and gathered again in orderly ranks at the rear of the house. Ten gleaming white beehives butted the side of the well-kept red barn; the blunt nose of a Chevrolet pickup peeked out of its gloomy interior.

Beyond the barn a couple of acres had been gouged out of the forest for a garden and assorted pens: dogs, chickens, hogs, and a small circular corral that housed at least two horses, one of which nickered softly as I parked and cut the engine. That woke up the dogs and they came charging out of box houses, whipping tails and muddy paws, at least six of them, rawboned and floppy-eared, doing what they did best: deafening cacophony.

I heard a door slam at the rear of the house, a shrill whistle, a yell; gradually the noise subsided, the dogs running the fence, whining in protest. One more yell and uneasy silence. I heard the rear door clatter again, the sound of voices. I got out and dodged puddles across the threadbare, muddy lawn. I reached the off-center front porch just as the door opened and a man stepped out.

He was short and wiry, hair the color of sand, eyes as black as tar chips. They glared at me, almost hidden beneath thick sandy brows, blared an unmistakable message of unbridled rage.

A shiver of coolness raced along my spine: too much reaction for disturbing his dogs.

I took an involuntary step backward as he advanced across the porch, stalking, slender right hand fanned over the bonehandled grip of a gun slung low on his thigh. Tied down and hanging low in the manner of old-time gunslingers, modernday fast-draw artists. Stalking me. Crazy. The son of a bitch was crazy.

"You come to gloat, you dirty scut?" he snarled through clenched teeth. "One word, just one word, and I'll blow a hole in you you could throw a cat through!"

Jesus Christ! Right out of *Wild West Weekly*—Max Brand, Zane Grey, Louis Whatshisname.

I must have done something, laughed, sneered, or given

him a smart-ass look. He bellowed a curse, wiggled his fingers, and I was looking down the barrel of the longest handgun I'd ever seen.

"No, no!" I said, my insides recoiling in shock, surging upward. "Look! I'm not gloating! My name is Roman, Dan Roman. Your daddy sent me!" I probably sounded shrill, but I got it out without moving anything except my tongue and my quivering stomach. It sounded so good I said part of it again. "Your daddy sent me, Mr. Beechum!"

A bloated second drifted by; another. He still looked the same, but something had changed, some subtle alteration in the cosmic balance of things. His eyes clicked shut, then opened wide, realization swimming in their dark wild depths. His hands trembled. The gun wobbled, too heavy for the slender wrist. He licked his lips and put out a hand to grasp a post. His eyes met mine, then flicked away.

"Jesus Christ," he said hollowly. "You're not from Glazier."

"No, sir. No, I'm not. I'm from your daddy. I'm looking for Sandy."

He sagged against the post, the big gun disappearing with a flick of his wrist. "My God, man, I almost shot you!"

"Really? I didn't notice." My stomach rolled, a bitter taste crawling into my throat. I wanted to vomit. What I did was stand there grinning like a fool. And swallowing.

"Dammit, why didn't you—" He broke off and shook his head. "I guess I didn't let you explain."

"I guess you didn't," I said, feeling a rising swell of anger, my usual reaction to fear and embarrassment and danger. I felt like picking the old fart up and slapping him silly.

"I'm sorry as hell about this," he said, his pale face gathering color. "They killed Glory and I thought you'd come to—they did it before when they killed the pigs, fired the barn, and burned Milly, when they snuck in here and trashed my wife Myna's new little Ford, and when they dropped a skunk in the well and shot out all the winders—"

"Whoa. Did what? I take it Milly was a cow or a horse, but who was Glory?"

He took a moment to get his breathing straightened out, a deep breath and a shudder. His hand twitched down around the gun again, an agonized expression crossing the pinched face.

"Glory was three-quarter redbone, best damn bitch in the county, mebbe all of Texas. I was offered two thousand for her mor'n once. Sweetest yodel, and she could outrun the best of them. Everybody in the county recognized old Glory's bay—"

"Why would anyone kill her?"

"Meanness! Pure damn meanness and spite. They want my timber and they're getting desperate. Curly Glazier's running out of wood in this part of the county and he's got all that investment in the mill and machines; besides, he lives here. I'm the only holdout and he can't stand it. Partly 'cause its me, partly because of the lumber." He looked out across the waving sea of green that stretched as far as the eye could see. A wintry smile crept across the lean features. "These are my woods and nobody's gonna cut a stick of timber long as I'm alive. Or Myna. She's tough like I am. They can't buy us out, and they can't scare us out. I reckon there's only one thing left for them." He turned the smile on me and it had undergone a subtle change, a mixture of embarrassment and apology.

"I guess you think I'm some kinda crazy old coot coming at you the way I did. But . . . well, every time one of these things happens, in a day or two some city dude would drop by and make me another offer. Not Glazier. No, sir.

He's chicken shit. It'd be some slicker in a sports car like you're driving there—''

"It's a rental Chevy," I pointed out.

He nodded. "I can see that now. A while ago I was blind. I wasn't seeing anything but old Glory strung out on that junction fence down there, eight or nine little bitty puppies laying dead on the ground." He stopped and sighed. "I guess I went a little crazy at that. I only found her a couple of hours ago. If I'da been thinking right, I'da knowed it was too soon. All I can say is, I'm sorry."

I couldn't bring myself to say it was all right. It wasn't. Something had changed. I had been on the brink, looked into oblivion, and would never again be the same. I wasn't at all sure I could forgive Jonas Beechum for that.

So I just nodded and accepted his invitation to sit.

"Something to drink?" he said, suddenly eager to please. "I got apple cider, some tea or table wine, and some beer. No hard stuff. We don't believe in it."

"Beer would be nice."

"Myna, could we have a couple of them Lone Stars, please?" He spoke gently through the screen door, a kindly loving smile creasing the weathered face, bringing a twinkle to warm dark eyes. "Then why don't you join us? We have company."

Old-time southern hospitality, the way it was when I was a kid. Heartwarming.

She was taller than her husband by a couple of inches. Willowy. As dark as Joline Coldwater. As a matter of fact, she looked like her.

She had the same dark eyes that all East Texans seemed to have lately, long black hair pulled back in a ponytail, clasped snugly at her temples with a golden headband. A round pretty face and softly turned lips, high cheekbones and a dimpled chin. Unless Beechum had somehow aged

46

to a different clock, she was twenty years younger than he.

They sat side by side on a wicker love seat facing me, fingers intertwined, Jonas's gaze meeting mine only occasionally, in fleeting passage. Myna looked at me steadily, somberly, as if searching for the craven heart beneath the amiable facade. She was three-quarters Comanche, or so Beechum told me before five minutes had passed.

"She's from West Texas," he explained proudly. "Plains Indian. Great horseman. She can ride good's any cowboy you ever saw. Bareback. That filly yonder is hers. You oughta see her ride. I ain't much for it, myself. All these trees, she feels smothered around here sometimes. We go out to Sweetwater, on up north to Lubbock, camping out along the way. Clean air out there. Don't smell like oil. She can breathe."

She nodded and smiled while he talked, turning to look at him occasionally, a soft light in her eyes. Once again I was struck by her resemblance to Joline Coldwater.

"Joline Coldwater," I said. "Could it be that you're related?"

She nodded and smiled. "Yes, she's my sister." Her voice was low and mellifluous, a faint trace of huskiness that gave it a pleasing resonance.

"Lives with that kooky bunch over around Burlwood. Living with a feller named Twill. Like man and wife. Myna don't hold with that, but you know how this younger generation is."

"What can you do?" I said, thinking that Joline looked only slightly younger than Myna, and that would put her in her early thirties; only a couple of years younger than me.

"I understand Twill brought your niece Sandy over here a few days ago," I said.

Beechum scowled. "Yeah, that's right. Tuesday I reckon it was, wasn't it, Myna?"

47

She nodded without speaking.

"Your father was worried about her. He wanted to make sure she was all right."

"Why wouldn't she be?" Beechum growled. "She's my niece. I wonder if he thinks I'd let something happen to her?"

"That was the problem. He didn't know where she had gone. Her husband wouldn't tell him anything. Your dad was getting concerned."

Beechum barked a short strident laugh. "You bet your ass he was." It was a strange thing for him to say and I waited for a follow-up. But none was forthcoming. He looked off, whistling through his teeth.

"She's no longer here," Myna said after a short uncomfortable silence. "Jonas drove her to the bus stop on Highway 45. We tried to get her to fly, or let us drive her home, but she said she needed the time alone to think."

"About what?"

"I don't know," she said soberly.

"When was that?"

"Thursday night," Beechum put in, back from his perusal of the verdant wood, his expression vague and unfocused.

Myna touched his hand. "No, honey. It was last night. This is Thursday. She only stayed one night. I had to work, remember?" She looked at me. "I work Mondays, Wednesdays, and Fridays at the hospital in Irondale."

"Yeah, that's right, ain't it?" Beechum sighed. "That'd make it Wednesday. She called that no-account husband of hers, told him when she'd be in. He said he'd pick her up."

"Well," I said heartily. "I guess that puts me out of work. I wish all my cases ended so well."

Beechum looked up sharply, then leaped to his feet as the dogs began barking furiously. Without a word, his face tight and strained again, he jumped off the porch and dashed around the corner of the house, hand fanned above the gun.

I turned back to find Myna watching me; she made a moue of apology and shook her head. "I'm sorry about what happened."

"You think he should be carrying that cannon? He seems a little bit too handy with it."

"I know, but . . . but it isn't loaded." She canted her head and gave me a sunny smile.

"Jesus Christ." I felt anger rekindle, a hollow spot behind my breastbone.

"I know. I'm sorry. I know how you felt."

"No, I don't think you do."

Her slender fingers worried the top button on her blouse. "He's not crazy. Really. He took the shells out himself. He's afraid of what might happen. He gets so angry. They've pushed and pushed for years, did things to us you wouldn't believe. But Jonas is a strong man, a stubborn man. This is his home. He loves these woods; they're the only thing he has except . . . me. He'll die before he'll give them over to the cutters." She stopped as Beechum's whistle sounded out in back. The raucous noise diminished.

"And there's more to it than just the lumber. Bad blood between him and Curly Glazier. Has been for years now. It's not just the timber. It's me. It's not a secret, Mr. Roman. I was engaged to marry Curly Glazier when I met Jonas Beechum. I soon discovered that I only liked Curly, admired him—I discovered that I loved Jonas." Her head lowered, a quiet smile. "I had to go to him. Curly was his friend. To Jonas that said it all. It was unthinkable to trespass." She looked up, her features soft, blurred. "I had to . . . to convince him." She laughed quietly. "He thinks to this day that he swept me off my feet, that he

49

betrayed his friendship. I can't convince him otherwise. Now, of course, it doesn't matter. Too many bad things have happened for them to ever be friends again.''

''It's a sorry situation,'' I said. ''How about the sheriff? Have you talked to him?''

She spread her hands. ''He's tried to help. His men have staked out our house a few times when we were gone. Nothing happened. And we can't prove anything. They're very careful. They respect my husband. They know if he catches them, he'll kill them.''

I lifted my eyebrows. ''With an empty gun?''

''Oh, he carries the bullets in his pocket.'' She glanced up at my face and broke into laughter just as Jonas came around the corner of the house, walking lightly now, his step springy.

He looked at his wife and smiled. ''She been telling you one of them smutty jokes they learn her down at that hospital? Dirtiest talking people I ever heard tell of.''

She laughed again and switched smoothly to a less contentious subject. ''You're just easily shocked. I was telling Mr. Roman about the deerskin blouse and moccasins Joline made for Sandy. Just like mine. Sandy was really pleased. What was wrong with the dogs?''

Jonas shrugged. ''Cat, I reckon. Didn't see anything, but there's dang cats running wild all over this county. We're gonna have to start shooting them.''

''Could I get you another beer, Mr. Roman?''

''No, thank you, ma'am. I need to be on my way. I appreciate your hospitality.''

Jonas bobbed his head and looked sheepish. ''Sorry,'' he said shortly. ''Hope I didn't scare you.''

''Nothing I won't grow out of,'' I said. I glanced down at the rig. ''What is that, anyway? I couldn't tell much from the hole in the end.''

He smiled and appeared to flinch and held out his arm,

the long revolver lying across his palm. "Colt .44. Usta be owned by Whiskey Sam Coble. You heard of him, I reckon."

"I think so. Outlaw or lawman?"

"Both," he said tersely. "Outlaw till he got caught and almost hung up in Oklahoma. He went straight after that, became a Texas Ranger. Died in a shoot-out in El Paso. Bunch of Mexican bandits crossing the border to steal. Sorry way to go. Shot in the back. They say he was faster'n any of them." He hefted the gun, ran his hand lovingly along the barrel, curled his small fist around the worn bone handle. "I don't know. All them old gunfighters, they wasn't really very fast. Mostly they stood out in the street and pecked away at each other until somebody fell or they run out of bullets. We've got boys now who coulda drawed, fired, and reseated before they coulda cleared leather. I'm not bad myself, and I can't hold a candle to some of them." He twirled the gun, dropped it into the holster.

"When I was a cop," I said, "we had a rule. Never pull a gun unless you need to use it; never use it without a damn good reason."

He looked at me silently for a moment, then shrugged. "Don't lecture me, boy. I told you I was sorry." He turned on his heel and went inside the house.

I looked at Myna. She was smiling faintly.

"Well, I guess I told him."

She chuckled. "Beechum arrogance. He's got his share of it. You don't know how hard it was for him to say he was sorry."

"I can guess. I was raised among people like your husband. More pride than good sense sometimes. Most of the time, actually."

We left the porch and walked toward my car, dodging puddles.

"You're a Texan," she said, more a statement than a question.

"Yes. Raised not too far north of here, as a matter of fact."

"You live in Dallas?"

"Close. Midway City."

"That's where Sandy lives."

"Yes. I've been to their house."

"Her husband, Peter. What did you think of him?"

"I couldn't make a fair evaluation. I only met him once for a short time." I glanced down at her as we reached the Camaro. "Seemed a bit . . . high-strung."

She laughed softly. "High-strung? Is that a nice way of saying bastard?" Her dark eyes gleamed, finely etched lips quirking at the corners. I sensed a depth of humor and wit not obvious in the presense of her husband. A woman of quiet surprises, serious turns, and funny twists.

"He's a womanizer, you know," she said seriously. "That's one of the reasons Sandy came down here. To see Jake Twill. He's sort of her guru, I guess you could say. They were lovers once, long before Joline, and they should have married. But Jake isn't the marrying kind and she finally gave up and married that joker Conrad."

"We all have illegal pasts, as a buddy of mine used to say. Let him who lives in a grass hut throw the first spear . . . or something like that."

She smiled briefly, a full flashing smile that lit up her face. "You're right. The Beechum case is closed for you, isn't it? Well, good-bye and good luck, Mr. Dan Roman. It was nice meeting you."

She extended her hand. She had a firm grip. Warm, and in no hurry to pull away. I didn't mind. Not at all.

"Your sister said Mrs. Conrad was suffering from a sickness of the spirit. What do you think?"

Her hand slipped out of mine. "Joline is living close to

nature almost in the old way. It has, oddly enough, made her more immature, more impressionable. She professes to believe in the old ways of our people, embraces their philosophy—their superstitions. Sandy was just depressed, I think, searching for something she can only find within herself. I think Jacob helped her."

I thanked her again and watched her lithe figure make its zigzag course to the house. I turned the car around and drove out to the road.

I felt vaguely disconsolate. No elation. No sense of a job well done.

It took a while to ferret out the reason for my malaise: I wanted to see Myna Beechum again. I knew I never would.

I was less than a mile away from the Beechum ranch when the black pickup loomed suddenly in my rearview mirror. Riding high above the Camaro on wide fat tires and a highsprung chassis, its engine rumbled and popped angrily as I instinctively decelerated and moved to the right so he could go around.

But he didn't pass. He hung there, riding my tail, so close I could see scratches on the heavy black bumper, dead bugs stuck to the massive chromework, a red light buried behind the grill that was just beginning to flash. A siren shrilled, whined down, shrilled again.

Cop. Damn! A county mountie looking for a score. I tried to remember how fast I had been going as I eased onto the shoulder, braked the little car to a stop. It didn't much matter, I thought glumly, city slickers were fair game, never a closed season. Budget-boosters, revenue-enhancers. Keeps the taxes down for the local folks. Call it a toll tax.

I lit a cigarette and stepped out of the car, turned to face the stalwart figure strolling leisurely along the shoulder toward me. No hurry now that the victim was secure, another statistic in this week's quota. I felt a weary blip of useless anger, a faint ripple of surprise as I got a better look at him.

He didn't look like a cop. Tall and wide shouldered, lanky, dressed in a cream-colored whipcord suit, glossy high-heeled boots, and a flat-crowned Stetson cocked at a rakish angle, he looked more like a West Dallas pimp or a wildcatter lately fallen on good times. Curly auburn hair grew almost to his collar, a fist-sized hank spilling across his forehead as he lifted the hat in a friendly greeting. No ticket book, no gun, none of the jingling accoutrements of a cop.

"Sorry if I scared you, friend," he said, smiling easily, a handsome smile as befitted the handsome bronzed face. He exuded self-assurance, an uncomplicated aura of superior masculinity that set my teeth on edge.

"Nothing I won't get over," I said. "Used to happen all the time back in high school."

He laughed. "Touché. I'll admit to a bit of grandstanding, but now and again I find it necessary." He took a silver cigarette case from his inside coat pocket, selected one, and lit it with what looked like a gold-plated Dunhill. Smoke spilled from elegant nostrils; the smile thinned. "What company are you with, friend?"

"What business is that of yours, friend?" I leaned a hand against the Camaro's roof and returned his meager smile, spilling some smoke of my own.

He shrugged genially. "Just thought you'd like to know the Beechum two thousand is spoken for, friend. All tied up. Thought I'd maybe save you a little trouble."

"Hmmmm. I understood there was only fifteen hundred."

"Two thousand. I oughta know. I lease everything around it."

54

"And you want it too, huh? Your name wouldn't be Hog Glazier, would it?"

His face tightened almost imperceptibly. "Glazier, yes," he said softly. "I don't believe I've heard that first part before. You just make it up?" It was a gentle invitation to battle, as clear to me as a backhand across the face, a gauntlet on the ground. I straightened and threw away the cigarette. I'd been scared spitless already today. I had something coming for that, and besides, once a day was enough.

"Maybe I misspoke," I said. "Maybe it was Dog Glazier instead." I couldn't make it any plainer than that without being profane, and for one long, overloaded second I thought we were going to fight. His face slowly turned copper, the wide-lipped mouth tightly crimped.

Before he could answer, a pickup came over the rise behind us, the bed filled with dark-skinned, unsmiling men. The driver honked and waved. Glazier waved back. The Mexican nationals stared at us without a change in expression.

I looked at Glazier. He lifted his hands, palms outward.

"Wally Starket," he said crisply, backing away from hostility with uncommon ease. "Got him a little tract over on the Neches. Taking on a few new men."

I relaxed. "Timber dying out around here?" I kept my voice neutral, even.

He shrugged. "Not dead yet, but it's got a bad cough. Pockets here and there. I keep a few good men busy."

He ambled around in a little circle, clearly not satisfied with what he had learned from me, just as clearly not certain how to go about finding out more. I stepped back to the door of the Camaro.

He stopped in the middle of a circle and looked at me. "Okay, well, look, I don't know what you've heard about me, nothing good, probably, but I ain't their enemy. Me

55

and Jonas Beechum usta be good friends. He's a lot older, but that didn't matter. Man, we usta hunt these hills and hollers—'' He broke off and finished the turn. ''But that's old news. We ain't that way no more, and I'm sorry for it.'' He looked across a narrow plowed field alongside the highway, pointed to a dark line of evergreen trees two hundred yards away. ''That's Jonas's timber.''

''You want this timber.''

''I do,'' he said bluntly. ''That I do. It'd keep me and my men alive for years. No clear-cutting; no, sir. Select timber. Jonas could pick it hisself.''

''I didn't think you could do that profitably.''

''Absolutely. When you're not greedy, when you're small like I am. Jonas wants it kept wild. We could keep it wild and still make him a rich man. Me too, for that matter.''

''Why won't he talk about it?''

He gave me a searching glare, then shook his head. ''There's other reasons.''

''Myna,'' I said.

His mouth tightened. He opened it, then closed it again to wait for another noisy, rattling pickup to pass. Another honk, another wave. He turned back to me, frown lines marring the smooth bronze forehead.

''For a short visit, you damn sure learned a lot.''

''That's my business.''

''I know it's your business and I ain't prying in it, but—''

''No, you misunderstand. It's my business. My name's Dan Roman. I'm a private detective.''

He canceled the frown and smiled faintly. ''A private detective. I guess I've never met one of you before.''

''We're an endangered species, like whooping cranes.''

''You a friend of the Beechums?''

''Something like that. My visit had nothing to do with timber.''

"They need some friends. Especially her. Jonas gets so damn crazy sometimes."

"Maybe he's got good reasons."

"Yeah." He carefully crushed his cigarette beneath a heel. "They've had their share of problems. Just being a Beechum and living in this county is a problem all by itself."

"Why is that?"

"That old man," he said bitterly, stepping out into the road to stare back the way we had come. "That old bastard almost ruined this county for timbering before he went off to plunder somewhere else. Mor'n fifty years ago. Lot of these places just coming back. Talk about your robber barons, man, nobody was worse than that old man."

"They always say the same about any rich man."

"Yeah, but this time it was true. My own daddy worked for him for twenty years. He wasn't much better, only not as smart. Not smart enough to get rich. Macomber Beechum was different. He was smart and crooked and cunning. He came out of the piney woods up north of here somewhere, came in here without a pot to piss in, with a wife and twin boys. Next thing anybody knew he had him a cutting operation going. Not mor'n three miles from where we're standing. Four thousand acres of some of the best pine in Texas, and he was going like a house afire."

"Where'd he get it?"

"Lot of stories about it, but the only one that's stood the test of time, and the only one he's never denied, is that he won it in a poker game down in Galveston. Some half-breed Indian. Don't remember his name, if I ever heard it. Story goes that he got the breed half-drunk, or whole drunk, and cold-decked him. Maybe true, maybe not, but Daddy always said he believed it." He made another aimless circle, pulled his coat together and buttoned it. "All I know is, folks, mostly old folks, still curl their lip when the Beechum name comes up."

"Why would Jonas want to stay?"

He lifted his eyes toward the line of woods again. "Same reason I do, I guess. Born here, close to here. Jonas was raised not a hundred yards from where his little house stands today. Usta be the camp boss's house long time ago when the big house was standing. It burned down twenty-five years ago. Miles and Jonas was twins. Miles hated the woods, Jonas spent all his time there. When it come time to leave, he wouldn't go. The old man finally gave up on him, settled this two thousand acres on him so he wouldn't starve to death, I guess. But Jonas refused to cut it, even a little bit. He lived off the woods, trapping, a little work around now and then. I've always figured the old man sent him money along. He always lived pretty good." He shook his head, an incredulous look crossing his face. "He's setting there on eight to ten million dollars. And all because he likes to coon hunt."

"Probably more to it than that. Some people's roots run deep."

"That's a fact." He straightened his hat, brushed off his coat sleeve, and took a step forward. He shoved out a hand, hesitantly, as if afraid I'd refuse to shake it.

"Sorry about the bulldozing. I get a little excited sometimes."

I pumped his hand and let it go. "What did you have planned when you stopped me?"

He made a mild grimace. "I was gonna whip your ass, I guess."

"What stopped you?" I asked, then added a little needle. "From trying?"

He looked at me thoughtfully, then shrugged and smiled. "I guess it looked like it was gonna be work. Basically, I'm lazy."

We exchanged nods. He went back to his pickup. I got into the Camaro. He made a U-turn and went back the way we had come.

I lit a cigarette and pulled onto the highway. I felt loose and easy, my ego salved, my manhood restored.

It was a vain and foolish feeling, but it felt good nevertheless.

6

I CAUGHT THE FOUR O'CLOCK SHUTTLE FROM HOUSTON to the Dallas-Fort Worth Airport, reached my house around six.

I took a hot shower before putting in the call to Peter Conrad. One tiny dangling thread and I could close out the Beechum case, close out the Beechums. I had to know if Sandy arrived home safely, if, against all odds, the bus had been hijacked to Texarkana, say, or Lubbock. Not likely, but thorough was my middle name, and I needed to know that she was safe in the bosom of her family before I reported that fact to Beechum.

It was answered on the second ring, a gruff "Hello" that I recognized, that dumbfounded me for an instant, made me wonder if I had absentmindedly dialed the wrong number.

"Homer?"

"Who is—Dan?"

"Yeah, it's me. Damnedest thing. I thought I was dialing someone else. I must have punched out your number without knowing it. Christ, I must have jet lag." I laughed a silly little laugh. "But from Houston? Forty-five minutes?"

"Are you finished?" His voice contained a note of impatience, hint of belligerence.

"Sure. Sorry I bothered you."

"Who you calling?"

"I thought I was calling a guy named Peter Conrad to see if his wife made it back from East Texas. Okay? Sorry I disturbed you. No need getting all sweaty and sticky about it."

"You called Peter Conrad."

"Yeah, that's what I said. I thought I called—"

"No, Dan, you called the right number. I'm at the Conrad home. What's this about his wife?" His voice had subtly changed, rough and terse and all cop.

"You're at—what the hell are you doing at Conrad's house?" But I knew the answer to that already, or thought I did, and I felt something squirm its way downward to my stomach.

"Why don't you come on over here and we'll talk about it. Fifteen minutes, okay?"

"Hey, wait a minute, Homer, who—"

"Fifteen minutes, Dan, or I'll send a squad car to pick you up."

"Dammit, Homer, don't order me around! I'm not one of your—shit!" I hung up. Not much point in talking to an empty line.

Being friends with Police Captain Homer Sellers wasn't always easy. He seemed to grow more cantankerous each passing year, more intolerant of the shortcomings of others—particularly mine. Born and raised in the same small Texas town, we were about as different as two men can be and still be civil to each other. Big, shambling, often unkempt, he had broad blunt features to go with his oversize body, a heavy thatch of mudcolored hair that never lay in the same direction twice in a row. Obstinate, perverse, downright slovenly when he was drunk, he was a fair-minded cop, always there when you needed him—what more could you ask from a friend? He believed in America and motherhood, the Cowboys and the cops, and never understood the change in me after I came back from Vietnam, never quite forgave me for quitting the department.

And now, seated on the arm of a velvet couch in the white room at Peter Conrad's house, he stared at me as if he had never seen me before, blue eyes teary and bloodshot from new contacts, as testy as a bear with a thorn in its nose.

Beyond his bulk, through an open bedroom door, I could see occasional flashes of light as two cops I didn't know snapped pictures. Near the door another cop in plainclothes paced nervously, another stranger, young and broad shouldered and athletic. He snapped the plunger on a small silver pen as he walked, and I found out his name was Chester when Homer yelled at him to stop, threatened to slap his ass back into a squad car. That probably meant he was a new addition to Homer's homicide department. Five detectives and Mitsi.

Beyond that, I knew nothing. Because of Homer's presence, I assumed a murder had been committed. But since he hadn't seen fit to tell me, I wasn't going to ask. I could be as stubborn as he could. Besides, I wasn't sure I wanted to know.

"Damn thing that gets me," Homer said suddenly, his voice as scratchy as sandpaper on a bell, "is the way the bastard killed her, making her kneel that way, shooting her in the back of the head."

Her. I felt a sinking sensation in my chest. Sandra Conrad?

Chester stopped, snapped to attention. "Execution-style. Maybe it's mob connected.'' Behind him, in the other room, a vacuum cleaner began its raucous hum.

Homer gave him an impassive look. "Made her get in that bedroom closet, kneel down, and then shot her. Big caliber gun, looks like.''

I suddenly realized that in his convoluted fashion, he was trying to lure me into the conversation.

"Maybe she was hiding,'' I said.

Chester gave me an annoyed look. Homer pursed his lips. "What I thought, too." He stood up, crossed to the bedroom door. "You guys about finished in here? How about you, Doc?'' I heard a chorus of unintelligible answers.

I turned to Chester. "Have you identified—is it Sandra Conrad?''

The annoyed look became a frown. He shrugged.

"Not unless she's a young Mexican woman,'' Homer said from the door.

The knowledge brought no relief; the load simply shifted.

"Chester, why don't you run out to the car, call in, get the wagon out here? They'll be finished pretty quick. Doc says he can work her in this evening. You can go along, witness the autopsy. You gotta learn sometime.''

Chester left, some of the spring gone out of his step, tanned face a little paler.

Homer looked at me and grimaced. "Got a lot to learn, that boy. Shoulda known better'n to take somebody out of vice. Good vice people never make good homicide people. Don't know why. You wanta see her before we move her?''

I shook my head, then thought about it for a moment and changed it to a reluctant nod. "Maybe I should at that. There was a young Mexican woman here the day I came to see Conrad. Presumably the cook, but she wasn't

63

dressed like any cook I ever saw, and her makeup was smeared. Do you have the Conrads downtown?''

''Why do you ask that?'' He took a folded handkerchief out of his pocket and dabbed at his eyes. ''You think they killed her?''

''I don't think anything. This is their house. I don't see them anywhere. It's a logical conclusion.''

He grunted. ''It's a wrong one. We don't know where they are.''

''Who reported the murder?''

''Gardener stopped by to get his pay. He couldn't rouse anybody and the front door was standing open. He got excited and went to one of the other neighbors he works for. They called in. Uniforms checked around and found the girl.''

''What're you doing here?''

He shrugged. ''Shorthanded. Melrose is on vacation, Lynville's sick. Beckett and Simms are working a killing down on South Peachtree.'' He dabbed his eyes again and sighed. ''That left Chester.'' He unfolded the handkerchief and blew his nose, peering owlishly over his cupped fingers. ''Okay, little buddy, tell me how you're mixed up in this mess.''

''I'm not mixed up in anything, Homer. Sandra Conrad's grandfather hired me to find her. I trailed her to Irondale, then to her uncle's place outside Crater. He told me he put her on a bus last night. Peter Conrad was supposed to pick her up at the bus station. That's it. I called over here a while ago to make sure she made it home okay before I called my client.''

''You talked to Conrad? When was that?''

''Wednesday morning.''

''What'd he have to say?''

''He said she wasn't missing, that she had left with an old friend, boyfriend actually, for East Texas. A man

64

named Jacob Twill. Twill sent me to Sandra's uncle, Jonas Beechum.''

"*The* Beechums?"

I nodded. "Macomber Beechum is her grandfather."

He whistled softly through his teeth. "And Conrad didn't mind her going off with an old boyfriend?"

Before I could answer a tall, lean man in a stained white jacket came through the bedroom door. He carried a small black bag and had a lined, cynical face that wasn't meant for smiling, a face that had seen too many hard choices and wrong decisions. His gaze flicked over me without pausing and centered on Homer. He kept walking, lifting a long arm to tap Homer on the shoulder. "Walk me to my car, Captain. I don't have much time if you want that autopsy report tonight."

Homer nodded and fell in behind him. He paused at the door. "Why don't you take a look, Dan? They'll be moving her in a few minutes." He gave me a quick smile and ducked out the door. He knew well my feelings about viewing dead bodies.

I smoked half a cigarette before going in—nicotine courage—disposing of the butt in a potted plant outside the door. There were three men in the room instead of two, as I had thought. One of them I recognized, a short stocky redhead with dime-sized freckles and guileless green eyes. He was on his knees beside the bed, carefully snipping carpet strands into a small glassine envelope. He looked up, did a double take, then straightened, grinning.

"Hey, Dan Roman, what the hell you doing here? You back with us again?"

"Hello, Ted. Homer wanted me to take a peek at the . . . victim. See maybe if I know her."

"Sure thing." He scrambled to his feet and dropped the envelope into an open bag on the bed. He wiped his right hand on his pants leg and held it out. "How you doing,

65

buddy? Long time no see." His handclasp was firm and warm. We had been partners once.

"Good to see you, Ted."

We nodded and smiled again, a little embarrassed by our fondness for each other. It was all a part of the peculiar bonding that occurs between men who face a common danger together, who like, respect, and trust each other. When it works, it works well; when it doesn't, it can be disastrous. We had ridden the streets together for two years, made detective at about the same time, worked together again in Robbery several years later. He had made sergeant and moved into the tech squad, I had eventually become a lieutenant in Homicide.

I followed him across the large room. Fully as ornate as the white room, it was easier on the eyes and the spirit, gold-toned furnishings and soft brown-and-beige carpet, two full-size water beds, one of which was in wild disarray. A pair of Indian moccasins peeked from under one of the beds, and a beaded buckskin blouse was thrown carelessly across a velvet chair. A small stack of magazines were piled on the floor beside the disheveled bed.

The girl lay half-in and half-out of the closet, her body clenched into a tight fetal knot, hands still clasped atop the bouffant hairdo as if shielding her head.

"She's still in rigor," Ted Baskin said. "Doc Paris laid her on her side to check for lividity. She was scrunched up there in the corner on her knees, leaning against the wall, kinda."

"Hiding?"

"I'd say so, yeah. Killer opened the door. She was too scared to look up and the son of a bitch shot her in the back of the head. Maybe she knew he was going to, maybe she was praying—shit! Bastard ought to be hung up by the balls."

"How do you know it was a man?" I could see half

her face; the bouffant hairdo, now matted with dark co-agulated blood, was the same, as was the dress. It was the girl I had seen with Peter Conrad on Wednesday morning.

"We don't, not for certain. But he/she used a pretty damn big caliber handgun. Not the size a woman would generally use. A .45, most likely. Maybe a .357."

"You haven't found the slug?"

"Just pieces. It came out through her cheek, left a hole like a teacup. You wanta see? We can turn her over."

"Not necessary." I turned away and reached automat-ically for a cigarette.

He gave me a sympathetic grin. "Don't blame you. It's not a pretty sight. I doubt we'll find enough pieces to get a positive weight ID on caliber. It went into the concrete floor and ricocheted into the corner there, hit a metal stud brace and came apart. We found the main fragment, but it's flatter'n a gob of cold spit."

"We're finished, Sarge." A slender man in faded jeans, a T-shirt, and a Bell Helicopter gimme cap stood in the open doorway. A camera dangled around his neck and he carried a large metal container that looked like a fishing-tackle box. His partner, resplendent in the latest drugstore cowboy fashion, slouched silently nearby, his fat face shiny with sweat, blank with boredom, gleaming snakeskin boots crossed at the ankles, one beefy hand propped against the handle of a vacuum cleaner.

"Take off," Baskin said. "I'll hang around—" He broke off and looked at me. "Did the captain leave?"

"Went outside with the doctor. I think he's coming back."

He nodded and turned back to the doorway. The two men were gone. He shrugged and smiled at me. "Damn hard to get good men nowadays. Everybody's an individ-ualist, the Big I, upwardly mobile. They wanta work nine

67

to five and still get to wear a big gun to wow the ladies. Everything's different, Dan.''

"Same old song, different words. Remember how they used to call us college cops panty-boosters, nooky-raiders, hippie-dippies? Same old refrain, different generation.''

We moved toward the door. I stopped at the brown velvet chair and looked at the buckskin blouse. Holding it by the tips of the shoulder seams, I spread it out across the back of the chair.

"Nice blouse,'' Baskin said. "Don't see many anymore, not like that. You think it belongs to her?''

"No. I think it may belong to the lady of the house, Sandra Conrad.''

"Maybe I should take it along.''

"It wouldn't hurt. You might run a gunpowder residue test.''

His eyebrows lifted. "You think she mighta—''

"I don't think anything.''

He nodded and fingered the soft material. "Good job.''

"Handmade,'' I said, bending to study the multicolored beading worked unobtrusively into the shoulder patches. It looked almost exactly like the one Jacob Twill had been wearing. It was the answer to something I had been wondering about.

Sandra had made it home.

7

HOMER SELLERS ROCKED GENTLY, STARING IN DISGUST AT the beer I had just given him. He glanced up at me, a funny look on his face, eyes mellow and slightly fuzzy now that he had removed the contacts.

"Whatever happened to that good scotch you usta give me? What's this beer shit? You getting cheap in your old age?"

"Getting smart. Came to myself late one night and realized I'd been having an in-depth discussion with a lampshade." I sat down in the rocker-recliner across from him and lit a cigarette.

"No kidding? I didn't know you'd been drinking that much."

"I didn't either, and that was the problem."

He sampled the beer and grimaced. "Well, if you can drink it all the time, I can do it once." He turned and looked at the small bar across one corner of my den, empty shelves and a hammered silver ice bucket. A milk white vase with artificial flowers. "Don't look right," he grumbled. "Usta look forward to coming over here just to get a nip of that scotch."

69

"Finally it comes out. You were only using me." I took a sip of my own beer and tried to hide a shudder; the first taste is always the worst.

He laughed, a short vague guffaw that meant his mind wasn't on the conversation. He stirred and peered at me owlishly across the fireplace hearth.

"Well, whatta you think, Dan?"

"About what?"

"This Conrad thing. The Gomez girl. It don't make much sense."

"Murder never makes sense, Homer."

"Come on, you know what I mean. Doc Paris said she'd been dead sixteen to eighteen hours he thought. That puts it somewhere around midnight last night, give or take an hour. That's about an hour after your lady friend would've been arriving at the Dallas bus station. If Peter Conrad picked her up, and if they came straight home, they should've been there when it happened. If that's so, where the hell are they?"

"You're asking me?"

He gave me a sour look. "I'm talking it out, Dan. The way me and you usta do."

"That's fine, Homer, but I'm not a cop anymore."

"You didn't give up your brains with your badge, and you're in this right up to your buns."

"Not likely, old buddy. All I did was follow the lady. As soon as I can reach Beechum and make my report, this case is finished for me."

He cocked his leonine head and squinted. "How so? You don't know for certain that she made it home."

"Certain enough. That was her buckskin blouse on the chair, her moccasins under the bed. They were given to her while she was down in East Texas. She left wearing them."

70

His eyes glimmered, reflecting the dancing flames in the fireplace. "You're dead certain about that?"

"Well, nobody told me in so many words, but her uncle can confirm or deny it. He took her to the bus station."

He shrugged thick shoulders, a disconsolate look on his broad face. "We already done that, thanks to you. She was wearing them when she got on the bus. Her uncle said so. You know they don't have a phone? We had to get the sheriff to send out a car—"

"Then what's your problem? I'm satisfied she made it home. That's it for me. I didn't contract to make a career out of keeping tabs on her."

"That don't help me a damn bit. Where the hell is she? Where the hell is Conrad? I told you, it don't make any damn sense."

"You put out an APB?"

"Now, why didn't I think of that?" He took a long drink of beer and forgot to grimace. He stared into the fire. "Only thing I can think of, and it don't make much sense, is that Peter and Carlotta Gomez had been playing a little grab-and-tickle while his wife was gone. She found out about it—maybe found Carlotta asleep in the bed or something like that—and lowered the boom on her—"

"You're right, Homer, you don't have a sensible idea."

"What's wrong with it?"

"Couple of things. Carlotta didn't strike me as being stupid, just passive. And I don't think Sandra Conrad is the type to lower the boom on anyone."

"Come on, Dan. You know anyone can kill if they're provoked enough. We've already picked up rumbles that Conrad is a womanizer. Maybe this was the last straw."

"Then where are they?"

He grunted and drank more beer. "That's the rub. Maybe after she shot the girl, she turned the gun on him—"

"Where's the blood, the body?"

71

"She coulda made him get in the car, drove to somewhere remote. Maybe she turned the gun on herself afterward."

"If maybe's were gold doubloons, Homer, you'd be a wealthy man."

"Well, what's your theory?"

"I didn't say I had one."

"You've got one," he said confidently. "Does a snake pee in the grass?"

"Okay, suppose they did a little more than kiss hello. One of the beds was mussed up. Maybe they had a coming-home tussle and decided to go out to eat afterward. The Gomez girl was there alone. Maybe she went in to straighten up the bedroom, somebody came in on her— remember, we've had ten young women killed this past year—"

"Don't fit. She wasn't molested."

"—in this area alone. Serial killings in her age group. And not all of them were raped. At least they haven't said so in the papers. It's a possibility, Homer."

He made a show of looking at his watch. "Kinda late to be eating. Almost midnight. Here it is over twenty-four hours later, and they ain't home yet. That'd make it one of the longest meals in history."

"You didn't let me finish. Maybe they came home and found her, panicked, and took off—" I broke off. It sounded stupid even to me. "Forget it."

He pushed to his feet and stood watching me, grinning. "I believe I will, if you don't mind. That is, unless you can come up with something better. You've slowed some since you left the department, son."

"Haven't we all. Just doing what you always taught me, Homer. Considering all the possibilities."

He ignored the sarcasm, rocking gently on his heels, lips pursed, a faintly ludicrous figure in too-tight pants and striped shirt. I remembered what Mitsi had said. "You putting on weight, Homer?"

The thoughtful look dissolved into a scowl. I had probed a tender spot. He had never been touchy about his weight before. Female influence?

"You ain't exactly the Thin Man yourself," he growled. He gave me a critical look. "But, at that, you're thinner than you usta be. What're you running, about two hundred?"

"One-ninety. I've cut down on my fluid intake."

He laughed. "That'll do it every time." He shuffled a few feet toward the door, his shoulders slumped. "Christ, I'm tired."

I got up and followed him. "I'd suggest a search of the grounds, Homer. Looks like they have eight to ten acres. Lots of room to hide a couple of bodies."

He was too weary to bother with sarcasm. He nodded heavily. "Yeah, we already done some of that. We'll pick it up again in the morning. You gonna come over?"

"No thanks. I have a busy day planned."

He mustered a sardonic smile and opened the front door. "Yeah. Well, don't overdo it."

"Take it easy, Homer. I'll see you later."

"Yeah, later." He lifted a big arm and crossed the lawn toward his aged yellow Plymouth. "Don't forget. Support your local police."

I went back inside the house and into the kitchen. I took the unopened bottle of Jack Daniel's out of the cupboard and placed it in the center of the cherry wood dining table in the bay window. I sat down and stared at it, trying to decide if I really wanted a drink.

Dead bodies always made me want a drink—reaffirmation of life, I supposed. Sex had always made me want a drink, too, nearly as much as a cigarette.

I picked up the bottle and shook it, watching the tiny

bubbles, the sparkle of light in the dark liquid. Entrancing, but the problem was, one usually led to another . . . and so on.

The only way to fight something was to stand up to it, look it in the eye. My grandfather had taught me that a long time ago. He hadn't been talking about drinking, he had been talking about fear, cowardice, greed, the other things that come along to test a man's honesty, his courage, and mainly, the power of his will.

He'd been right, of course, my grandfather—he was always right—and over the years I had turned it into a game, a comic game to everyone but me, a way to test my own inner resolve.

Sometimes I won and sometimes I lost.

That night I won, but winning was getting harder all the time.

I was stowing the breakfast dishes in the dishwasher the next morning when I heard a car door slam out on my driveway. I dumped soap granules into the triangular slot, slammed the door, and punched the buttons. I reached the living-room doorway in time to see a shadow pass across the draped windows. One shadow. Someone wearing a cowboy hat. And cowboy boots. I could hear them cracking on the pebbled concrete walk. I crossed the room trying to think of someone I knew who wore a cowboy hat and boots. Offhand, I couldn't think of a one.

I was waiting in the entry-hall doorway when the door bell rang: four notes of "Moonglow," the theme from *Picnic*. My choice. My dead wife Barbara had wanted the theme from *Dragnet*.

I lit a cigarette and let the chimes chime again before I opened the door. Another small quirk of mine: never answer a phone or a doorbell on the first ring. It has something to do with fear of rejection, according to a local pop-psychology column in the newspaper. I've never been sure why. They dispense wisdom, they don't explain. Maybe that's why it's called pop psychology, after soda pop, popcorn, anything light and fluffy, or sticky sweet.

As I had suspected, he was a stranger, neatly turned out in a two-piece western-cut suit, tan with brown stitching across the pockets, a string tie with a chunk of turquoise as large as my palm. He wore four silver-and-turquoise rings, two on each hand, something that looked like a silver wedding band in his left ear. Reptile-skin boots. By the time I got around to the long handsome face, the sandy hair, and the colorless eyes, I already knew I wouldn't like him.

"Mr. Roman. My name is Claudell Beechum." He paused, as if waiting for applause. When I said nothing, did nothing, he went on: "You work for my grandfather, I believe—"

"Worked," I said. "Worked. The job is over. Your sister returned home Wednesday night. I relayed that information to Victor Starling over an hour ago."

He looked perplexed. "But we still don't know where she is."

I relaxed a little: the time for shaking hands was over. "Look, Mr. Beechum. Your grandfather hired me to locate your sister. He wanted to bring her back home. She returned of her own accord. That officially terminated my employment."

He shifted his feet, looked off across my lawn as my next-door neighbor, Hector Johnson, backed his pickup into the street. Hector honked the horn and waved. I waved back.

Claudell brought his pale eyes back to me. "I'll rehire you, then."

"No," I said.

Edward Mathis

He looked perplexed again, a little disconcerted. "Well, why not, may I ask?"

"The job is over, Mr. Beechum. And, right now, I expect your sister is a grade A number one suspect in a murder. An accomplice, at the very least. I don't get involved in murder cases."

He waved an imperious arm, his long face swollen with rage. "This whole thing is ridiculous! Sandy is a businesswoman, for Christ's sake! The top executive for Macomber Beechum Enterprises. Why would she kill some silly little Mexican girl—"

"I take it the police have been to see you?"

"Yes. A rude bastard named Simms and another one. They got me out of bed this morning. It soon became clear they think Sandy is involved in some way. It seems obvious to me that bastard husband of hers killed the girl and has done something with Sandy—"

"Why would Conrad kill the girl?"

"How the hell would I know? But it's the obvious conclusion. He was balling her. Everyone knew that except Sandy—"

"That doesn't make her look too smart, does it?"

"Who?" He looked startled.

"Sandy. If everyone knew it, then it must have been pretty obvious. I understand it had happened before—Conrad cheating, I mean. That kind of thing usually tends to make a woman more suspicious than not."

"Sandy's gullible about some things. Naive. She believed that bastard's song and dance about—"

"A savvy businesswoman like her?" I said, interrupting for the fourth or fifth time, something I didn't ordinarily do. But I was finding that my snap judgment had become a self-fulfilling prophecy; I didn't like Claudell Beechum worth a damn.

"Look, who the hell's side are you on, anyhow?"

76

"Nobody's side, Claudell. I'm what you might call a disinterested spectator at this point."

His eyes flashed angrily, the dull brown stain creeping back into his cheeks. He pushed the felt cowboy hat upward with a thumb and leaned forward, lips curling. "Would more money perk your interest?" His left hand slipped inside his jacket and slipped out again, holding a long black billfold. He flipped it open, exposing a sheaf of hundred-dollar bills. He leaned forward and riffled—actually fanned the damned things in front of my nose.

But even that wasn't as bad as the arrogant sneer, the condescending look on his equine face, his blithe assumption that his money would make the difference, send me into a fever sweat of helpless greed.

I smacked my lips ecstatically and he grinned.

I moved a little closer; he laughed.

I reached out and grasped his hat brim firmly on the sides, snapped downward smartly; the rough rider crease popped out as the crown rounded; Claudell's face disappeared all the way to his open mouth. I could barely see the silver earring.

"You probably didn't notice," I said, "but the sign there says no solicitors. Good-bye, Claudell."

I backed through the door and closed it on his one-handed struggle with the hat.

To give him credit, he didn't curse. Not even once. Not out loud.

No tolerance, I thought. Homer would say I had no tolerance.

Maybe he was right, but life was too short, time too precious. There were just too many good people to waste time on the fools.

8

MY FATHER DIED A DISMAL DEATH. DRUNK AND ALONE, frozen to death fifteen yards from the door of a hunting cabin he and I had built during my fourteenth summer.

A secret tippler for years—nothing heavy, never drunk—my mother's death when I was eighteen had set him off, loosed him like a blue tick hound on some wild and exotic scent. And he had never stopped running, or drinking, not until the tail wind of a Texas blue norther sucked the life out of him with its icy blast. Accident, or by design? Nobody ever knew for sure.

He had left no money, but he had bequeathed me other things: a deep respect for the law, a propensity for all things alcoholic, and four hundred acres of marginal woodland surrounding a cabin.

My feelings for the law, along with Homer Sellers's influence, had lured me into the cops, the same feelings that drove me away ten years later when I could no longer abide the faltering system. My liking for alcohol had long been a continuing problem in my life, and the four hundred acres of land had eventually brought me enough money from lignite coal that I could pick and choose my cases without consideration of fee, a measure of independence I cherished, a fact of life that allowed me to avoid defectives like Claudell Beechum.

But sometimes having a little money is like having a little knowledge, it makes you too hasty, too cocky, too quick to assume that you have a handle on your life, that you control your fate.

Arrogance and decisive action had worked well with Claudell Beechum. He had retreated quietly to lick his wounded ego and sulk, perhaps to vent his frustration and anger on some hapless employee.

But Claudell had been easy, a piece of cake, nothing at all compared with the Beechums who showed up on my doorstep a couple of hours later.

Two of them. Honey-toned skin and bright blue eyes—four of them. Black designer jeans and low-heeled shoes, yellow silk blouses. Rounded figures and breasts—more than their fair share. They had sweet oval faces and flashing smiles, a captivating sensuality that impinged on my senses before they said a word. Thick masses of wheat-colored hair rounded out the images they undoubtedly wanted to project. It all worked well for me.

"Mr. Roman?" Her voice was low and sultry, a faint hint of irrepressible sauciness beneath the surface. The other one watched, smiling, exuding charm.

"Yes, ma'am," I said. I had already guessed who they were; what I didn't know was what they were about.

"Our name is Beechum," the second one said. "I'm Hope and she's Mercy. You'll have trouble until you get to know us better." She didn't offer to shake hands.

"I'll be fine," I said, "as long as you don't change places." I stepped back a pace. "Would you like to come in?"

"Oh, yes," Mercy said. "That was the idea. We want to talk to you about our sister."

79

I ushered them into the den, keeping my eye on Mercy for purposes of identification. They settled on the couch, two petals from the same rose, exactly alike yet subtly different in some indefinable way.

"Did Claudell send you?" I settled into the rocker-recliner across from them.

"No," Mercy said quickly, gathering a handful of hair and flipping it back across her shoulder. "Claudie's a . . . a wimp. We came of our own accord. We talked to Granddaddy this morning and he told us you had quit your job—"

"I didn't quit. The job was over."

"No, it isn't," Hope said earnestly, leaning forward, blue eyes round and anxious. "We still don't know where she is, and it's even worse now with poor Carlotta dead like that. Something bad must have happened to her—to Sandy, I mean." Small brown hands lifted from her lap like startled doves, gathered at the impeccable lips.

"How could it hurt?" Mercy made a similar gesture, then allowed her hands to drift aimlessly back together in her lap. "You could still go on looking for her. It's very important, Mr. Roman."

"I'm sure it is. But you have to understand. Your sister is caught up in a murder investigation now, the police—"

"Oh, the police said it would be all right. Captain Sellers. He's in charge. We saw him this morning. He said it would be all right as long as you stayed out of his way." Mercy's face brightened.

"That's what he said, huh?" I tried to picture Homer saying no to anything these two proposed.

"Oh, yes," Hope rushed on, sensing victory. "He said that ordinarily he wouldn't tolerate a private detective nosing around, but that since he remembered you from the old days, he'd make an exception in this case."

"It's nice to be remembered," I said, buying time with a cigarette, getting away from bright predatory eyes, a force field of sense impressions overwhelming logic, subverting common sense.

"We can help," Hope said breathlessly. "We know all her friends. We'd do what you told us."

"Anything," Mercy added succinctly, her voice scaled down to low and sultry again.

They were overdoing the hard sell a bit, but somehow it didn't seem to matter. They were obviously deeply concerned with their sister's continuing disappearance and the undeniable fact that she was a prime suspect in the murder of her husband's lover. That was enough to make anyone act a little dingy, if in fact the twins needed prompting in that direction. And maybe I had acted a little hastily in closing out my case based on the circumstantial evidence of the buckskin jacket and the moccasins—and, of course, the dead woman. I felt a faint stirring of self-disgust. Had I let the murder scare me into quitting prematurely? I cleared my throat.

"All right. I'll talk with the police and see what they've come up with. Sandy's a suspect in a murder, and if I should find her I'll have to inform them."

"Of course," Mercy said. "We understand that, don't we, Hope?"

We looked at Hope. She nodded slowly and wet her lips. "Maybe you could let us talk to her first . . . for just a minute?"

"It may not be possible. It would depend on the circumstances."

Mercy nodded, clapped her hands, and stood up and stretched, high breasts pushing against the yellow fabric, full body limned by the glare from the patio door. She looked around the room. "You have a nice place, Mr. Roman."

"It's . . . okay," I said, feeling a little defensive, seeing it through alien eyes for the first time, the Sunday paper where I had thrown it on the fireplace ledge, overflowing ashtrays, a jumble of magazines on the floor by the chair I now occupied, beer cans on the end table, the coffee table—

"It could stand a good cleaning," Mercy said, a warm guileless smile on her face. "I take it you're not married."

I shook my head.

"No live-in girlfriend either," Hope said—a statement, not a question.

I shook my head again, wondering where this was leading.

"We'll come over and clean it up for you," Hope said, matching Mercy's warm smile. "You men." She stood up and linked arms with her sister.

"I have a woman comes in on Fridays," I said, and pushed to my feet.

Mercy grinned broadly. "Not this Friday, she didn't."

"Not for a couple of Fridays, I wouldn't think," Hope said and, as if by tacit agreement, they drifted apart and surrounded me, one on each arm. They walked me to the door.

"What can we do?" Mercy wanted to know, squeezing my arm like an old cherished friend.

"You can make up a list of her friends. Try to think who she would go to if she found herself in trouble; list those first. You could do the same for Peter."

"We don't know Peter's friends that well . . . we don't know Peter that well, either."

"It's more than likely that wherever they are, they're together."

"Why do you say that?" Hope squeezed the other arm. We stopped at the door and they crowded around in front of me, staring intently at my face; I felt like a breadstick engulfed in butterscotch mousse.

"It's logical," I said, easing out of their grasp and

opening the door. "We know her uncle put her on the bus, and we're almost positive her husband picked her up in Dallas and brought her home. The Gomez woman was killed around that time. It seems reasonable to assume a connection, and that they either left together or . . . or were taken."

"Taken? You mean kidnapped?" Mercy looked at her sister, lower lip caught between her teeth.

"You mean like for ransom?"

"I don't know. I'm only theorizing, but you see, we must consider all the possibilities." I was sounding more pompous by the second. A few more minutes and I'd be telling them how I caught mass murderer Angie Divorack all by myself—just to see the blue eyes widen, the delectable lips pucker with awe.

"We'll make up that list right away," Hope said, taking my right hand in both of hers. "And one of us will bring it over."

"If I'm gone, drop it in the mail slot in the door—"

"Oh, no," Mercy said, capturing my other hand. "We'll call first." She raised on tiptoe and kissed my cheek. "We'll have to get in to clean up."

I chuckled. "That really won't be necessary."

"Yes, it will," Hope said, kissing my other cheek. "That's part of the deal, isn't it, Mercy?"

Mercy nodded, smiling. "We always keep our bargains, Mr. Roman." She pressed my hand firmly, then turned it over and traced my palm with soft fingertips. "You have great hands, Mr. Roman."

"I noticed that, too," Hope said. "Big and strong."

"I take no credit," I said. "They came with the body."

They smiled politely and simultaneously released my hands, barely in time to prevent a sensory overload.

Momentarily disoriented, I stepped outside ahead of them, turned in confusion, and caught a glimpse of two low-slung cars parked end-to-end in my driveway. Porsches. Red with white stripes. Identical, as far as I could tell.

I turned back to the twins, no longer certain which was which. "Two cars?"

The one in front laughed. "We make each other nervous driving. We always go together, but we each like to drive. Besides, we never know when one of us might want to stay . . . somewhere." She wrinkled her nose, eyebrows cocked coquettishly.

"Makes sense," I said.

"It simplifies our lives," the other one said. "We don't have to worry about rides, breakdowns, and things like that."

We said good-bye again and I watched them trip lightly out to their cars. They drove sedately to the corner, stopped, made the turn, then let out the tiger, ripping the peaceful morning wide open with the scream of tortured rubber, the howl of whining engines.

I lit a cigarette and went back inside.

Kids will be kids, I thought fondly.

"How about Conrad's car, Homer? Is it missing?" I spooned a glob of chili into my mouth and held it immobile, waiting for the bite of the peppers. Blue fire seized my tongue, and my eyes began to water. I chewed cautiously.

Homer Sellers grunted and shook his head, grinding methodically on a chunk of hamburger and bun, a limp strip of fried potato. He took a drink of tea and swallowed.

"Nope. He's got one of them little BMW's and a Fleetwood. They're both in the garage."

"How about the woman's? Maybe he drove her car to the bus station."

"Nope again. She's got a Ferrari. It's there too."

84

I quenched the fire with a taste of tea. "That makes you wonder a little?"

He took another bite of hamburger and talked around it. "Just a tad."

"And?" I tried another spoonful of chili; it hardly burned at all.

"And what?"

"And what's your conclusion?"

"Don't know as I've come to any conclusions. I've got an opinion." He waved down a roving waitress carrying a large pitcher of tea, gave her a benevolent smile as she filled his glass. "Don't get too far away, honey, I like lots of tea."

"Yes, sir," she said and drifted away without an appreciable change of expression.

Homer looked after her, a baffled look on his broad face. "I don't understand women nowadays. You can't even be friendly."

"You called her honey, Homer. That's a sexist term."

"Honey? How can that be sexist? Women call men honey all the time."

"That may be, but some women think it's condescending, sorta like calling a grown man boy."

"Hell, I call you boy all the time." He looked up and grinned. "Does that bother you?"

I shrugged. "What's your opinion, Homer?"

"I don't think it does. You know I don't mean anything—"

"I'm not talking about that and you know it. What's your opinion on how the Conrads disappeared?"

He chewed on the last morsel of hamburger, his gaze absently following the waitress around the room. After a while, he swallowed, washed it down with tea.

"You know the answer to that as well as I do. They didn't just walk off, or fly. So there had to be someone

85

Edward Mathis

else involved. Somebody with a vehicle. Elementary stuff. So far we haven't come up with anybody, neighbors or anybody else, who saw another vehicle. Far apart as them houses are, all the woods and everything, I'd be surprised if we did. People around there tend to mind their own business, for one thing. They're kinda preoccupied with their own selves. People with a lot of money are like that.''

''You didn't turn up anything on the grounds search?''

''If you mean dead bodies, no. But we haven't finished it yet. Conrad has ten acres there, most of it in woods. It's a pain in the ass.''

I stirred the chili, undecided about another bite. ''The buckskin blouse. Anything there?''

He poked the last limp french fry in his mouth and gave me a bleary look, blue eyes swimming in moisture. He unfolded his napkin and dabbed at each one tenderly.

''Funny thing about that blouse. Good idea you had about gunpowder residue test. How come you thought about that?''

''Just a hunch, Homer. Why not? It never hurts to fish. Are you saying it was positive?''

He squinted, lips pursed. ''Nope, not a trace.''

''How about the Gomez woman? Anything there?''

''We're checking family and friends, ex-boyfriends. Doesn't seem to be a current boyfriend. Maybe Conrad had the market cornered for a while. No record on the girl. Mexican national with a card. Been around a couple of years. Good family in Mexico City. Spoke excellent English, I understand.''

''Yes, she did.''

''Hell, I don't know. Maybe you had the right idea there at first, a random killer working this area. Maybe he got scared off before he could rape her or whatever.''

''Dumb idea, Homer. Where are the Conrads?''

He glowered at me. ''Well, that could fit too. He musta

86

had transportation. You don't walk around in that area, not for long. So if he had transportation, he coulda taken the Conrads with him. Who the hell knows? Maybe he dumped them somewhere, dead. Or he might be holding them, waiting awhile before trying for ransom.''

"Sounds good to me. Hang on to that thought." I stood up and placed one finger on the bill lying in the center of the table. "Let me get this."

"Sure," he said readily, and looked up at me and grinned.

"One of these days you're going to fool me and I'm going to flat out have a heart attack." I picked up the bill and dug into my pocket for a tip.

He threw up a hand. "No, let me get the tip," he said grandly, standing up and producing a crumpled wad of bills. He selected a one-dollar bill and dropped it on the table. He drank the last of his tea, then glanced toward the waitress with the tea pitcher. An odd expression crossed his face. Without looking at me, he dipped into his pocket again, came up with a palm full of loose coins. He selected one, dropped it on the table, and picked up the dollar bill.

He came around the table before I could react, herded me toward the cashier.

"What the hell was that, Homer?"

"A nickel. Now that, by God, is sexism."

9

Some weeks there are days when I don't have a visitor. Lazy days when I catch up on my reading, hit a lick or two out in the yard, lounge around on the patio and watch my three resident squirrels caper about in the trees. Tranquil days, restorative but dull. Sunshine, a beer now and then, a great deal of quiet introspection.

Friday, March 15, was not one of those days. Before my early lunch with Homer Sellers, I had already had three visitors: Claudell Beechum and the scintillating twins, Mercy and Hope.

My fourth visitor was waiting for me, squatting on his heels beneath one of my oaks, his mud-spattered, battered, three-quarter-ton Dodge pickup disgracing my driveway.

Victor Starling. Lean as a hickory limb, probably as tough. An inscrutable face that remained expressionless as I parked the Ramcharger and nodded at him through the open window.

He nodded back and rose effortlessly to his feet, neat and trim in a denim suit and a pale blue western shirt. His hat rode squarely on his head, a cream-colored Stetson, flat crowned and narrow brimmed. He looked younger than he had before; I attributed it to the city clothes, a different environment. I had guessed his age at sixty-five the first time; now I wasn't sure.

I took my time getting out of the pickup, lighting a cigarette, wondering about the reason for his visit. I had made my report to him over the phone, and we had agreed that my job was finished. Now he was here, only a few hours later. Something had changed. What?

"Howdy," I said, using a word I hadn't used since I once made a trip to New York City to pick up a prisoner.

"Mr. Roman," he said. He met me halfway and we gripped hands briefly. He stepped back and slipped a long-fingered hand inside his jacket. He extracted a white envelope and held it out. "Your fee," he said tersely.

"Well . . . thanks, but you didn't have to bring it to me. The mail would—"

"I know, but I was coming to Midway City, and anyway, a man likes to get what's owed him. The mails aren't always too reliable."

"That's a fact." I took a step toward the house. "Come on in, Mr. Starling. I'll see if I can't scare us up a beer or something."

"No, thanks," he said politely. "I only stopped by to deliver your money." He paused and smiled. "And to confirm something the twins told me earlier this morning." The smile broadened into a grin. "That they had hired you to continue the search for Sandra." The grin lit up the somber face, revealed a surprising depth of emotion, a hint of inexplicable glee.

"Yes . . . well, it isn't all that cut-and-dried. I told them I would talk to the Midway City police and do what I could to help. It's probably a waste of my time and their money. The police are looking for her—along with her husband—and they outnumber me fifty to one. Even if I

89

found her, there's still the Gomez woman's death to contend with.''

''If they think she did that, they're crazy. I realize the police have to work with what they find, what they can see, but Sandra isn't the killing kind. If she was, she'd have killed that husband of hers a long time ago.''

''How long have they been married?''

''Five years or thereabouts. And he's cheated on her almost from the beginning.''

''I don't understand that. She isn't dumb. She couldn't be and run the Beechum companies. Is she blinded by love? Someone said she was naive. I find that hard to believe, also.''

''No, she isn't dumb. She knew, I think, almost from the start. I just don't think it mattered to her all that much.'' He took off the hat and turned it slowly, smoothing the soft inside band. ''I don't believe she ever loved him.''

''Then why keep him around?''

He shrugged. ''He's good at what he does. He was head of accounting at MCB when Sandra met him. She made him a vice president in charge of administration. He's done a good job.''

''So could a thousand other men.''

A smile as thin as a rapier slash crossed his lips. ''I gave up trying to understand women a long time ago.''

''I'm still working on it,'' I said.

He turned his face toward me, the glimmer of humor back in the dark eyes. ''What did you think of the twins, Mr. Roman?''

''I'm not sure how to answer that, not sure that I should try. I don't know them well enough.''

''As women, I mean. As sex objects, shall we say, since that seems to be their primary goal in life.''

"If that's their goal, I think they're ready for graduation."

He laughed dryly, a sneaky, lascivious laugh that somehow surprised me. Had I been wrong about him? Was he just another dirty old man, after all, a closet lecher?

His next words dispelled that notion. "If they were mine I'd cut them off. Not one more cent until they straightened out, got married, had some kids, settled down." He slapped the hat back on his head, the narrow face rigid with righteous indignation. "Mac's always been too easy on his family, gave them too much, trusted them too much, and it's damn near been the ruination of him. Ever since his stroke ten years ago, when he thought he was going to die and turned everything over to Miles, it's been all downhill—" He broke off, his weathered face looking older again, and paler. "But that's his business, his money," he said sharply, as if rebuking me for prying.

"Right," I said. I took out a cigarette and lit it, wondering where he fit into Macomber Beechum's life, wondering at the edge of bitterness in his voice.

"I've been with him thirty years," he said, as if reading my thoughts. "Thirty damn years, good and bad, thick and thin. His right-hand man, the only one he could ever trust all the way. I've done things . . ." His voice faded and he made the knife-slash smile appear again. "Them kids don't know anything. Not even Sandy, and she's the smartest of them all."

"Smarter than her dad?"

His head inclined slowly. "Smarter than her dad, yes. Miles was smart, but he was a gambler, reckless. The whole thing was a big game to him, and he fancied himself a master player. Something was missing in Miles." He stared past me, down the curving street to the small park a city block away, his dark eyes widening as if with dawning knowledge. "All of them. All of them except the old

91

man. Something missing . . .'' He looked back at me, his face as tight and hard as it had been the first time I saw him, the black eyes flat and emotionless. ''And he turned it all over to them—first Miles, then Sandy, and now . . .'' He let it drift again, something like a shiver rippling through the slender body. He stood up straight, buttoned his coat, touched his hat, and moved the thin lips in a tortured smile. ''I'm glad you've reconsidered, Mr. Roman. Don't worry about your money. If the twins don't pay you, I will.''

''I'm not worried,'' I said. ''And I'm also not sure there's anything I can do.''

''Please try,'' he said, and crossed the short strip of grass to the driveway and his decrepit pickup.

He drove off without looking at me again, without waving. I watched him go, feeling an odd kind of detachment, a vague sense of déjà vu. So far I had met five of the Beechums and, other than a definite lack of class, a certain amount of eccentricity, I had not found them much different from other wealthy people I had met.

But maybe that was my fault, a lack of insight. It was a melancholy notion, and I went inside wondering if I should consider another profession after all, something simple and mundane and having nothing to do with people. Sheepherder was the only thing that came to mind.

I passed through the den on my way to the kitchen and a beer. The red light on my phone answering system was blinking. I flipped the review button, turned up the sound, and went on to the refrigerator. I was pulling the tab on a can of Coors when Homer's rumbling bass came on the line.

''In case you're interested, little buddy, I just got a call from Simms out at the Conrad place. They found a body in an old well on the back of the property. A man. Matches the description of Peter Conrad. It's one o'clock and I'm just leaving, so if you want—'' The end of the cycle cut him off. I let it run, but he didn't come back on again.

I reset the machine and sat on the arm of the couch for a moment staring at the fireplace, an accumulation of charred ends and dead ashes.

Peter Conrad. Dead. Alone. If Sandra had been found with him, Homer would have told me. I felt a curious prickling along the back of my neck, up behind my ears.

Sandra Conrad. A killer after all? First her husband's lover, a cold-blooded execution. Then her husband, just as coldly, perhaps. Marching him at gunpoint through the blackness of the woods . . . Was that the way it had happened? Undoubtedly. He would have been too heavy for her to carry and, besides, they had found no other signs of violence in the house or surrounding grounds. Sweet, sensible Sandra. A depth of determination no one had suspected. Determination and . . . what?

I felt a shiver work its way along my nerve endings, crawl across my back to nestle at my spine. Women were gentle creatures, givers of life, nurturers—not killers.

I shook myself like a hound on a riverbank and chugalugged the rest of my beer.

I glanced at my watch: one-twenty.

Plenty of time.

But I had reckoned without the heavy Friday afternoon traffic, the propensity of normally sensible human beings to become daredevils behind the wheel of a car. A five-car pileup on the Airport Freeway. Caught between exits, on an overpass, there was nothing I could do but shut off the Ramcharger's engine, get out, and exchange platitudes with other indignant motorists, our eyes shiny, voices high with the secret relief that we were only spectators in today's passion play on our highway.

It took forty-five minutes of apparent chaos, harried cops and tow-truck drivers, three ambulances and a fire truck standing by. Gobs of people coming from everywhere. Word flashed up the line; two dead, a half-dozen injured. Enough blood to start a bank.

We looked at each other and shook our heads. Damn fools didn't know how to drive. Probably some wild-ass kid started it, or some old man too old to be driving, some old lady too feeble to handle today's machinery—more likely, though, there was a drunk somewhere in the pile. Drunks cause 50 percent of all accidents, you know. We clucked our tongues and looked innocent.

They finally got it sorted out. We mounted up, revving our engines and driving slowly past the awesome spot, glittering bits of glass and a piece of metal or two, firemen hosing down the blood, their faces impassive, policemen waving at gawkers, their faces irate and impatient. All in a day's work. Move along, stupid.

By the time I reached the Conrad estate in Sunnyvale they were cleaning up their own little tragedy. The cop on the gate passed me through a small group of onlookers, several of whom had press cards dangling around their necks. A Channel 5 mobile-unit truck crowded one edge of the wide driveway and a tall man carrying a video camera stooped and blazed away at my stern visage—just in case I turned out to be somebody.

I parked where the cop had told me, alongside two green-and-white prowl cars, empty, their lights still circling lazily, motors chugging. The house was thirty yards off to my right, stately and graceful among the towering elm and stunted oak. Straight ahead I could see movement through a parklike expanse of trees, the short-nosed boxy frame of an ambulance wending a tortuous path through the woods, Homer Sellers's ancient yellow Plymouth not far behind.

I got out and lit a cigarette. A smell of burning oil wafted by, the sound of a rumbling belch as one of the police cars loaded up and backfired sluggishly. I walked around my truck and turned off the motors of both cars, flicked off the lights. There were sometimes good reasons for leaving a patrol car running unattended; offhand I couldn't remember what they were.

The ambulance picked up speed as it reached the black-top driveway, went by me with a noisy susurrus of tires, a puff of smoke as the motor shifted up.

Homer pulled up across from me, gave me an annoyed, crabbed look, then turned to say something to the man riding with him. They exchanged nods and climbed out. Homer looked at him across the dingy yellow roof.

"Appreciate your help, Mr. Haskell. Don't you want me to have someone run you on back home?"

Mr. Haskell lifted a long hairy arm. "No, no, Captain. I need the exercise. Glad to be of service." He gave me a cheery grin and a nod and pumped his legs up and down a few times as if priming his body for action. "Just a nice short run." Sixtyish, dressed in tennis shorts, he had thinning silver hair and knobby knees, a concave chest with a dense mat of hair that bulged his T-shirt like the padded crotch of a rock-and-roll star. He bounced up and down a couple more times, grinned, waved, whirled, and scampered off across the pedicured lawn.

"Titus Haskell," Homer rumbled. "Neighbor. Gave us a temporary ID on Conrad. Belongs to the same country club. Played handball with him a lot, chess, like that."

"Hate to see a grown man grieve like that," I said. "Sad thing to watch."

He brought back the crabbed look. "What the hell, Dan? Some men don't show things. Anyhow, you're a good one to talk. The Sphinx ain't got nothing on you." He pulled a plastic-tipped cigar out of his shirt pocket and stripped off the cellophane. "Where the hell you been, anyway?"

"Watching your stalwart minions referee today's game of freeway pinball."

"Another wreck, huh? Well, we're due; it's been a couple of days." He lit the cigar with a kitchen match and flipped it onto the yellowish green lawn. He squinted at me through a rising cloud of smoke.

"Two," he said, as if in answer to a question. "One right through the old kazoo—" He reached out a stubby finger and prodded my chest in the vicinity of my heart. "And one right about here." He stabbed the finger between his eyes. "Either one woulda done the job, but our killer wanted to make sure, I guess. We kinda figger she shot him in the heart first, then when he didn't fall as fast as she thought he should, she followed up with the head shot. Maybe not. Maybe there was a lot of rage and one wasn't enough."

"She?"

"Slip of the tongue," he said blandly, sucking on the cigar. "Just seems natural somehow to say *she* under the circumstances. Whatta you think?"

"I don't think anything, Homer. I don't know what happened. You want to tell me?"

He nodded soberly, thumbing the corner of each moist eye, then leaning against the Plymouth and folding his beefy arms.

"Some things we know and some things we're guessing at. One thing we know is that she—or somebody—marched him down from the house to the well. Barefoot. His feet were all beat up, cuts and scratches, looked like saw briers and maybe some thornbushes. Anyhow, barefoot, and in his pajama bottoms. Hands tied behind his back. Tight. Doc didn't take them off, but you could see the swollen flesh, discolored, even a little blood where he musta tried to get loose. The killer walked him to the well, took off the cover, and made him sit on the edge of the housing. Or maybe just kinda lean, since it's only about three feet high. Then she shot him.''

"What kind of well, Homer? I thought wells were small drilled holes with pipe—''

"An old well, that's what kind. The kind they usta dig before they invented drilling rigs, I reckon, or unless you couldn't afford a drilling rig and wanted to dig your own. Way they explained it to me, you start off with a three-foot-diameter tile, three feet high. You set it where you want the well, get inside, and start digging. The tile drops as you dig, and when it's even with the ground you pile on another one. And so on until you get water. Sounds simple, but it's damn hard work. Anyhow, it was about forty feet deep, three feet or so of water in the bottom. Conrad went in backward, all doubled up. Top of his head and his feet were all that was showing above the water.''

"Time of death?''

"Educated guess from Doc Paris puts it somewhere around the time the Gomez woman got it.'' He sneezed, then produced a handkerchief and blew his nose lustily, the blue eyes glistening at me over his cupped fingers. "Now whatta you think?''

"How can you be so sure he was shot at the well?''

"Blood patterns on the surrounding bushes and grass, on the well cover itself. Both slugs went through clean— well, not clean, but they went on through and they left tracks.''

"You didn't find them.''

"We will,'' he said confidently. "Ted Baskin was plotting trajectory on Simms when I left. Unless they ricocheted off somewheres, Ted'll find them.''

"Big caliber?''

"Looks like it. Paris thinks so, and so does Ted. I ain't

no ballistics expert, but that's how I saw it, too." He fell silent and went back to puffing on his cigar. I could feel his eyes, knew without looking that the makings of a sardonic smile would be edging his lips. He was as predictable as next year's utility hike, and usually just as frustrating.

I lit another cigarette, feeling the prickling on the back of my neck again, trying to understand what human emotion could sustain such an arrogant, methodical taking of life. Hatred? Rage? Fear? Love? Any one, or all, I thought, plus there was simple greed, self-preservation, pride . . . the list went on.

"You think she did it? You think she killed both of them?"

He made a one-shoulder shrug. "I'm tilting in that direction."

"That brings us back to one of the same problems as before. How did she leave? You think she just walked out of here carrying her handgun? It's at least two miles to a store, Homer, or a service station, and I'm sure you've covered all of those already."

"That we have, and nobody saw her. But that don't mean she didn't have some help, somebody with a vehicle. Maybe she called someone from the house and they come picked her up."

It was entirely possible, even likely, and I knew it. Claudell and the twins lived in Midway City, only minutes away; Victor Starling and Macomber Beechum, perhaps forty-five minutes at that time of night. Plenty of help within a reasonable period of time. Perhaps a friend, someone I'd never heard of. But on the other hand, how many people could you trust to aid and abet a double murder? Unless, of course, they weren't aware at the time that the murders had been committed. Another thought came booming in: why would the Beechums hire me again if any one of them had been involved in aiding Sandy?

"By the way," Homer said. "We have a woman who heard the shots. A widow woman named Elsie Conagle lives on the adjoining property to the east. She told us the other day she heard two shots sometime Thursday morning early, around one o'clock. We didn't pay much attention since there was only one shot in the Gomez killing and chances of her hearing that were pretty slim. But now with Conrad killed it begins to make some sense. We'll have to talk to her again." He pushed away from the Plymouth and ran a hand through his unkempt hair. "You wanta run down and see the well?"

"I don't think so, Homer, I wouldn't want to get in your way, take advantage of your good nature just because you remember me from the old days."

He gave me a startled look, then slowly formed a grin. "Them twin dollies been to see you, huh? Ain't they something? Made me feel young just looking at them."

"Mid-life crisis, buddy. Next thing you know you'll be wearing designer jeans and chains, driving a BMW, and blow-drying your hair."

"I tried that blow-drying shit," he said glumly, fingering a swatch of hair. "It just made it look worse."

"I doubt that," I said, and dodged away from a descending arm. I crossed the driveway to my truck. He followed, smiling amiably.

"They got you to change your mind, huh? Hired you back?"

"Yep," I said, and climbed inside the truck. "But don't expect me to help you. With your mind-set on this thing, it'd be too much like bounty hunting. I'm not going to find her just so I can turn her over to your tender care."

The smile broadened. "That's assuming you can find her."

"Oh, I can find her. If she's alive and not stuffed in some other well somewhere."

The smile vanished, segued into an irritated frown. "You really believe that's the case, or are you being your usual ornery self?"

"What I believe doesn't matter, Homer. It's all pure conjecture at this point, anyway. You don't have a single scrap of physical evidence linking her to the murders."

"We've got the deerskin blouse and the moccasins—"

I interrupted him with a shake of my head. "That doesn't prove a thing and you know it. The only thing the blouse proves is that she was here sometime during the night, and even that isn't beyond-a-shadow-of-a-doubt conclusive."

"I have to go with what I've got, Dan. Right now I've got nothing that proves she was taken out of here by force. Dammit, it's a classic triangle, wife and lover and husband. The husband and lover wind up dead. Guess who's left. Even Chester knows that much and he's dumb as pig fat."

I climbed into the pickup and closed the door. We looked at each other through the tinted glass. I rolled it down. He stood scowling, hands on his hips, a disheveled Sidney Greenstreet, the weeping blue eyes giving him a curiously vulnerable look.

"You know what your problem is, Homer? Well, I'll tell you. You've got about as much imagination as a stump." I started the engine, regretting not so much my words but my tone of voice. I smiled to take the sting out of it. "Happy hunting, Sherlock." I let the Dodge ease forward.

"Quitter!" He spat the word at me like an epithet, but an epithet without rancor, only regret. For a while there it had seemed like the old days, the two of us working together the way we used to, using each other as a sounding board, talking it out, bickering, but more times than not coming up with something significant to the case, a new direction, sometimes a solution.

I understood his feelings, sympathized with them, a sort of low-grade nostalgia. But every profession has its limitations, its laws. Mine had only two important ones, and they were self-imposed: don't take people where they don't want to go, and don't fool around with murder.

So I was breaking my own rule in searching for Sandra Conrad, suspected killer. But what the hell, rules were made to be broken, as they say, and I was far from convinced of her guilt.

When the time came, if it ever did, I could always back off and leave her to the tender mercies of the law, let the will of the people have its way.

But in order to find her I had to know where to start looking, and to know where to start looking I had to be absolutely, positively certain that she had in fact rode home from East Texas on a Continental Trailways bus.

10

It took an hour of my time, a drive to Dallas, and thirty dollars to learn the bus driver's name and address. James Bishop Parleigh. A tall rotund man with patent-leather black hair, a bristling mustache, and gold-flecked green eyes shot with blood.

He lived in a production-line frame house in Oak Lawn that had a concrete porch with wrought-iron railings, twin gables, a steeply pitched roof, and a drooping TV antenna guyed with wires.

I found him half-asleep on a combination glider-lounge on his front porch, a can of Coors clutched in one long-fingered hand, a soggy unlit cigar in the other. He wore shapeless cotton pants and a multicolored sport shirt with two buttons missing and a frayed collar. He had splotches of freckles everywhere there was skin showing, and a brown-speckled, disarming smile.

He was a widower, he said, that's why he dressed so sorry, why he hadn't shaved since he got in off his run. No point to it no more. His three grown boys were off gallivanting around the country and his girls never come to see him, anyhow. He had five more years to retirement,

102

and then he was going to sell this mother and move to Florida, California, someplace like that where he could lay on the beach in the sun and not get sun cancer like you did in this damn Texas state. Did I know that freckles were a form of cancer, that most women freaked out over a freckled dong?

"No, I didn't know that," I said. "How nice for you."

He chortled and slapped a thigh. "It's a fact. It fascinates them."

He went on to tell me that he had seniority now and could just about pick his runs, that he had a pretty nice stash of money in the bank, some CD's, and was thinking about opening one of them IRA's for retirement. Man couldn't have too much money when he retired if he wanted to live halfway decent with a nice mobile home and maybe a new Ford or Chevy.

I agreed with all of that and showed him the picture of Sandra Conrad. "Do you ever remember seeing this woman before?"

He studied the photo for a moment, his lips pursed, eyes narrowed. "Man, I'm not sure. I see so many . . . She supposed to be one of my passengers, or what?"

"I was hoping you could tell me."

"She looks kinda familiar, but, man, I just don't know—"

"Try picturing her in a buckskin blouse, deerskin with fringe on the arms and patches of different colored beadwork across the front of—"

"Hey, yeah! Houston to Dallas. Last Wednesday. Yeah, sure, I remember. I picked her up somewhere north of Houston, Spring, I think it was, the stop at the Dixie Queen restaurant. Had a kinda yellow scarf on her head. Only picked up three, four passengers. Yeah, this lady was one of them, all right. Real friendly, too. Had a ticket to Dallas."

"You're sure it was her?"

"Oh, yeah. Long black hair, pretty. We talked a minute about the schedule. I said something about her blouse, and she said it was a gift from a very dear friend. She turned so I could see the fringe on back and everything. You don't see them kind of clothes much anymore."

"About what time would that have been?"

He closed one eye and chewed thoughtfully on the cigar, spat a bit of tobacco over the railing. "Had to be eight-thirty or thereabouts. Yeah. We was due in Dallas at twelve-thirty, and I don't never miss my schedule by much." He took a drink of beer, made a face, and set the can on the porch railing. "Hot. Say, I ain't being very neighborly. You want a can of beer?"

"No, thanks. Did you make your schedule?"

"Right on the button," he said proudly. "I ain't never off mor'n a couple of minutes either way—barring a jam-up on the highway, that is."

"Do you remember seeing her at the Dallas station, someone picking her up, maybe?"

His face screwed up again. "No, I didn't. Funny thing. I was just thinking here a minute ago, I ain't all that sure she went all the way to Dallas. I sure didn't see her there and I usually stand by the door until most everybody is off. I like to thank them for riding with me, you know; it's good public relations and the company tells us to do it anyhow—"

"How about her luggage? Wouldn't it have been in the storage bin?"

"She didn't have any as I remember. Just one of them tote bags like some women carry, you know, everything in it but the kitchen sink. She kept that with her."

"Maybe she fell asleep on the bus, or waited until everyone was off."

"Well . . . it's possible, I guess. I don't always wait on

the stragglers. Some of them take all day getting off. The old ones, usually, creeping along . . .'' His voice faded and he shifted positions on the lounge. ''I was just trying to remember the last time I saw her—Corsicana, I think. We had a ten-minute stop. I saw her out on the sidewalk talking to some woman. Not one of the other passengers, at least I don't think it was. Probably somebody waiting on another bus.''

''What did she look like?''

He passed a hand across the stubble on his jaw. ''I just flat don't remember. Just some woman. Fairly young, I think. I didn't pay much attention. Wouldn't have noticed her at all, probably, if it hadn't been for her blouse. It looked a whole lot like the one your lady had on.''

''Buckskin?''

''Well . . . I couldn't swear to it. Them windows are tinted pretty heavy and I didn't get a good look. It just looked like about the same thing. Maybe they was comparing them or something.''

''You don't remember seeing her after that?''

''No, I don't. But that don't mean much. I was in the john when they loaded up for Dallas. We picked up eight or ten more passengers. We was loaded by then, every seat taken and some young guys standing. Don't usually allow that no more, but they was only going to Ennis.'' He handed me the picture, a quizzical look on his round face. ''This lady your wife or girlfriend or something?''

''Or something,'' I said. ''She's not where she's supposed to be.''

He nodded. ''Probably run off somewheres. Women do that all the time nowadays. Kids too. Men always have.'' He shook his head. ''Man, I can remember times when the kids was little, eight mouths to feed on a bus driver's salary. I thought about taking off many's the time. Just packing it in, taking off, and starting all over somewheres.

105

Jesus. Then I'd think about them six little kids, my old lady, and I couldn't do it. I ain't been much of a success, maybe, but we didn't miss a whole lot of meals.''

''Success is a matter of opinion,'' I said. ''Getting by can be success. Depends on where you start.'' I put away the picture and stood up. ''If you raised six kids, Mr. Parleigh, you don't have to stand short around any man.''

We smiled at each other and shook hands. I thanked him and left, trying to think how it must have been living in a house with six small children. Constant cacophony. Fights and tantrums and fingerprints on the walls. Odd odors and obscure diseases, hungry mouths.

It sounded terrible but probably wasn't. As an only, lonely child, I had no conception of life in a large family beyond my imagination, beyond the movies and TV sitcoms where all the kids were cute and witty and solved grown-up problems by the end of the last commercial.

I had been raised on a working ranch with the usual complement of animals, a half-dozen ever-changing ranch hands, and deeply religious parents who never seemed to understand that little kids need love more than theological doctrine, need demonstrations of affection more than Christian piety and discipline.

Not that they had been unjust, or abusive, or even mean. They were reserved and noncommunicative, repressive by virtue of their own strict upbringing. I was born ten years into their marriage, a startling, disruptive development, and they never seemed to recover, never quite understood that I had unique emotional and physical needs not readily fulfilled by twice-weekly injections of religion.

The cowboys taught me about life, each in his own fashion, and it wasn't at all surprising that I grew up with somewhat distorted, if quixotic, views of a man's role in the scheme of things. Cowboys are loners, dreamers, fiercely independent, and prideful to a fault. They work long and hard, a killing pace that spits out greenhorns like confetti and tolerates neither malingerers nor fools for very long.

As a result I was lost for years between their ideas of the world and what I perceived it to be, a gray area as diffuse as the dead zone between daylight and dark. Eventually I came to understand that life was nothing more than a complicated mosaic of personal triumphs and tragedies, of chance encounters and random couplings, and that we no more controlled our fate than the rabbit ruled the hound. The road was already there, the course charted; about the best we could do was give it a nudge once in a while, try our best to keep from crossing the center line.

I drove home across Dallas only partially satisfied. Parleigh's identification rang true, but his knowledge was limited. I still didn't know for certain that she had been picked up at the Dallas bus station by Peter Conrad. A logical assumption but, like most logical assumptions, not based on irrefutable fact.

It was beginning to look, I thought glumly, like the only way I could find out was to locate Sandra Conrad and ask her.

I ate steak for dinner. Charcoal-broiled porterhouse and baked potato. Lettuce. Green onions and Italian bread. Corn on the cob and butter, real butter. Iced tea. A simple meal, one of my favorites, one we had had often during the years before my wife and my son had died.

Barbara had died at thirty-three, the victim of a leukemic-type cancer that had developed almost without warning, escalated to a critical stage with unbelievable speed. One of life's calamities, death's unexpected gambit in a game that man can never hope to understand.

Tommy had died a year later, at fourteen. Tall and straight, handsome in a way his father had never been, he had solved his problem with life by smashing it against a bridge abutment on a lonely county road. Two boon companions, a stolen car, and one too many hits of speed. He had lost his way chasing hallucinogenic dreams; I had almost lost mine chasing the man who had sold him the drugs. Police brutality is what they had called it and, for once, they had been right. The dealer didn't complain; he felt lucky to be alive.

I ate in the den in front of the TV, listening to the day's accumulation of trauma: murder and rape, and mutilation on the highways, a rehash of the Gomez slaying, the introduction of Peter Conrad's—pictures of the well, the blood-spattered metal cover, Conrad's black-bagged body being loaded into the ambulance, Homer looking foolish, saying, "No comment at this time."

Henry Lee Lucas was in the news again, recanting all but three of his self-proclaimed total of six hundred serial murders. Some two hundred and ten cases closed solely on his confessions were being looked at again, and a lot of law enforcement officers' faces were stained a permanent red.

Ten new AIDS cases in Dallas, two in Fort Worth, bringing the year's total in the Metroplex to fifty-one. Almost an epidemic, according to Dr. Sean McMarthy, director of communicable diseases in Dallas. He went on to say that it was no longer just a homosexual problem: no one was safe. He called the viral infection "the kiss of death," adding that out of some eighty-eight hundred cases in the United States as of March, forty-three hundred had died.

When the camera suddenly panned in on a heart transplant operation, I turned off the set. There's only so much I can take while I'm eating, and open heart surgery ranks way down on the list.

I turned it on again after I finished eating, switched to

Channel 24 and *Crossfire*. Raucous wrangling, four grown people yelling at each other over the bombing of abortion clinics.

I turned it off again and settled back in my chair. I had a decision to make. Sandra Conrad. I had to either call in my dogs, piss on the fire, and quit, or get out there and get with it, find her before Homer did. And then what? Ask her if she did it, committed two cold-blooded murders? And if the answer was no, ask her why she had been hiding out if she hadn't?

Another question that cried out for an answer: why had Conrad's killer taken him to the well? The logical answer to that would be to hide his body. But why? To what purpose? Anyone with the IQ of an uneducated armadillo would know the police would search the premises and eventually find the body. Delay? Punishment?

I opted for the second. Being shot in the comfort of your own bedroom was one thing; being hauled out into a storm, marched on bare feet to a dark hole in the ground, and deliberately murdered there was something else again. Revenge? For what reason?

A woman scorned, perhaps. An ex-lady love, Carlotta's predecessor?

I shook my head over that one. It was difficult to imagine Conrad inspiring that kind of unreasoning passion, the intensity of emotion necessary to sustain two premeditated murders and quite possibly a kidnapping. A man known for casual affairs, today's woman would know what to expect from him, exactly nothing beyond his own needs and desires.

And therein lay my problem with Homer's theory that Sandra had killed her husband and his paramour in a fit of vengeful rage. The consensus I had gleaned from the Beechums and others clearly indicated that she had known about Conrad's indiscretions and simply didn't care. Not enough to do something about it.

Furthermore, having just come home from a week in the Big Thicket with an old boyfriend, she had damn little room to complain.

So, goddammit, where was she? Who was hiding her, feeding her, protecting her? Again, the logical answer was one of the Beechums, maybe *all* of the Beechums.

But that didn't make sense either, I thought ruefully. The Beechum twins had hired me to find her. Claudell had tried. Even Victor Starling had approved, and he would certainly know if the old man was harboring a fugitive from justice.

That left the Jacob Twill enclave in East Texas, the Jonas Beechum ranch a few miles away . . . and God only knew how many other loyal employees and friends I didn't know about.

Feeling defeated, I carried my dishes in to the dishwasher. I found a can of Bud in the refrigerator. I lit a cigarette and reclaimed my seat, flipped on the TV again.

Jimmy Stewart's face flashed on the screen; the camera cut to Grace Kelly's pristine beauty. Jimmy Stewart's leg was in a cast and he was holding a pair of binoculars. He looked annoyed.

Rear Window. One of my favorite golden oldies. I chased the Beechums out of my mind and settled back to watch.

11

THE TINKLING NOTES OF "MOONGLOW" ROUSED ME, brought me struggling out of the hypnotic twilight zone better known as dozing. Jimmy Stewart had exchanged the binoculars for a telescopic camera lens, and Grace Kelly hovered over his shoulder, her lovely face anxious. Thelma Ritter fidgeted nearby.

The doorbell rang again. I came up to full alert, yawned, and reached for my cigarette in the ashtray, found nothing but a cold filter and a line of dead ash.

I lit another, yawned again, and padded to the door just as the chimes went off a third time.

I yanked it open, stood blinking into the wide blue eyes of Mercy Beechum, or the wide blue eyes of Hope Beechum, I had no idea which.

"Where *were* you?" she said, a note of mock reproach in her voice, a shapely pout disappearing beneath a dazzling, white-toothed smile.

"I was asleep," I said.

She glanced at a tiny watch on her left wrist. "At seven-thirty! I've heard of going to bed with the chickens, but this is ridiculous. It isn't even hardly dark yet."

111

"I'm like an old hound. I get still, I go to sleep."

"That's too bad." She looked past my shoulder and made an impatient gesture. "Well, are you going to invite me in, or are we going to stand out here discussing your sleeping habits?"

"Come on in," I said. "Don't pay any attention to the mess. I haven't had time—"

"That's why I'm here," she said tersely, stepping inside and closing the door. "I'm going to do something about the mess."

"You're kidding!"

She looked startled. "Of course not. Remember, it was part of our deal? We'd clean up your house for you and you'd find Sandy for us—and we'd pay you too, of course."

"This isn't necessary," I said, my voice sharper, a little haughtier than I had intended. I wondered if I should be offended.

She gave me a wispy appealing smile, and wrinkled her nose. "You're not going to be stuffy, are you?"

"That's not the point. I have a cleaning lady for that. I'm not going to allow you to waste your time."

She sat on the arm of the couch, looking deflated. "Well . . ." She let it drift and gave me an enigmatic look. Her face brightened. "Oh, I'm forgetting the main reason I came." She slipped a hand into the rear pocket of her jeans and came out with a folded paper. "The list you wanted. That first one is Sandy's second in command, Nelson Morrow. They're also good friends."

I glanced at the list: a half-dozen names, three of which appeared to be MCB employees. None of the names was familiar, but that wasn't surprising; we moved in different circles.

She stood up abruptly and looked around the den. "The least I can do is pick up a little in here." She looked at me and turned on her smile full wattage. "But if you don't mind, Danny, I'll wait and do it in the morning." The bright eyes caught mine, fused, held me mesmerized while she spoke the next words clearly and distinctly. "Before I leave."

I stared at her, stunned beyond permutation of cause and effect, replaying her words for misinterpretation, fearing the very real possibility that my overheated libido had imploded and punched holes in the fabric of my sanity.

"Before you leave . . . where?"

She smiled her answer and came to her feet in one fluid movement. By the time she reached me, I was standing, feeling myself tense as an old familiar escape mechanism made itself known, some ragged remnant of manly pride left over from the ancient chauvinist days when men pursued and women captivated. Maybe that made me an anachronism, but I still liked it that way.

I captured her hands on their way up my chest to my neck, the full lips only inches away, parted in startled wonder. We stood that way for an eternity, blue eyes reflecting in blue eyes. The silence thickened as the hiatus grew. I began to feel foolish again, began to feel the heat of her lush body pressing against mine. I wondered if I could get out of it gracefully, then wondered if I could get out of it at all, and whether I really wanted to. "You're melting my VISA card."

"What on earth's the matter with you?" she said, her tone light and amused, a marvelous bit of deception that might have fooled me completely had I not been watching her eyes. They no longer twinkled, or sparkled. They glittered, cold and shiny with anger, a fleeting glimpse of glacial blue before descending lids shuttered them.

She pouted prettily, stood on tiptoe, and kissed my cheek. Only then did she ease the pressure of her body against mine; she backed away with a flip of her ponytail.

"I only wanted to kiss you good-bye," she said crisply. "You must have misunderstood."

"I'm like that," I said. "I'm hopelessly vain."

"I wasn't sure when I first met you if I liked you. Now I know why, you prick."

"Why you weren't sure, or why you didn't like me?"

She turned back to face me, hugging her arms. "B-b-both." Her face was pale and set, the stammer as surprising as the pass had been. "You in-in-insufferable a-a-ass."

"Are you sure I'm ready for that? I haven't been a prick very long."

Her features loosened and I thought she might smile, but they were only in transition from cold and hard to soft and hurt. Her chin quivered; the big eyes clouded with moisture. I began to *feel* like an insufferable ass.

"Look, Mercy—Hope, this is silly. I'm sorry if I've hurt your feelings. I didn't mean to. You're a very lovely woman. I—any man would be tickled to death to . . . uh . . ." There was nowhere I could go with that, so I started over. "Look, everybody gets turned down now and then. It's no big—"

"Are you implying," she said icily, "that I made a pass at *you*?" No trace of a stammer, and she tagged a snotty little laugh on the end of it. I felt something ripple and slide behind my breastbone, warmth creeping into my face.

"Maybe not," I said, forcing humor into my voice, "maybe it was the other one. Somebody damn sure made a pass at somebody. It wasn't me."

The blue eyes blazed. "You bastard!"

"There you go again, giving me another promotion."

She snatched up her purse from the arm of the couch, slung the strap across her shoulder, and whirled toward the door, her spine as stiff as a metal post, injured dignity spinning off in palpable waves. She marched through the entry hall and yanked open the door. I followed her, feeling a seeping rill of anger of my own.

"Does this mean you won't be cleaning the den?"

She whirled again, the purse swinging wide, and for one charged second I thought she might hit me with it.

Instead, she crimped her lips tightly, then hissed through clenched teeth: "Don't push your luck, mister. I'm trying my best to keep from firing you!"

She turned and ran.

I stared after her, stunned, unable to assimilate her meaning into the theme of our conversation so far. By the time I recovered, she was climbing into her Porsche.

I leaped across the porch and onto the lawn.

"Don't do me any favors, lady! I quit!"

The Porsche's headlights stabbed the dark; the engine roared, tires screaming in astonishment as she peeled rubber backward out of my drive. Barely pausing, she yanked the little car around, tromped again, and went through the stop at the corner at no less than sixty miles an hour. I watched her taillights swerve, wink, and disappear around the curve beside the park and wondered just how in billy-blue hell I had managed to blow the guts right out of this fine spring evening.

I went back into the kitchen and opened a beer. I was debating whether to go to bed or sit outside for a while when the phone rang. I picked it up on the second ring.

"Hello."

"I'm sorry, Mr. Roman," a soft voice said. "I acted like a child. I'm afraid I don't handle rejection well. Will you forgive me?"

"Nothing to forgive," I said. "My act wasn't so great, either."

"Not at all. I think you were a gentleman under the circumstances. It's just that I . . . well, I'm not used to . . . I have this terrible temper."

115

"Forget it. It never happened."

"That's what I was worried about. You won't say anything to her?"

"To her—who? Sandy?"

"No, my twin."

"How am I going to know? I don't know which one you are."

"That's what I mean. Don't mention it to either one of us. Now, do you see?"

"Yeah . . . sure, I guess. Okay, done."

"And you won't quit?"

"No, I won't quit." I struck flame to a cigarette. "Where are you? You couldn't possibly have made it home even the way you were driving."

She laughed softly. "No, I'm at the shopping center at Highway 157 and Airport Freeway. I really appreciate this, Mr. Roman." She paused. "Good-night."

"Good-night, Ms. Beechum."

I hung up slowly and took a gulp of beer. Rich people. Neurotics. No, too tame. How about crazies. All crazies of one kind or other. Maybe it was the strain of all that money, of always being on guard, a surfeit of luxury that softened the sinews and eroded the soul. I had been holding out hope for the twins, but now it seemed they were as screwed up as all the rest of them. Maybe even more so. At least one of them.

I finished the beer, showered, and went to bed, wide-awake and restless. I finally went to sleep, the threat of tomorrow and more of the Beechums hanging over my head like a sentence of death.

12

NELSON MORROW FIT WELL THE ROLE OF SECOND IN COM-mand of MCB: quick and sharp beneath an overlay of oily and smooth. Mr. Fix-it with muscles. Tall and athletic in sparkling white tennis togs and blue Adidas, he greeted me warmly on the veranda of his pretentious mansion a mile or so north of the Conrad home. He had a square handsome face, close-cropped black hair, and dark watchful eyes. He smiled easily and laughed often. At everything, at nothing, a low cultivated chuckle that was pleasing to the ear and, after a while, vexed the soul.

A survivor, I thought. A man who could change directions in midsentence, switch allegiances the way other men change expressions. Although he was urbane and sophisticated on the surface, I sensed an element of raw aggressiveness beneath the veneer. But most of all I sensed insatiable hunger for success, its accoutrements. It was there in his meticulously groomed person, the Philippe Patek watch, two diamond rings, and a band of hammered gold around his wrist; in the Olympic-size swimming pool, tennis courts, and low-slung stables along the back line of his five acres; in the house itself, modern-excessive, opulence for its own sake, as pretentious as the three-year-old Rolls-Royce I had seen on the way in, the Maserati, the Ferrari with the crushed fender and dented bonnet, the stretch limousine that had lady-of-the-house written all over it. For a simple working man, Nelson Morrow had a lot of things.

He offered me scotch or bourbon or vodka. I declined. He offered me a beer, which I accepted. A trim young blonde in a blue-and-white uniform dashed off to fill our order, and we sat down at a circular umbrella table near the edge of the sparkling pool. Out on the courts two boys and two girls batted balls at each other with more energy than accuracy, more catcalls than compliments. A four-letter word drifted to our ears. Morrow turned in his seat and looked at them and laughed.

He turned back, spread his hands, and grinned expansively. "Kids today, eh? Know everything by the time they're ten. Done everything by the time they're fifteen. Don't care about anything but having a good time, girls, cars, getting high. Them two boys out there, they're seventeen and eighteen. Never done a lick of work in their lives, and don't want to. Hell, they don't even like to work on cars. I thought all boys liked to work on cars. Not mine, no sir." He leaned back and produced a crumpled package of cigarettes from his pants pocket. "You got any kids, Mr. Roman?" He patted his other pockets and frowned.

"No," I said. I produced my own cigarettes and lighter. I reached across and held flame to his cigarette. "No, I'm not married."

"Phew," he said, exhaling a cloud of smoke. "You don't know how lucky you are. Women . . ." He trailed off into his meaningless laugh.

"They're different," I said.

118

"From us, yeah. From each other, not much." He laughed again.

"Sandra Conrad," I said. "I hear she's different."

He sobered instantly, the tanned face closing down on humor, exuding concern, a mercurial change that reinforced my snap judgment of him earlier. "You heard that right. Sandy's one in a thousand—hell, no, one in a million. Not many women I'd work for, let me tell you. She's smarter than any man I know, tough as an old boot, and can read a stand of timber better'n anybody I know."

"Timber? Is that a big part of your current business? I thought MCB had diversified, spread out into all kinds—" I broke off as the girl reached the table with our drinks. She dropped a small cork coaster on the table in front of me, added a napkin and my beer, a bottle of dark-hued German brew that I hated.

"Thank you," I said, and she gave me a surprised sidelong glance.

"Get us an ashtray," Morrow said brusquely, taking the scotch from her hand.

"Yes, sir." She stepped two paces to our left and brought an ashtray from the adjoining table. I didn't look up.

"Will that be all, sir?"

He waved her away without answering, tasted his drink, frowned, then caught me watching and grinned ruefully. "They never make it right."

I nodded, wondering how you could mess up scotch and rocks.

He leaned forward on the table, his face earnest again. "If you want me to talk freely, Mr. Roman, you'll have to give me your word that what you hear won't be repeated."

"Anything that pertains to your business, I can guarantee that. I can't guarantee you anything as far as Sandra

119

Conrad's concerned. I'm sure you know by now that she's a prime suspect in her husband's murder. I won't withhold information from the police, and anyone who helps her, hides her out, or whatever, is an accessory after the fact.'' I stopped and met the dark eyes squarely. ''That's ten to fifteen years' hard labor.''

He slapped the table and laughed explosively. ''So that's why you're here? You think I'm hiding her?''

''No, not exactly. You're her friend, or so I've been told. You worked with her right up until she went to East Texas. You may have seen something, heard something that might help me find her now. I understand that she was exhausted, perhaps ill, when she arrived in East Texas. Can you shed any light on that?''

He sipped his drink and mashed out his cigarette. He stared into the blue-green pool water and held his chin in one manicured hand.

''Not ill, I don't think. She was tired, ground down. We've been having some business . . . problems lately.'' He stopped and laughed, the sound hollow, meaningless. He looked back at me and shrugged. ''I think she was dreading it more than anything.''

''Dreading what?''

He breathed deeply. ''Her uncle, Jonas Beechum. The two thousand acres of land he owns—or thinks he owns. He does own it, I guess, but what he didn't know, hasn't known all these years, is that he doesn't own the timber and mineral rights. Macomber Beechum withheld that bit of information from him when he turned the land over to him.'' He shook his head. ''That old man. He could never really let go of anything.''

''And Sandra was going to tell him?''

He nodded heavily. ''Yes. I advised her to let the legal people handle it, write him a letter, or whatnot. But she felt it would be wrong to tell him that way. She said it was her job, she'd have to do it in person. Dammit, I told you she had guts.''

''But why tell him? After all the years he thought it was all his, why drop it on him now?'' I thought I knew the answer to that, but I wanted to hear him say it.

''We need the money,'' he said bluntly. ''And not only the money, we need the work. Macomber Lumber Company is still the biggest company we own, the best producer, the best cash flow. Ordinarily. But we're running out of trees. We've picked up a large tract west of Jonas's land, but by itself it isn't enough to justify the new equipment we'd need to buy, the movement of personnel, old equipment—'' He broke off and shrugged again. ''We have to have Jonas's land. There's no getting around it.'' He shifted uncomfortably and cleared his throat. ''Or the whole shebang may go down the tubes.''

''Are you talking about the timber lease—''

''I'm talking about MCB,'' he said grimly, a pained look on his face. He raked it with a hand as if he could wipe it off. ''Look, Mr. Roman. It's not all that big a secret. MCB is in deep shit. We have been since that son of a bitch Miles almost dumped us in the silver market back in '79 and '80. That and oil. He set up an investment company and went into oil the way a bear goes into a honey tree. Then came the glut and OPEC crapped in its pants and the world was floating in the damn stuff. Right on top of that came Reagan's damn depression. We had to close some businesses and liquidate others. I guess you know Miles killed himself. That was why. He managed to gamble away a hundred and fifty million dollars in less than two years. Silver and oil. He had visions, he said. We'd be as rich as Howard Hughes on his best day. When silver hit a hundred dollars, we'd buy out General Motors and build us a Beechum car. He had visions all right. Loony tunes. He was nutty as a pecan roll and nobody could make his old man see it. We lost twelve companies before we were able to slow things down a bit. Sandy and I did that, most of it. We're down to six and they're all tied to the lumber business in one way or another. Not big companies, but still viable if we can keep them producing. That's why we must have Jonas's land. It'll give us a breathing spell and some much needed cash flow.''

"Did you talk to her while she was in East Texas?''

"No, and that wasn't like her. Her uncle don't have a phone, I understand. He's Miles's twin, you know, and personally I think the old coot is an ounce or two shy of a pound. He carries a gun, for Pete's sake, like he's Wyatt Earp or somebody.''

"He seemed smart enough to me," I said. "A little hasty, maybe.''

"I thought she'd call. There must be pay phones down there even if it is the asshole of nowhere.''

I took my time lighting a cigarette. "You ever been to East Texas?''

"I've flown over it a lot of times. Looks like a damn jungle to me.''

"Where you from?''

He hesitated. "Oklahoma. Why?''

I nodded and changed the subject. "Have you been contacted by the police?''

My change in direction caught him off guard; he had been all set to defend Oklahoma, the wide open spaces where you could breathe, where the sky went on forever, and a man could find oil by driving a golf tee into the ground. I had heard it all before—from both sides of the border.

"Yeah. A detective named Simms and his partner. They asked a lot of questions, some of them pretty damn stupid.''

"Stupid? How so?''

"Well, for instance, they wanted to know what would happen if Sandy never showed up. Who would be in charge, who would inherit the company?"

"A typical dumb cop question. Who would?"

"Hell, I don't know. I'm executive vice president. I'd be in charge until . . . well, until whatever the rest of the Beechums decided. The old man and the twins and that twerp Claudell. And Victor Starling, maybe. Who the hell knows? The old man hasn't been right in the head since his stroke ten years ago. If he had been, he'd never have put Miles in charge." He shifted in his wrought-iron chair, an icy edge of bitterness turning his voice cold, brittle. "Only halfway smart thing he's done since he got sick was turning it over to Sandy, and he didn't have any choice in that since he's so damn set on having a Beechum running the company." He barked a short humorless laugh. "If she shouldn't turn up for some reason, he'd have himself one hot choice between Jonas, the twins, and Claudell."

"Maybe he'd appoint one as the titular head," I suggested, "and let you run it."

He gave me a pitying look. "It's plain to see you don't know the Beechums."

"As much as I want to," I said, thinking he was undoubtedly right. With the possible exception of Jonas—who would never leave his beloved land, anyway—it was difficult to imagine the Beechums in a subordinate role to anyone.

He gunned the rest of his drink and fished the last cigarette out of his crumpled pack, his tanned face openly morose, the first evidence of honest emotion I'd seen.

I couldn't help but wonder if it stemmed from his own untenable position or from Sandra Conrad's dilemma.

I lit his cigarette and pushed to my feet.

"I appreciate your time, Mr. Morrow, and your candor."

"Yeah, sure. Glad to be of help." He made no move to rise, or to shake hands.

I touched him lightly on the shoulder. "Keep your seat. I can find my own way out."

He nodded absently, looking across the pool toward the tennis courts. I had obviously been dismissed from his thoughts, from his insulated world.

But that was all right. I'd always wanted to say that, and this was the first time I'd ever had the chance.

13

HOMER SELLERS LEANED BACK IN HIS SWIVEL CHAIR AND scratched a small red bump on his heavy jaw. He had gone back to his old glasses, thick bifocals that caught the light and expanded his cerulean eyes, giving him the look of a myopic sea lion. He poked the last bite of his hamburger lunch into his mouth and chewed methodically, staring through me, digesting what I had told him along with the food.

I lit a cigarette and waited, knowing from experience that it would be useless to hurry him. Like an old hound with a long-forgotten bone, he had to nuzzle and sniff and paw, stand over it and hike his leg a couple of times before he was satisfied with the smell.

Finally, he rolled forward, swept the residue of his lunch into the wastebasket. He folded his arms on the desk and looked at me, his face as bland as a lump of dough.

"Okay. So what's your conclusion?"

"I didn't say I had one, Homer. I was just bringing you up to date. As it happens, I do, however."

"And that is?"

"I have a feeling she's dead. We could be chasing a ghost."

"Reasons?"

"Somewhere between eight and ten million of them, depending on whose estimate you believe. Her uncle Jonas's land in East Texas. She went down there to tell him it really wasn't all his, that they were going to cut the timber."

"You think he might have killed her?"

"I don't think anything. You asked for reasons, I'm giving you reasons. There are other people interested in that timber. A man named Curly Glazier took a run at me because he thought I was trying to buy it out from under him. That's two. With Sandra dead the company would be up for grabs by one of the other Beechums. That's three. The old man's dying. He wants a Beechum at the helm. He only has four choices left, actually only three since I don't think Jonas would take it. He turned it down once before."

He picked up a long yellow pencil and beat a rapid tattoo on the back of his hand. "Them's good reasons, all right. You have any idea where we might find the body?" He was baiting me, but it was all a part of the ritual of our peculiar relationship; he needled me and I disappointed him. I ignored his question.

"What if Conrad didn't pick her up at the bus station?"

"Then how'd she get home?"

He shrugged. "Lots of ways. Taxi service ain't so great, but it's there, and she coulda called somebody else."

"Why, when she'd already called her husband and he was going to pick her up? It don't make a lot of sense. Have you checked the taxi companies?"

He nodded, looking grumpy. "Yeah. Nothing." He gave me a quick glance and a crooked grin. "That was just an example. Dammit. We don't know for sure that

Conrad brought her home. Nobody at the bus station in Dallas could identify him—or her either, for that matter.''

"Too many people. Those bus stations fill up and empty out in a matter of minutes sometimes.''

"Claudell and them twins,'' he said, and sighed. "They swear they didn't pick her up, or haven't seen her since—so hell, maybe you're right. Maybe she's dead.'' He looked up, scowling. "You got any more reasons?''

"No, but it occurred to me that we only have Jonas's word that she called Conrad. Or her word secondhand if Jonas didn't actually hear her make the call. That's something you could check easily enough. The call would have been made from a pay phone somewhere in a little town called Crater. Probably collect.''

"Okay. Good idea.'' He brought back the lopsided grin. "You still have one now and then, I see.''

"Well, hell, Homer, I are a detective after all.''

"You were a detective. I'll even go so far as to say you were a good detective. Now, you ain't nothing but a hound dog chasing footloose men and discontented women.''

"It doesn't rank up there with heart transplants, Homer, but it needs to be done. And don't forget the kids I find.'' I spoke lightly, but it was a tender spot he poked at every so often; out of frustration, sometimes pure damn meanness. It was part of the price I paid for being his friend, and it wasn't all one-sided. I had faults, too. Not many, but some, and a few of them rankled him deeply. To make him fighting mad all I had to do was vilify the Cowboys, disparage the President—any President—and slur the cops. It made things interesting, if a little tiresome at times.

"Every hog to his own wallow, I always say,'' he said, ripping the cellophane from a plastic-tipped cigar. He made a ritual of lighting it, talking jerkily through puffs of blue-white smoke.

"Got the autopsy report on Peter Conrad, by the way.

About what we expected. One in the ticker and one in the brainpan. Killed him dead.'' He huffed a cloud of smoke in my direction and smiled. "He had AIDS," he added casually.

"AIDS?"

"AIDS." Homer's eyes glistened like shiny blue marbles. "You know what AIDS is, I guess. You'd damn well better, the way you're always catting around."

"Yeah, I know what it is. He didn't look sick to me. A little pale, maybe."

"He wasn't sick. Not the way you're thinking. Seems he had the virus, coulda had it for up to four, five years before the symptoms showed up."

"They found it in the autopsy?"

He shook his shaggy head. "Nope. Doc said they wouldn't have found that in an autopsy. They done the routine stuff, but there wasn't much question about what killed him. Doc Paris found it out from one of his partners in that clinic down on Plainview and Slocum. Conrad had a complete physical back in January. Article I read said AIDS was gonna be an epidemic if they didn't find a cure. Trouble is, people can have it for years, spread it around and not know it. Typhoid Mary all over again. Thousands of them, maybe millions. Hell, it's enough to make you give it up."

"Give what up, Homer? Why don't you say the word? It won't bite you."

He glowered, his broad face slowly turned red. "Ain't no sense in talking dirty when you ain't mad. Too much of that shit going on around here now. These young cops can't put together a sentence without using four-letter words. I guess they think it makes them sound tough."

"Shocking," I said.

He slapped the desk, the frown segueing into a stingy smile. "Yeah, ain't it. Go on, get your butt out of here and find that Conrad woman for me. When you do that, first thing you do is pick up the phone and call me. I'll pin the hero medal on you myself—me or the mayor. He's getting a little tacky about this whole thing, by the way. He gave me a lecture just this morning on the adverse effects of unsolved crimes on society.''

''Show him your new decoder ring, Homer.'' I stood up and lit a cigarette. ''I suppose it's occurred to you that if Conrad had AIDS, then in all likelihood Sandra has it too.''

''It had.'' He remade the wintry smile.

''Just thought I'd make that little point.'' I grinned and ambled toward the door. ''I figured you might want to check with her doctor.''

He snapped his fingers. ''Gee whiz, now why didn't I think of that?''

I opened the door. ''You can't expect to pick it up all at once, Homer. Hang in there, you'll make it. Hell, look at the stupid Cowboys. They've been trying for years to get it right.''

He straightened, the color rushing back into his face. ''Now, looky here, Dan—''

I stepped through the door and closed it. I nodded at Mitsi and got out of there before he could start using nasty four-letter words. Mitsi didn't like it when I made him mad; she thought it was hard on his heart.

I spent the rest of the afternoon checking the list of Sandra's friends supplied by Mercy and Hope. Two were out of town. One, an MCB employee named Sarah Routte, an industrial engineer, was on a business trip to Atlanta. The second was also an employee of MCB. Mark Wilhelm, manager of accounting, was somewhere in California on vacation, due back in three days. The third MCB employee, Tracy Johnson, supervisor of the computer department, assured me she knew nothing about her boss's disappearance, had not, in fact, known that she was missing at all. She had heard about the murders, of course, but since she did not read the papers and watched very little TV, she knew none of the details. She had thought about calling Sandra and offering condolences, but had decided to wait rather than give the impression that she was prying. Sandy was so . . . so *funny* at times and she wasn't always sure how to take her.

She was an earnest, nervous little woman in her mid-thirties, with upswept hair and a thin pretty face that appeared to be aging before its time. Petite and meticulous in a peasant blouse and skirt, patent-leather pumps, she met my eyes without hesitation and passed my inward polygraph with flying colors. I left her with the feeling that Diogenes would have loved her.

Cynthia Melrose was a different story. Tall, willowy, a bottle blonde with predatory green eyes, she professed to be Sandra Conrad's best friend as well as her neighbor and, with very little prodding on my part, confessed to various indiscretions in company with the chief executive of MCB. Sandy and she dined together, she said, several times a month. Only the best restaurants, of course, usually in Dallas, sometimes in Fort Worth when they felt wild and reckless. Afterward, they would visit the singles bars—only for the dancing, of course, and stimulating repartee, a drink or two and a little harmless flirtation. Only once . . . or perhaps twice, had it gone beyond that . . . which, of course, was all right for her since she was divorced, but, really, she had been a little shocked at Sandra. Not that she blamed her. Absolutely not. Sauce for the goose, you know. That husband of hers . . . well, she didn't like to speak ill of the dead, but he had been a proper son of a bitch, worse even, than her own ex-asshole. At least her ex hadn't flaunted it, rubbed her nose in it the way Conrad had Sandra's.

I let her talk it out, wind down, her voice rising as she went into a recital of her ex-husband's failings, as a husband, as a father, as a man. After a while, during a lull in which she made a fresh drink, I asked her if I could take a look around the premises.

She threw me out.

14

THE NEXT DAY DAWNED COLD AND RANCOROUS, A SEAM-
less sky the color of dirty gray wool hung glowering just
above the treetops, and the saturated air covered everything with a fine patina of damp.

A great day for a funeral. Peter Conrad's funeral. I decided to go at the last moment. I wasn't sure why, although the thought of seeing Myna Beechum again lay
curled up in the back of my mind like a soft furry kitten,
brought a gentle acceleration of my heartbeat.

I jeered at my image in the mirror while I shaved,
scoffed as I dressed in my best suit, a lightweight, dark
blue worsted, 20 percent silk. A maroon tie, white shirt,
and my new black boots rounded out my ensemble. I felt
like a dandy, looked so much like a North Dallas Yuppie
I decided not to go, then went anyhow, paying no attention
to my foolishness.

I decided against the pearl gray flat-brimmed Stetson—
too much. Besides, I wasn't at all sure *she* was going to
be there. I made the short drive to the cemetery in a state
of mild anxiety and fluctuating expectations.

She was. Along with all the other Beechums with the

exception of the old man. Victor Starling stood tall and lean and somber off to one side of the family huddled together beneath a small canopy erected above the grave. A large group of men in business suits stood just outside the covering—fellow workers, I guessed—and a handful of curious onlookers milled quietly a hundred yards down the slope of the hill. I blended with the business types, slowly worked my way toward the front.

A voice droned monotonously, a litany of Conrad's accomplishments, a recitation of his virtues, a lament for his precipitous demise. Nothing was said about fornication, infidelity, general cussedness; nothing was said about the method of his untimely end.

Jonas, standing between Myna and Joline, looked uncomfortable in a three-piece black suit, hat twisting in his gnarled hands, features caught in a curious mixture of solemnity and disdain. Without the gun, he looked smaller somehow, more fragile, older.

Myna and Joline wore simple black dresses with no adornment, no makeup, dark eyes cast downward as they listened to the sanctimonious eulogy.

Claudell was there, resplendent in a burnished gray suit and a pale pink tie. He was bookended by the twins, Mercy and Hope, dressed inappropriately, I thought, in red blouses and black designer jeans, their faces wearing identical looks of bemusement, as if they shared secrets beyond the ken of common folk. I studied their lovely features and lush bodies and wondered at my own stupidity, still unable to decide which one had been my would-be lover.

The ceremony ended. A moment or two of silence, and two smooth-faced men knelt beside the flower-draped coffin. It began to move, to descend. Nobody said anything. No sobs, no murmurs of regret, no tears that I could see. Somebody cleared his throat, somebody else blew his nose. Nobody stepped forward and threw dirt on the coffin, a custom the movies have taught us to expect, as barbaric as it seems to me.

The coffin stopped, only the mounded flowers still visible. The two smooth-faced men stood waiting. The crowd stirred, began to shuffle their feet. Cigarettes appeared and lighters clicked. Voices came muted and solemn, reeking with artificial piety and false sorrow. That Peter Conrad had gone to his grave unmourned was plain for all to see, and a few of the more charitable ones obviously felt called upon to mouth empty platitudes in an attempt to bring warmth to this cold, final act of man, to justify his existence.

I wended my way toward Jonas, surrounded now by Myna and Joline and the twins, still looking slightly unfinished without the gun around his slender waist. His roving eye caught mine and, for just a second, his face seemed to darken before breaking apart in a smile. He nodded at me, slapped the hat on his head, and stepped out of the clutch of women to shake my hand.

"Appreciate you coming, Mr. Roman. Right nice thing to do."

"Not at all," I said limply, wondering what he would think if he knew I had come mainly to see his wife.

He turned to the women. "Reckon you all know Mr. Roman. Myna, Joline, I know you do. You twins, if you don't, then this is Mr. Dan Roman—"

"We know him," they chorused, four bright guileless eyes meeting mine as they presented soft warm hands to be shaken, identical smiles to be assessed. I turned to Myna's amused smile, knowing no more than I had before.

"Mr. Roman. I agree with my husband. It was thoughtful of you to come."

I clutched her hand briefly and repeated my lame denial,

the warm strength of her hand doing little to aid my equanimity, the dark eyes, clear of artifice, making me feel like a lecher. Daunted but not repentant, I dropped her hand and turned to Joline.

"Nice to see you again, Mr. Roman," she said, unsmiling, the dark eyes remote.

"Good to see you again," I said. "Mr. Twill couldn't come with you?"

"Yes, he came, but he doesn't attend funerals. He's waiting for us."

Jonas snorted. He lifted the hat, then reseated it firmly on his head again. "Man has to do some things in this life he don't want to do."

"Not Jacob," Joline said serenely. "He's gone past the necessity for saying and doing things just for the sake of appearance. Jacob is the only truly free man I've ever known." She paused, looked at me. "And the most generous man I've ever met as well."

Jonas cackled, his right hand wandering restlessly to his hip. "He can afford to be. All them idjits turning over their money to him like he was some kind—"

"Jonas, Joline . . . please. Mr. Roman isn't interested in family squabbles." Myna made a humorous face, but her eyes were flashing and there had been an edge to her voice that neither of the combatants ignored.

Jonas squinted at her, then nodded sourly. "Yeah, reckon you're right." He lifted a hand. "Nice seeing you again. I'll wait at the car." He angled off down the slope, short choppy steps in his high-heeled boots, back ramrod straight. A small man, I realized suddenly, who had always wanted to be big. Maybe that explained, in part, his obvious antagonism for Jacob Twill, a big man in stature if not in accomplishment.

Mercy and Hope had been surrounded by the men in business suits. No longer subdued, their flashing smiles and lilting voices gave the somber proceedings a sudden festive air.

Claudell hovered on the perimeter of the group, his face petulant. Farther up the slope, two men in khaki work clothes waited beside a yellow backhoe. Victor Starling had disappeared.

We moved away from the grave site. I lit a cigarette and tried to remember what it was I had wanted to ask Myna. Joline walked ahead of us, slender and lithe in the black sheath dress. Viewed together, the resemblance between the sisters was not nearly as remarkable as I had thought. Joline was taller by two inches, more angular; she had strong attractive features as opposed to Myna's more softly rounded face that could escalate from merely pretty to beautiful with no more effort than a change of expression.

"You should wear blue more often," she said, slowing almost to a stop, allowing Joline to pull farther away. She half-turned toward me, a teasing note in her voice. "You're very handsome in blue."

"Lord, don't tell me that. My head's too big the way it is."

She laughed softly. We continued walking.

"Black isn't your best color," I said, being my usual tactful self. "But it doesn't matter. Nobody faults a rose for the color of its vase."

She made an inarticulate sound that may have been a giggle. "I think there's a compliment in there somewhere. But, you're right, I'm too dark to wear black."

"Dark? You're not as dark as I am."

"Yes, but yours is from the sun, mine is from my Indian blood."

"Maybe so, but that's no reason to brag. For your information, I've always thought I have some Indian blood. I'm always getting this irresistible urge to go pee in the woods."

136

She clapped a hand to her mouth—not quite in time. One lilting peal rang across the hillside, the parking lot, raising heads and questing eyes. Out at the edge of my peripheral vision, I saw Joline turn and stand staring; off to my right I saw a pickup door open, a slender compact figure in a black suit step down and clap a cowboy hat on its head.

I put my arm across Myna's shoulders. I looked at Joline and shook my head. "She'll be all right. It just suddenly hit her, I guess. Death. It does that to some people." I patted her shoulder tenderly. "There, there, Mrs. Beechum, it'll be all right." I snapped the handkerchief out of my breast pocket and gave it to her and lowered my voice. "Here, you can hide behind this. I think they're coming."

Her shapely head bobbed; she snatched the handkerchief the way a drowning man grabs a straw, bunched it around her face as Joline drew up beside us, her eyes bright and suspicious. Jonas zigzagged around parked cars, still twenty yards away.

"What happened?" Joline said curtly, taking over my backpatting chore.

I shook my head ruefully. "Golly, I don't know. We were talking about Sandra, about her being missing and all, and she just suddenly went to pieces. Does she do this often?" I avoided the dark punishing eyes by busying myself with a cigarette.

"Not often," Joline said dryly. Her arm tightened around her sister's still-shaking shoulders. "Come on, honey, let's go to the car." She wasn't buying it, that much was clear, but she wasn't about to betray her sister with her husband pounding gravel a few feet away.

Jonas ground to a stop, breathing hard, his little eyes flicking from me to Myna and back again. "What the hell happened?"

"She's just overwrought, Jonas," Joline said matter-of-

137

factly. They were talking about Sandra,'' she added, giving him a knowing look, raised eyebrows, and a pained expression.

He took a deep breath and shook his head, looking almost pleased. ''Well . . . look, I'm sorry, Mr. Roman. Appreciate you taking care of her that way. Oughta knowed better'n to leave her like that. Oughta knowed she'd be tore up after all this. My fault, I shoulda stayed right with her.''

''Quite all right,'' I said.

Myna wiped her eyes, head still bowed. I caught one glimpse of wet flashing eyes before she turned away under Joline's guiding hand. We watched silently as they made their way among the cars. I puffed on the cigarette and tried to think of something pertinent to say.

''Too bad,'' I said finally.

''Naw,'' Jonas said. ''Women, they need to cry. Makes them feel good. Myna don't cry like she ought to. First time I ever remember her really cutting loose like this. I guess she thinks more of Sandy than I thought.''

''Probably.'' I suddenly remembered what it was I'd wanted to ask Myna. That was definitely out for the time being. Jonas would have to do.

''I understand Sandra brought you some bad news when she came to visit.''

His head whipped around. ''What bad news?''

''About the timber on your two thousand acres. That they were going to cut it.''

He nodded, scowling. ''She mentioned something about it. But she knowed better. I told her to forget it.''

''And she accepted that?''

He shrugged, his face darkening beneath the frown. ''She didn't have no choice. My land, I have the say on what happens to it. No way they could cut that timber without my say-so.

"How about the timber rights?"

"Ain't no such thing. That's surface rights. I ain't got the mineral rights, but I got the surface rights and that includes the timber. Somebody don't know what they're talking about. I could lease out the timber rights, but I damn sure ain't going to do that." He gave a baleful glare, black eyes glittering. "You sure don't know much about owning land."

"Not much," I agreed.

He took off the hat and ran a hand across his head. "We had us a little argument about it, all right. But I got that young lady straightened out real quick. I told her to go back and tell that sonuvabitching husband of hers to go suck eggs." He whirled and glared toward the grave where the two smooth-faced men were removing flowers from the casket. "He was a conniving, greedy bastard. No wonder somebody put holes in him. Sandy oughta done it a long time ago, 'cept she couldn't kill anybody and—" He stopped and breathed deeply, his face suddenly empty, slack. "And she needed him too much."

"Needed him? From what I hear, he chased everything in skirts that came along."

He nodded and settled the hat firmly on his head. "Love wasn't what she needed him for, Mr. Roman." He looked up, staring at me soberly. "She needed him to run the company for her."

Shock shuddered in my stomach like a dying bird; a tiny rill of adrenaline spurted. I hid my confusion behind a cigarette. By the time I got it going, I was back in control again.

"I thought she ran the company," I said, my voice as casual as a yawn.

"So'd everybody else," he said, a hint of irony in his voice. "The bitter truth is, Mr. Roman, Sandy ain't any smarter than the rest of us Beechums. And that ain't none

139

too smart. She had a little more learning, a couple of years of college, one of them junior colleges. But that didn't make her any smarter. It only made her realize how dumb we really are. Even Pa. Pa's cunning, and he's a thief, but he ain't really very smart. If he had been, he'd never have put Miles in charge. Even I'da known better than that. Miles wasn't any smarter'n me or any of the others, he only thought he was. And Miles was greedy. I always knew that. When we was kids he always got the most and best of everything, cheated and stole when he had to.''

"About Conrad,'' I said, getting him back on track. "I understood he was only a vice president—''

"That he was,'' he interrupted brusquely. "He wanted Nelson Morrow's job, but Sandy knew Pa would never hold still for that. Pa didn't like Conrad worth a damn. He thought Conrad married her for her money. But that was only partly true. Sandy needed him more than he needed her. He must have been smart, I'll give him that. According to her, he helped pull them out of the mess Miles made of things. Not all the way out, but he kept their heads above water. Sandy admits she would have lost everything a long time ago if it hadn't been for him.''

"Nobody seems to know that except you,'' I said. "Not even Nelson Morrow.''

He shrugged. "I don't know about that. I only know what Sandy's told me over the years. She used to come down regular after her daddy killed hisself.''

"It didn't bother you that Miles was losing the company?''

"Nope. Thirty-odd years ago I made a choice. I gave up all rights for two thousand acres of trees. I don't wish them any bad luck, but I won't let them cut my timber to save their damn company either.''

"And you're sure about the timber rights?''

He gave a cynical grin. "Son, I've been around this timber business all my life."

"You think it was Conrad's idea to cut the timber?"

"She told me it was. Don't reckon she lied."

"How could they be wrong about a thing like that? Land and timber rights and lumbering is their business."

"Don't ask me questions I can't answer. I don't know nothing about what they thought or didn't think. I only know what I know. That timber's mine and I ain't cutting it." Truculence had crept into his voice, and his eyes roamed across the rapidly thinning parking area restlessly. "Myna and Joline are waiting for me," he said, buttoning his suit coat. He took a step away, then turned and held out his hand. "Thanks again for coming, though I'm beginning to suspect you had your own reasons."

"The usual," I said. "Paying my respects to the dead."

"Yeah . . . well." He gave me another friendly smile and turned toward his pickup. "Gotta go. We got a coon hunt coming up tonight. I can't be late, I've got the dogs."

I watched them drive off the almost empty lot. I lit a cigarette and walked to my pickup pondering a curious fact: none of them, not a single one, had asked me how my search for Sandy was coming along.

15

ON THE DRIVE BACK HOME, I THOUGHT ABOUT WHAT JO-
nas had told me, trying to fit his revelations into the shadowy portrait I had been forming of Sandra Beechum, of
the Beechum family as a whole. They wouldn't fit. Like
drops of water in boiling oil, they skittered around the
surface and tried to leap over the edge.

For one thing, he was the only one I had met who
thought of her as anything less than an extraordinarily
gifted entrepreneur, clearheaded and decisive, smart as a
whip. Macomber Beechum thought so, as had Victor Starling. Her husband, Peter Conrad, and Nelson Morrow, her
executive VP, had also concurred that she was highly intelligent and capable. And they were in a position to know;
they worked with her every day.

Only Jonas said no. An uncle who lived some three
hundred miles away and saw her infrequently. An eccen-
tric himself, to put it in the kindliest terms I could think
of, a self-avowed ignoramus, a stubborn old man who
cared for nothing beyond his beloved forest, his dogs, and
his wife, quite possibly in that order. Paranoid, belligerent
to a dangerous degree, his very name made him an outcast

142

in his own homeland, if Curly Glazier could be believed. A psychological grab bag of neurosis, he was undoubtedly a bit dotty when judged against the standards of civilized behavior, a bit short when measured against the yardstick of normalcy.

If that were so, I thought, wheeling the Ramcharger into my driveway and shutting down the engine, then why was I beginning to believe him?

I made good time, grabbing a hamburger and malt near Buffalo, Texas, eating while I drove, averaging more than sixty-five miles an hour despite the heavy Highway Patrol presence on the interstate highway. But, even so, it was late afternoon before I pulled onto the wide parking apron at the restaurant bus stop near Spring, Texas. The sky still glowered, but the threat of rain had vanished from the air, replaced with a faint petrochemical smell that grew stronger the closer I got to the coast.

I shook the kinks out of my muscles and gassed up the tanks. A young boy with wild brown hair and zits covering the lower half of his face washed my windshield and wrote up my MasterCard ticket. He gave me my receipt and I handed him Sandra Conrad's photograph.

"You remember seeing this lady? About ten days ago. Caught a bus here for Dallas."

He stared at it without much interest, idly squeezing a lump on his jaw. He shook his head. "I don't think so. If I did, I don't remember her."

"She wore a deerskin blouse. Very colorful. And actually, it was a week ago last Wednesday."

He shook his head again, slowly. "No sir. I don't remember. If she caught a bus they might remember inside. Go in there and see Carrie Barnes. She's the blonde with the big boobs." He grinned and cupped oil-stained hands a foot away from his chest to show me how big.

143

"That big, huh? Maybe Carrie missed her calling."

He thought that was funny and proved it by laughing, a nasty, sneering little laugh that didn't make me feel particularly witty.

He wanted to know if I had checked my oil lately. I told him no, and left him rooting around under the hood, still chortling.

Inside, I had no trouble at all finding Carrie: a short wait in front of a small counter jammed in one corner of the big room, a sign that said BUS TICKETS.

I lit a cigarette and leaned on the counter, and in less than thirty seconds a short stocky blonde appeared in a doorway and made her way across the floor toward me, bouncing on the toes of white jogging shoes, jiggling only a little, not nearly as big as my gas jockey had led me to believe. She had big blue eyes and a Nordic face, fine cornsilk-colored hair.

"Yes, sir. Can I help you?"

"Yes, ma'am," I said, my tone as positive as hers had been, and went into my little routine with Sandra's photo, marveling at her fair unblemished skin as she scanned the picture closely and slowly began shaking her head.

"No, sir, I don't remember ever seeing her."

"Do you work this counter all the time?"

She nodded, still looking at the picture. "On my shift, I do. That's every day from four to midnight except Sunday."

"A week ago Wednesday. Early evening. She was wearing a deerskin blouse—"

Her head popped up, the blue eyes opened wide. "Deerskin blouse? I remember a deerskin—did it have dark patches on the shoulders here . . . and beadwork?" She traced a triangular pattern on the front of each sturdy shoulder. "And did it have leather lacing and fringes in front and back and on the sleeves?"

"That's it," I said. "You have a great eye for detail."

She smiled, the pale skin blooming a dull rose. "I have a great eye for faces too, and I don't think this was the lady wearing the blouse." She canted her head, sand-colored eyebrows lifting quizzically. "The lady I remember had a narrower face, a little prettier, and her hair was longer."

"Are you sure?"

She puckered her face and looked at the photo again. "Pretty sure. I remember her real well. I'd never seen a blouse like that before outside of the movies and TV." She nibbled at her lower lip. "I could be wrong, I guess. I was looking at the blouse more than I was at her."

"Maybe that was it. She did buy a ticket to Dallas?"

"Yes, I remember that for sure. I remember I had to hurry, the bus was about ready to leave."

"Did you see anyone with her? A short, wiry man about sixty?"

"No. I didn't notice anyone else. But it was late dinnertime and we were pretty crowded." She wet her lips and smiled. "Are you her husband, or her boyfriend or something?"

"No, I'm a private investigator—"

She squealed and clapped her hands, and I realized she was younger than I had thought. In my peripheral vision, I saw heads lift, heard a chair scrape as someone turned to look.

"Really? Like Magnum? Like Simon and Simon?"

"Not exactly like them, no. Close, I guess."

"A private eye!" she said, and clapped her hands again. "I really didn't think—oh, could I see your thing?"

"My what?" I said, unable to stop a grin.

"Oh, you know, your . . . oh, my God!" Her face flamed. She covered it with her hands, peeping at me through her fingers, the tide of crimson flowing down across her neck.

"You mean my ID, I'll bet," I said, and took my wallet out of my pocket. I laid the plastic rectangle on the counter. "There. That makes all these questions legal."

She regained her composure quickly, but the blood looked as if it was there to stay. She picked up the identification card and read it calmly, ignoring me, ignoring the muted ripple of laughter around the room. The people at the nearby tables had been close enough to hear our little exchange, and Carrie knew as well as I that her innocent slip of the tongue would soon become "that night that Carrie Barnes asked that private eye to see his thing." It would become a part of the folklore of the tiny town, and I could tell by her expression that she was resigned to it, would, I hoped, know how to handle it with aplomb.

She laid the card on the counter and gave me a cool look. "Yes, that's what you are, all right."

I nodded and gave her a rueful smile, wishing there was some way I could turn it around, take it on myself. It wasn't a big deal in the overall scheme of things, but to someone her age it didn't have to be. Already the murmur of laughter was swelling as the story traveled around the room.

"I'm sorry," I said.

She shook her head and smiled, her pink face filled with knowledge beyond her years. "Don't be, Mr. Roman. It wasn't your fault." She hesitated. "It *was* funny."

I nodded and smiled again, and left.

I stood at the door of the Ramcharger for a moment listening to the rumble of traffic on the interstate, smoking, disgruntled. Very little return for a lot of effort. Carrie's identification lacked conviction; James Parleigh's was positive. So where did that leave me? Not much better off than before. I still didn't know for certain that the woman who boarded the bus had in fact been Sandra. A preponderance of the evidence, Jonas's word, the buckskin blouse, Parleigh's identification, told me it was. That would be a logical assumption to make. But logical assumptions were nothing more than a form of guessing and could be just as unreliable.

Through the café window I could see Carrie talking to a group of teenagers. I couldn't see her face, but they were all laughing and I wondered if the razzing had already begun. I sighed and tossed away the cigarette, started the truck and drove off the lot, trying to decide what to do.

I could go home, a four-hour drive, or I could rent another motel room, spend a restless night listening to the walls rustle and murmur about the sights they'd seen, the lies they'd heard.

There was a third alternative: I could visit the Beechums. Friendly faces in an alien land. A fifty-minute drive would do it, maybe an hour at most. A cold beer and the rusty old swing, questions I had forgotten to ask before, a few more now that I had talked to Carrie Barnes. It made a lot of sense. A good detective kept on plugging, unrelenting, resourceful. Ask enough questions and you eventually get the right answer. If detectives had a creed, that would be it. Talk, talk, talk. Listen.

It took an hour and twenty minutes. Strange roads after dark. I loafed along, bemused. A local could do it in an hour easy. An hour there and an hour back. Two hours for Jonas Beechum to drive his niece to the bus and return home.

The house looked dark at first glance, small and somehow forlorn beneath the massive live oak and lofty pines. A dusk-to-dawn light mounted on a pole cast eerie patterns on the asbestos siding, and a headless-rooster weathervane limped around in a circle. I began to wonder whether my brainstorm had been such a great idea after all—but only until I saw the light, a soft yellow glow around drawn draperies, an instant beacon, irresistible and electric, proof positive to my overheated imagination that she was there. Alone. My stomach fluttered at the thought. A part of me, the cynical part, jeered with derision. Another part squirmed with embarrassment.

I got out and walked to the porch, stepped across the squeaking boards, and rapped lightly. The faint sound of canned TV laughter ceased abruptly. I fancied I heard footsteps. A short pause and the door swung open; we stood looking at each other through the screen door.

"Mr. Roman!" Surprise added a note of husky harshness to the mellifluous voice, a quizzical expression to the lovely face. She wore a yellow nylon robe and pajamas, a pair of shiny silver house shoes.

"I was in the neighborhood," I said, the feeble attempt at humor sounding flat and hollow. "I wanted to talk to Jonas about Sandy."

"Jonas isn't here," she said. "He and Scrub Marlowe and Fess Tinker are out running the dogs." She paused, her eyes in shadow. "They'll be out there all night." She reached up slowly and unlatched the screen door. "Won't you come in?"

I treaded water for a moment, trying to read her expressionless face. "Maybe for just a minute," I said, stepping back and gesturing toward the swing. "Maybe we could sit out here. It's a warm night."

She nodded and pushed through the screen door, turning to press it closed against its pneumatic control. She turned back again, and I had moved. We were close, closer than I had any right to be.

We looked at each other some more; I reached out and put my hands on her shoulders—slowly, slowly, giving her time to move, to shrug them away. She didn't move. Or

148

shrug. She stood passively, a faint smile working at her lips, the dark eyes alive and shining.

"I'm lying," I said. "I came to see you. I knew Jonas would be gone with the dogs. He told me at the cemetery."

Her head inclined. "I know. His voice carries. I heard him this morning."

"You're not angry?"

"No. Should I be?"

"I don't know. I don't know what the hell I'm doing." My fingers touched the smooth curve of her neck, moved gently with a will of their own.

The smile broadened, the dark eyes grew wider. "The next step, I think, would be to kiss me, Mr. Roman." Light sprayed across her face as a car whistled down the highway, the brief illumination sparking fire on the convex surfaces of her eyes.

I cupped her cheeks in my hands and leaned forward, stopped. "I can't possibly kiss anyone who calls me Mr. Roman."

"Dan," she said, her voice oddly muted, submissive, as if she had cast off all womanly restraint. "Danny," she whispered. "Is that what she calls you?"

"There is no she."

She clucked softly and came against me, arms sliding inside my jacket and around my waist. "There must be a she somewhere for such a he," she said, and laughed softly, taking the initiative right out of my hands, stretching on tiptoe to press our mouths together lightly, the warm caress as soft as a baby's kiss.

Another car whooshed by, almost unnoticed. She broke the kiss, murmured against my lips. "We should go inside. They can see us from the highway." Her voice was heavy, rich with promise, long lashes drooping, dark crescents on her cheeks. The skin on her face felt warm, feverish; her lips looked swollen, the lithe body clinging to mine, fluid and boneless.

"Right," I said, and when she gave no indication of moving, I picked her up and carried her through the door.

16

I BROKE FREE OF HER EMBRACE, WRENCHED MYSELF AWAY from the quicksilver clutch of her body. I rolled to the edge of the bed and swung my feet to the floor, feeling disoriented, fevered, a little crazed.

"What's wrong, Danny?" Her voice came from a long way away, startled and concerned, slumberous with the weight of desire.

"Nothing. I don't know." I pawed through the pile of clothing beside the bed, found my shorts, and put them on. Not without difficulty.

"I don't understand. You were . . . were perfectly fine." I felt the bed move as she changed position behind me. "What's the matter?"

"I don't know." I found my shirt, the sleeves turned wrong side out.

"Don't keep saying that! Something must be wrong. Why did you stop?"

"I don't know, Myna, dammit. I'm sorry."

"But you were perfectly . . . you weren't . . . you were doing great. I don't understand, Danny."

"The problem isn't between my legs, Myna. It's between my eyes."

I got the shirt straightened out and slipped my arms into the sleeves. I hit my forehead with the palm of my hand, a melodramatic gesture worthy of any third-rate thespian anywhere. "Here, right here. I guess it's called a conscience."

She moved again, came against my back, pressing tightly, warm breasts and warmer loins penetrating the thin material of the shirt. "You're being silly, Danny. We're not doing anything wrong, not really. Jonas and I haven't made love for ages, two years at least. You forget he's sixty-one."

"I don't think that changes it a lot."

"Then why did you—you started this, Dan Roman. You came here, lured me out on the porch and kissed me, got me all fired up and now . . ." She let it fade, breath pumping in my ear.

"I know, and I'm sorry. It's not easy to explain. It's just that every so often I run into something I can't handle, can't do the way I thought I could. Coming into a man's house and making love to his wife behind his back is one of them, I guess. I thought I could skydive too, but once up there, they couldn't pry me out of that plane."

"This is ridiculous," she said, her tone peevish for the first time, a note of petulance creeping in. "I'm burning up and you're talking about airplanes. And you're still—" Her hands slipped around my waist and down before I could catch them. "—perfectly hard."

"That's not the point, Myna." I captured her hands, wrapped one hand around both small wrists. She struggled silently for a moment, then suddenly relaxed and fell against my back and bit my ear.

"We could go to a motel, then, or out to your pickup."

"I don't think that would change things basically. You'll

still be married to a man I know, and I'd still be sneaking around behind his back."

I felt her stiffen, a hot jet of breath against my neck. "My God, what do you think *I'm* doing? I've never done *anything* like this before, never so much as *kissed* a man since we've been married." She stopped, breathing hard. "My God, what you must think of me!" She jerked her hands free and pushed away from my back, sobbing.

I whirled and caught her before she could retreat to the other side of the bed. She was nude and utterly desirable and it was one of the most difficult things I'd ever done, but I cradled her in my arms like a crying child and rocked her until the sobs subsided, faded into ragged breathing and an occasional hiccup. Tears of frustration, I decided.

"It has nothing to do with being bad, Myna. It only has to do with me. What we almost did is not necessarily bad in itself. It's just that I think I'd feel bad about it later. I've got too many things to feel sorry about already. I don't need anything more. This wouldn't have happened if I hadn't come here deliberately hoping for something like this. You were an innocent bystander."

"I was willing," she said, her voice small and child-like. "I liked you from the beginning."

"I knew that, or thought I did. I felt the same attraction and let it blind me to reality. The reality is that you're married and I've got no right to interfere in that. I have enough trouble living with myself the way it is."

"I think you're making too much out of it."

"Maybe so. I do that sometimes. I get hung up on things that never seem to bother other people. I'm not sure what that means. Maybe I was born out of my time."

She blinked up at me from her nest in my arms, her face solemn. "Maybe we met in the wrong life."

"Right. Maybe next time."

She squinted her eyes in critical appraisal of my face. "You look like an old soul."

I chuckled and eased her back to the bed. She had calmed, and the feel of her body and the view were rapidly growing too difficult to bear. Regretfully, but with a distinct feeling of relief, I leaned down and kissed her, then slid off the bed and resumed getting dressed, suddenly anxious to be gone, out of temptation's way.

"I guess this is the weirdest night of my life," she said, humor returning to her voice, lifting the edges of her lips. "The closest thing I can remember is the night of the senior prom in the backseat of Denny McCall's old sixty-one Chrysler. He left me high and dry, too."

"For different reasons, I hope."

She smiled. "Yes. He was what Jonas calls a hair-trigger Harry." She hugged her knees against her breasts and watched me light a cigarette. "Did you really have something to ask Jonas, or was that just part of your . . . your cover? Isn't that what you call it?"

I nodded and averted my eyes as she swung up on one knee and stepped out of the bed. She gathered her pajamas and robe from the floor where I had thrown them and nonchalantly began to dress.

"I wanted to ask him," I lied, "if Sandra had told him they were going to cut the timber on his land."

She looked at me through the V in her pajama top, then let it slide down. "Yes, she told him. They had a terrible argument. Sandy said they had to, to save the company. Jonas said he'd shoot the first man who broke bark on his land."

"Why would he threaten them if he could legally keep them off? It's his land, isn't it?"

"It's his land, but he isn't sure about the timber. He hasn't the faintest idea what was in those papers he signed thirty years ago, and he has no idea where his copy is. To tell you the truth, he's been worried sick about it. We've turned this house upside down, but no papers.'' She belted the robe around her slender waist. "Jonas has always been too careless with legal papers. He usually leaves them lying around and finally throws them into an old shoe box on the closet shelf. There's no telling what happened to the land papers.'' She shrugged and smiled. "He had nineteen years to lose them before we married.''

"They must have made up; he took her to the bus.''

"He had no choice about that. I had to work. I'm not sure if they made up, though. Joline came by to bring Sandy her deerskin blouse sometime after I left at two-thirty, and she said they were still at it. She said Jonas was drinking, something he almost never does because he never knows when to stop.''

"Alcoholic?''

She gave me an annoyed glance. "No, I don't think so. It's just that when he gets started he always drinks until he passes out. Is that an alcoholic?''

"Don't sound like it. How was he when you got home?''

She smiled briefly. "Passed out.''

"What time was that?''

She frowned, the look this time straight and steady. "Why?''

"I'm trying to find Sandy,'' I said quietly. "I need to establish a timetable on her movements.''

"Oh, she got on the bus all right.''

"How do you know?''

"Well . . . Jonas told me.''

"If he was passed out when you got home around midnight—''

"Not midnight. I had to work an extra shift. Dolly Marvin was sick. I got home around seven the next morning. I woke him up.''

"See how painless that was?''

"You tricked me."

"No, I just led you through the back door. Us detectives are sneaky. You gotta watch us every minute."

"I know," she said fervently, and made a raunchy smile. "I should have watched you a little closer a few minutes ago. Maybe I wouldn't be humming inside like a high-voltage wire."

"I said I was sorry. I don't know what else to say." I stared down at the rumpled bed for a moment, then looked back at her. "There are a couple of other ways—"

"Oh, hush," she said. "I was only teasing. I guess now I know how the boys back in high school used to feel."

"Humming like a high-voltage wire," I said, and she laughed, combing tangled black hair with her fingers, the fevered glow still in her eyes.

She walked me to the door and out into air that had grown markedly cooler. I followed her footsteps across the yard, avoiding the puddles, watching the trim figure move beneath the whispering nylon and wondering when I had become psychologically unsound. The old Dan Roman had never run away from a beautiful woman in his life, and here I had done it twice in less than a week. Born-again, I thought, a damned born-again idiot.

At the truck she showed me how mean-spirited she could be; she rose on tiptoe and kissed me, a real kiss, lips, teeth, tongue, and everything, something to remember, a living memento of what I had missed. It had an air of finality about it, of goals not achieved and chances gone, of faint-hearted fools and fair maidens forever lost.

I waited until she went back inside the house. I lit a cigarette and climbed into my small steel cocoon, safe at last in the knowledge that I had done all the damage I could do for one night.

17

I SPENT THE NIGHT IN THE SAME MOTEL IN CRATER. DIF-
ferent room, same clutter and sleaze. I slept even less than
I had that first night, lying in the penumbral silence, chain-
smoking, asking myself questions I couldn't begin to
answer, formulating answers for which there were no
questions. Berating myself. Feeling sorry for myself, for
Myna. For Jonas.

Somebody was lying.

Understatement of the year. Almost everybody was
lying, at least in part. Starting with Macomber Beechum
himself when he had lied to me about the cigarette. Lying
seemed to come easy to the Beechums. Part of their nature? Conditioning? Environment? Maybe a prerequisite
for acquiring and holding on to vast sums of money, big
houses, fine cars, sleek women?

Jonas had been lying about the timber rights to his land.
That much was clear. Myna's story had had the crystal
ring of truth, and it was inconceivable that Sandra and
Nelson Morrow would not know the true status of the surface rights. In hindsight, Jonas's confident declaration of

total control had had an air of sheer bravado, wistful thinking.

On the other hand, I believed what he had said about Sandra, about Conrad calling the plays behind the scenes, making decisions for which she took credit. I wasn't sure why except that it would explain in part her failure to take him to task over his infidelities. Almost from the beginning, I had had trouble buying the idea of Sandy Conrad, lady genius. And, once again, I wasn't sure why, beyond the fact that she was a Beechum and I had come to expect little from a Beechum. A biased viewpoint, and grossly unfair since I hadn't met her. She might well stand head and shoulders above the rest of the clan. I had an uneasy feeling that I would never know for sure.

The bed had a clammy feel, lumps, and smelled faintly of pepperoni pizza and sex. I dragged the room's only chair to the window, opened the drapes, and sat watching Crater nightlife on the strip. Garish neon and precious little stirring. Weeknights were for sleeping; Friday and Saturday nights would be a different story. An occasional pickup rattled among the potholes, and every hour or so a freight train thundered along clattering tracks fifty yards behind the motel.

I watched the midnight news on a snowy Houston station and dozed through an hour of silly sitcoms. Halfway through a fluffy bit of nonsense called *The Brain Connection*, I decided I would try the bed again, catchy odors and lumps and all.

I smoked a final cigarette and mashed it out. I was reaching for the drapery cord when the Buick turned into the motel parking lot.

It moved slowly, dark and gleaming in the artificial lights. I saw four silhouettes as it passed in front of the office, the brief flare of a match or a lighter. It looked new, showroom shiny, and moved almost soundlessly behind my pickup parked in front of the door, hesitating only a second, a small puff of white escaping the exhaust as it resumed its creeping speed, advanced another thirty feet along the aisle, and stopped.

The lights went off, the exhaust kept chugging smoke. Three doors opened and three men got out. Big men. Baseball-style gimme caps and dark shirts. Levi's and boots. Each one carried a club. Nonchalantly, as if they carried clubs often, they took practice swings.

A peeled limb as big as my wrist, longer than my arm. Hickory probably, or oak. An ancient weapon for which there was only one use. Primitive, effective, plentiful, and very painful. I watched them look toward my cabin and wished I had one; all I had were a couple of guns, and I didn't want to kill anybody. Dammit! Not tonight. I already had a headache and the hassle would take forever.

They either had a key or slipped the lock with a credit card. I heard clicking noises at the door seconds before it burst open, a momentary jam of shadowy figures before one of them found the switch and flooded the small room with light.

Two of them hung suspended over the bed, clubs upraised, staring at each other, the hasty bundle of bed-clothing I had raked together not fooling them for more than an instant.

"Shit! He ain't here—"

I stepped halfway through the bathroom door, leaned forward against the doorjamb, looking at them along the short section of wall that housed the shower.

"Bathroom!" The other one whirled, stopped, his broad face a ludicrous mixture of surprise and chagrin as he spotted me and the small automatic in my left hand. His partner, coming around the end of the bed, slammed into him before he could stop. Over by the door, the third one made a strangled warning sound.

"Hidy," I said. "You guys the plumbers I called for? Them's mighty funny looking snakes you've got there. I don't want the toilet all busted up, I just want it unplugged."

"Godammit," the second one said, pawing at his partner's shoulder. "Go on, Leo, that's just a popgun he's got there. He ain't gonna—"

"I'll go you one better," I said. "It's only a .22 and it only has rat shot in it. That make it easier? Guaranteed to kill a rat at fifteen feet, blow a man's balls all to hell at ten. Whatta you think now, partner?"

Leo dropped his club on the bed and gave me a sickly grin.

The second man, still hiding behind Leo, brandished his club and cursed. Over by the door, the third man cleared his throat.

"You gotta consider what he's got in his right hand. Stands to reason he's got something a little bigger in there—ain't you?" He directed the last part at me, his expression more curious than frightened—after all, he was by the door.

"You have to pay to see," I said. "That's the rules of the game."

"I fold," Leo said, raising his hands palm outward and backing into his buddy, still grinning his idiotic grin. He snarled out of the corner of his mouth. "Get out of my way, asshole!"

"No, no," I said, and waggled the little gun at them. "The game's not over. You lost, friend. When you lose, you pay. It's a lot like blackjack. You remember blackjack, everybody has a hole card." I waggled the gun again. "I'm calling you with this, so now I get to see your hole card."

The second man cursed and threw his club over Leo's head. I stepped back out of the way. It caromed off the wall and clattered to the floor. I stepped back into the doorway.

The third man was gone. The second was heading for the door. Leo stood frozen. I shot the second man in his right buttock.

He stumbled and screamed, caught himself on the door-jamb, and lurched outside. He let out a stream of curses and Leo and I looked at each other and listened to his hobbling footsteps recede.

"I guess it's down to me and you, Leo."

Leo looked pale. "My God, you really shot him!" He sounded horrified. He had dark red hair and a serious overbite, bulging brown eyes.

I moved out into the small alcove fronting the bathroom. I showed him the .38 in my right hand. "Your buddy was right, you know. I had something bigger." I slid along the wall and closed the drapes, crossed in front of the window, and kicked the door closed.

"Now, where were we? Oh, yeah, you were getting ready to tell me who sent you to operate on my sinuses. I'm guessing it was the fourth man in the car, the guy who owns the Buick. How close am I, Leo?"

"Hell, man, I don't know who he is." He shifted uneasily and ran his tongue all the way around his mouth. "We was just down at Pinto's playing some pool and this guy comes in and first thing you know we was stripping bark off'n them limbs. He said there was a hundred apiece in it and some fun—"

I lifted my hand and he stopped. I nodded and dropped the .22 into my coat pocket. I walked a couple of steps to his left and sighted carefully down the barrel of the .38. He was wearing yellow and gold needle-nosed boots. I shot the toe off the left one.

161

He screamed louder than the other one had. I watched him hop around.

"You probably already got your hundred, Leo. That was the fun part." My voice sounded strange and far away in the vacuum of concussion. "I don't want to have to blow off your other toe; bullets cost good money. You want to tell me now?"

He fell on the bed, hugging the foot to his belly, tugging gingerly on the heel, a look of intense concentration on his face as his foot slipped out of the boot. He wore no socks and his toes were still intact. He squeezed them in one scruffy hand and looked up at me, the silly grin back on his face. "Them mothers are still numb, man. I thought you'd shot them off."

"Shit," I said, and pointed the gun at his other foot.

"No, wait! Look, I heard Jellison call him Curly. I've seen him around before; somebody said he runs some kinda lumbering outfit out north of town somewheres."

"Curly Glazier?"

"I don't know, man. Maybe that's it."

"Describe him."

"Tall, good-looking bozo, curly hair, looks purty strong." He stopped, his head lifting as the sound of a siren penetrated the thin walls of the cabin.

"Company, Leo. Somebody called in those shots." I eased back the drapery and looked out. The Buick was gone. I grinned at Leo. "Your friends are gone." I sat down beside him. "In about two minutes a cop of some kind's going to knock on that door. Probably a deputy sheriff." I picked up his club and hefted it in my hand. "This ought to be good for assault with a deadly weapon."

"Hey, man, I didn't lay a hand on you."

"Not for lack of trying. But that don't matter, Leo. All I have to do is say you touched me with it and you're gone, man. Plus you're in here illegally, so that adds breaking and entering. I can't tag your friends because they're gone, so I guess you'll have to tote the load all by yourself. Five to fifteen, Leo, depending on how good a lawyer you can afford to hire.''

"Aw, shit, man, I ain't got no money for some—''

"Okay, Leo. Maybe we can make a deal. Do you know how to get in touch with Curly?''

His head bobbed. "You bet, man. Jellison'll know for sure.''

"Is Jellison the one I dosed with bird shot?''

"That what that was? I thought you said it was rat shit or something.''

"Was he Jellison?''

"No. Jellison was the young guy at the door. Chicken-shit bastard.''

The siren wound down with a weary bloop. Headlights flashed across the window. I heard an excited female voice rattling like a machine pistol. I dropped a hand on Leo's shoulder.

"Tell the cop you were looking at my .38, and like the dummy you are, you almost shot your foot off. Got that.''

He nodded wordlessly, practicing looking dumb, making it appear easy. I picked up the mangled boot and tossed it in his lap, the steel-capped toe dangling by a slender thread of leather. I dumped the cartridges out of the .38, all except the empty. I tossed it on the bed beside Leo just as the knock sounded on the door.

18

HE WAS TALL AND SPARE, NARROW-SHOULDERED, A THIN, beaked nose and piercing black eyes, long arms, and a chest rounded like a pouter pigeon's. He wore a crisp tan uniform, a white hat, and somewhere along the line, nature had frozen his face into a permanent scowl. He stood ramrod straight, right thumb hooked in the well-worn gun belt slanted across his flat midriff. The heavy gun hung low on his right thigh, looking, at first glance, like an exact replica of Jonas Beechum's.

Another one, I thought disgustedly, another cold-eyed cowboy cop so conscious of his own self-image he thrummed like a guy wire in a high wind. I had dealt with men like him most of my adult life, but it never got any easier.

"Officer," I said, giving him a toothy grin and an avuncular chuckle, keeping my hands in plain sight, moving them as little as possible. "I'll bet some citizen called in about the shot—right?"

He stared at me without speaking, looked past me at Leo grinning foolishly on the bed, the injured boot cra-

164

164

dled in both beefy hands, held out before him like a burnt offering.

"Shots, she said." He moved into the room. I gave ground. "A little one first and then a big one, she said."

I creased my brow and puckered my lips. "No, sir, don't know anything about two shots. Only one shot. Old dumbo Leo there tried to shoot off his toe. Can you imagine that?"

"Who owns the gun?" he asked casually. His voice was deep, resonant, no trace of a drawl. He came to a halt in front of Leo, leaned down, and picked up my gun.

"Mine," I said.

He popped out the cylinder and dropped the empty casing into his hand. "Only one load?"

"I thought I'd unloaded it," Leo said. "I dumped the loads and went to check the action and . . . and blowed off my toe." He looked at the deputy and giggled, a particularly foolish giggle that spoke volumes, and I began to see steel bars and hard cots, long-distance telephone calls, and a long hard night ahead of me.

"One of the cylinders hangs sometimes," I said. "Little buildup in there, I reckon, gunpowder residue blowing back—"

"You have a permit?" he asked politely.

"Don't need one," I said promptly, wishing I could bite off my tongue as something surfaced in the pale eyes, flickered, and disappeared. "I'm traveling out of my county," I went on lamely, "and the law says—"

"I know the law," he said. "You don't have a permit?"

"I didn't say that." I took out my wallet, slipped the PI identification card out of its plastic holder. I gave it to him along with a courteous nod.

He studied it at length, rubbed it between thumb and forefinger as if checking for authenticity, turned it over, and inspected the back. He handed it back to me and shrugged. He tossed my gun on the bed.

"Don't I know you?" he said to Leo. "Don't you work out at Curly Glazier's sawmill? Yeah. You're the feller who cut that four-by-twelve beam for me a couple months ago. Remember? You were having some trouble with your saw."

Leo fidgeted, almost looked at me, but caught himself in time. "Yeah, yeah, by gum, I think I do. Cedar, wasn't it? You was building a cabin or something."

The deputy swung toward me and held out his hand. "I'm Deputy Wally Hendricks, Mr. Roman. I'd appreciate it if you'd take a little more care with your gun while you're in my county." He spoke pleasantly enough, but there was no doubting his sincerity. "A man's gun is a very personal thing. I don't even allow my wife to touch mine." He said it with a straight face and I had no choice but to assume he was serious.

"Really? That's a shame. That's an interesting looking piece you're carrying. I was about to ask to see it."

He smiled and twitched his shoulder and held it out across his palm. "Look all you want to, Mr. Roman. Just don't touch it, please."

"Jesus Christ," Leo said. "Did you see that? Man, that was *fast.*"

Hendricks shook his head. "No, that was slow. Eight, nine hundredths of a second probably. Three hundredths is fast. My best time is four."

"No kidding," I marveled. "Four hundredths of a second. Golly, I can't blink my eyes that fast."

"The record is just under three," he said flatly, the pale eyes tight on my face. "Man out in the Dakotas somewhere."

"That's incredible," I said, straightening from my visual inspection of his gun. "That looks like a Colt .44, made back in the late eighteen hundreds sometime." As far as I could see, it was exactly like Jonas Beechum's.

He gave me an approving nod. "You know your guns. It used to be owned by old Whiskey Sam Coble, Texas Ranger—"

"Not the same Sam Coble who got shot in the back down in El Paso?"

"That's the one. I bought it off a feller who got it from a cousin of old Whiskey Sam's." His eyes looked a little warmer. "You know your Texas history, Mr. Roman."

"Some," I admitted modestly. "The old gunfighters, the Alamo, San Jacinto, you know, things like that."

His head bobbed in affirmation. "You bet. Those tough old bastards built this state, this country, in fact. Man ought to learn about his roots. My great granddaddy was scalped not fifty miles from this spot. Scalped and strung out over an anthill, honey poured all over his pecker and balls." He paused, his face flushed, a line of acne marks along his jaw standing out like rabbit tracks in new snow. "And not by Indians. My great granddaddy was a Texas Ranger, you see, one of the first ones back when it meant something." He stopped and looked from me to Leo and back again, breathing deeply, his eyes alight with pride.

I nodded admiringly. Leo made an inarticulate sound. I lit a cigarette and wondered how I was going to stop this now that I'd got it started.

"How about a beer, Deputy Hendricks? Leo here was just about to run across the road and get us a six-pack when he started fiddling with my gun. Won't take but a minute."

He turned abruptly to the door. "On duty, thanks all the same. Maybe some other time."

"That'd be great," I said. "Maybe you could give me some pointers on fast drawing—you know, some tricks of the trade."

Once again his gaze crawled over my face. "There's some," he said. "But mainly it's in the wrist and practice, practice, practice."

I followed him through the door. His blue-and-white cruiser was parked crosswise behind my pickup, lights off, motor quiet.

"I can tell you about practice," I said. "It took me almost a month to learn how to play the piano."

He turned, a smile edging thin lips. "You're full of bullshit, Mr. Roman. But that's all right. We all have some of that. Just don't go shooting off your Smith and Wesson in my county anymore. Okay? That asshole in there couldn't find his boot toe, much less shoot it off. Anyhow, the bullet went into the toe cap at the wrong angle for that. I can't force you to tell me what's going on, but I can come down on you like a drop hammer if you break any more of my laws. Understood?"

"Loud and clear."

He nodded crisply and I had to shake his hand again. He was, I thought, a little limp-wristed for a man who could pull and fire a gun in four hundredths of a second.

19

Leo was still sitting on the bed, looking injured, sawing at the dangling toe cap with a small penknife. He stopped and watched while I reloaded the .38 Airweight. I dropped it into my overnight bag and pulled the zipper. He looked relieved until I took out the little .22.

I pulled the chair over in front of him and sat down. I lit a cigarette. I offered him one. He shook his head.

"Them things will kill you."

"Not as quick as this," I said, and touched the end of his nose with the .22.

He moved his head. "Hey, man, come on now. I backed you up with the cowboy cop, didn't I—"

"You didn't have a choice, Leo, that I could see. I don't think he was too impressed with you the way it was. Did you screw up his piece of lumber?"

"I backed you up, man, and you owe me something for that. I coulda turned you over for shooting Fred Broome—"

I rapped him on the kneecap with the flat of the gun. "Shut up, Leo, before you make me mad. Bullshit time is over. You work for Curly Glazier, so don't tell me you

169

don't know what he looks like. You either start talking straight or I'm going to find out something I've been wondering about for a long time.'' I puffed smoke at him and waited.

"What?'' he asked finally, swallowing noisily, trying to close his mouth over his big teeth.

I hefted the small gun. "Rat shot. I've always wondered if it'd penetrate a pair of good boots. Personally, I don't think it will—it's bird shot, after all—but I'll bet it would smart like hell.''

"You ain't scaring me,'' he said sullenly. "I ain't afraid of no bird shot. But them bastards went off and left me, and I'll tell you all I know. Which ain't nothing much.''

"It was Glazier?''

"Yeah, him and Broome and Jellison come by a little while ago. They wanted to know if I wanted to have some fun and make a little money too. Glazier drove us over here and pointed out your cabin, gave Jellison a key and . . . and that's all there was to it.''

"Did Glazier happen to mention why?''

"I asked him that,'' he said earnestly. "I was curious myself. He just laughed and said he didn't like the way you drove a car.''

"What exactly were your instructions?''

He looked confused. "Instructions? Oh, you mean—well, we was just supposed to roust you around a little, maybe bust a couple of bones—''

"Like in my arms and my legs.'' I got up and walked away from him, a shiver rippling in my stomach. I looked out the window; the Buick was nowhere in sight.

I watched Leo's reflection in the window and visualized my body twisting and curling under the clubs, vicious laughter and animal grunts as hard wood smashed flesh and cartilage and bone. A little fun and some money, too.

I whirled on Leo, rage boiling in me like an unwatched pot.

"Get out of here, man!"

He looked at me and blinked.

"Out! Get the hell out of here. You find Curly. You tell that son of a bitch I want him here at eight o'clock in the morning—"

"Man, I don't know where—"

"Shut up! Don't talk, listen! He'll find you. He's out there now, watching. He'll have to know what happened to you, stupid. Tell him exactly eight. Not one minute before, not one minute past. You got that?"

"Yeah, but, man—"

"Don't talk, goddammit! Just get out of here before I change my mind!"

He stood up cautiously and limped to the door, the boot dangling in his hand.

"Tell him one other thing. Tell him if he brings a gun, I'll kill him, and if he doesn't come, tell him I'll come after him." My voice was shaking, but it no longer mattered; I had Leo's undivided attention. Right up to the time he backed out and closed the door.

The wake-up call came at seven forty-five, yanked me out of half-sleep into almost instant awareness, my first sight of the dingy room triggering a chain reaction of recollection. I put the Airweight on the night table by the bed and lit my first cigarette in two hours, yawning away fuzziness, shrugging off fatigue.

I went into the bathroom and splashed water on my face, rinsed my mouth, propped a hand against the nondescript wallpaper above the commode, and awaited developments.

At three minutes to eight I unlocked the door and moved

the chair to the middle of the room. I sat down and lit another cigarette and awaited further developments.

The knock came at precisely eight o'clock by my watch. And that surprised me: no two watches keep the same exact time.

"It's open," I said, "but you better come in easy."

The door swung inward. Curly Glazier stood there. Grinning. Dressed in tight leather pants and a T-shirt despite the early-morning chill. He held his hands at shoulder height and twirled slowly, doing a little bump and grind as he came to face me again. Funny, he thought it was funny.

"Okay? No gun, see?"

"Come in and close the door."

He did as ordered, then looked over his shoulder. "Want me to lock it?"

"No point. A ten-year-old could kick it in."

He nodded. "It's a shame what they sell you nowadays." The humor was back in his voice, his face, his eyes.

"You think this is funny?"

He shrugged. "Isn't it? Three bruisers like Dahl and Jellison and Broome, and you run them ass-over-teakettle with a little popgun with bird shot. I think it's hilarious."

"Ask Broome. I don't imagine he thinks it's hilarious."

"No, matter of fact, he don't. You tore his ass up pretty good. He ain't griping too much, though; he'll be getting sick pay for a few days." He laughed again and scissored his fingers. "How about giving me a smoke? I was afraid to bring any."

"Go to hell, Glazier. There's nothing funny about any of this. Up close rat shot can kill you. A little closer and hickory clubs can do the same thing."

"Aw, come on. They weren't supposed to do you any real harm. Bruise you up some, scare you."

172

"Why?"

The humor bled out of his face, leaving it cold and set, the bronzed skin slowly growing pale. A thin white line ringed his mouth; his nostrils flared.

"I told you that day out on the highway. Stay away from the Beechums. I want that land."

I studied his face while I lit a cigarette. "That's bullshit, Glazier. You know who I am, what I'm doing here. There's another reason and I don't think it has anything to do with the land. Tell me something, do you spy on the Beechums all the time or only when Jonas is out with his dogs?"

He stared at me silently, his face under control, but there was little he could do about the burning eyes, the galvanic response of a single nerve at the corner of his mouth.

"You saw us on the porch," I said softly. "You saw us kiss. You saw me pick her up and carry her inside. It's the woman, isn't it? You still want the woman?"

He broke eye contact, then threw back his head and barked a short humorless laugh. "I don't have to wait around, man. I can have any woman I want."

"Except this one. Except the one who got away, the one you wanted to marry. I don't blame you. I'm pretty high on her myself."

"You son of a bitch!"

"I can't deny that, I guess. You saw me with your own eyes."

"You were in there an hour!" He spoke through clenched teeth, his resonant voice suddenly rough and ugly.

"Not an hour," I said, "but long enough. So, what business is it of yours, Glazier? She's not your wife. She turned you down for another man. Face facts, man. She's been married to him—what, ten years? That's over thirty-five hundred nights, knocking off a few for coon hunting.

173

What do you think they do in that little house when the lights go out? A chaste kiss and good night, sweetheart?''

"You're a real son of a bitch, you know that?''

"I can be, yeah. I can be a mean son of a bitch when somebody keeps reminding me of it. I've let you get away with it twice now because I know how it feels to want a woman you can't have. But you've gone beyond that. You've let it become an obsession. Ten years. I have a hunch all these things that have been happening to Jonas Beechum don't really have anything to do with his land at all. They have to do with his woman.''

He didn't answer, didn't look up, the handsome face a curious shade of mottled gray.

"It won't work, Glazier. You can't scare her into leaving him if that's what you've been trying for, and I think it is. She loves him, man, and—''

"She don't love him!'' The words spewed from somewhere deep inside him, thick and constricted, almost unintelligible. He dropped to a seat on the foot of the bed, slumped forward, elbows on his knees, his expression pained, defeated. "That's what makes it so . . . so damned hard.''

I watched him warily. His distress seemed genuine, his pain real, but he had sent three thugs to break my bones and I had no desire to make things easy for him.

"Bullshit, Curly. I've seen her look at him. I've seen them look at each other. I suppose next you're going to tell me she married him for his money, the life of luxury they live out there in that mansion, all the fine cars, the servants—''

"No, goddammit, that's not it! It's the land!''

"The land,'' I echoed mechanically. "You mean the money for the timber—''

"No . . . the land, the land itself—'' He broke off,

174

looking as if he had just tasted something foul, his mouth stretched into a tight white line.

"Myna wants the land? Why, so she can coon hunt? Make sense, Curly. I understand your need to believe she had some reason for marrying Jonas besides love, but I think you're reaching a little, partner. Myna doesn't even like the forest. She loves the wide open spaces, West Texas, North Texas, anywhere but here where you can't see mor'n a half-mile in any direction. I know that much, and I've only known her a week or so."

"It's the damn truth," he said sullenly.

"I guess she's waiting for Jonas to die, huh? Well, I hear he's sixty-one and, since most old folks are living into their late seventies, early eighties, that means she's only got twenty more years or so to wait. Does that sound reasonable, Curly? Living like a dirt farmer's wife for thirty years just to inherit a lot of land you hate. Now, maybe, just maybe, I could understand her wanting the money from the timber—"

"You don't know anything," he said, his tone argumentative, filled with scorn, his belligerent expression straight off a ninth-grade school yard.

"What don't I know?"

"She never loved Jonas. Not ever. She liked him. It usta be hard not to like Jonas. Christ, I oughta know, he was my best friend. She was my girl. I introduced her to him. Sorriest damn day of my life the way it worked out. Jonas flipped over her. I could tell even though he tried to hide it. And that was funny in a way because he was sour on women. He got married once when he was twenty. It only lasted six months. He swore that was enough of that. Never happen again, he said. And it didn't. Not until he met Myna. He was fifty, I guess. She was twenty-six. She was hostile as hell at first. I thought it was just because she didn't like him for some reason. But then I found out—" He gave me a jeering smile. "This ain't really none of your business."

"Then forget it, friend. It's your story." I glanced at my watch and started to rise.

He threw out a hand. "Hey, don't be so touchy. Hell, I'm just trying to make a point here."

"Then make it. I've wasted enough time on you."

He grimaced. "Well, I finally got her to tell me why, and it wasn't Jonas so much as it was the Beechum name. She grew up hating the Beechum name. You remember the story I told you about the poker game in Galveston, Macomber Beechum and the Indian he created? Well, it did happen, purty much as the story goes. Jonas himself admitted that to me—"

"And Myna is the long-lost daughter of that Indian."

He gave me an annoyed look. "No, not exactly. She's his granddaughter."

"And she sacrificed herself to an old man to get the land back for her people."

"Dammit! You gonna let me tell this or not? That wasn't the way it happened at all. Nothing woulda happened if Jonas hadn't had another heart attack—"

"*Another* heart attack. Nobody's mentioned the first one."

"I told you, you don't know shit. The first time wasn't really a heart attack, I guess. He had rheumatic fever when he was a teenager. Screwed up his heart some way. A year or so before all this happened, he had a real bad attack. Spent some time in the hospital. Even had some kind of surgery, leaky valves or something like that. Anyhow, the doctors told him they couldn't do anything more, that he might last a couple of years if he took it real easy, laid around, didn't get excited, shit like that. Well, you know Jonas—or maybe you don't—but he wasn't having any of that crap. As soon as he got his strength back, he went right back to coon hunting, working around here just like he had always done.''

"Myna knew about it, huh? Decided a couple of years wouldn't be a bad investment—'' I broke off, withdrawing the needle at the sudden look of pain on his face.

"No,'' he said quietly. ''I can't lay it off on her. It was all my idea.''

20

I LIT TWO CIGARETTES, HANDED HIM ONE, GIVING HIM A little time to organize his thoughts. Eventually, when he showed no inclination to continue, I prodded gently: "You must have wanted the timber pretty badly."

He barked a short grating laugh. "Bad enough. I was being crowded out by the bigger companies. I needed it then as much as I need it now. I knew Myna felt like the land rightfully belonged to her family and—" He crumpled the butt against the heel of his boot, let it drop to the tiled floor. He stared at me, his face strained, a remote look in his eyes. "Jonas said the doctor said . . . no sex. When I made my pitch to Myna and to Jonas, that was my understanding. I knew Jonas was crazy about her, that was easy to see, and after a while Myna began to warm up to him. I figured a year, two years—it was the only way either one of us would get what we wanted. Jonas had no wife or kids. The land would revert back to Macomber Beechum or one of the other ones. They had their own lumber company. I also knew Jonas didn't want them to have it. He didn't like any of his family much, except maybe Sandy. He went into it willingly. I guess I didn't think about them—or wouldn't let myself think about them—sleeping together. I don't know. We never discussed it, not even me and Myna. I just assumed . . ." He paused. "But it wasn't long after they were married that I began to realize that they were—I saw them one day in Crater. I could tell. Jesus. I could see it in their faces. I wanted to kill him on the spot."

"Tangled webs," I said.

"What?"

"Never mind. Obviously he's still alive. Ten years. How inconsiderate of him."

"Almost eleven," he growled.

"No excitement, huh? Is that why you've been killing his horses, hogs, and his best dog, shooting out his windows—"

"I don't know nothing about that." He stared at me defiantly, his face cold and hard. "A few days later I caught him alone and faced him with it. The son of a bitch admitted it, said he didn't know what I was talking about, no sex, said it was the best thing ever happened to him, that he felt twenty years younger." His face looked suddenly swollen; a thick vein in the center of his forehead pulsed. "The dirty bastard said he didn't tell me the doctors said he only had a year or so to live. He said I must have dreamed it."

"Disinformation," I said. "The Soviets are experts at it. Jonas apparently isn't bad."

"I'da killed the little bastard, but he'd already started wearing that damn gun of his and I couldn't go up against that. He'd be fool enough to shoot you."

I clicked my tongue. "A gun against a hickory club. That wouldn't be fair."

"Goddammit! This ain't funny!"

"No, it isn't," I agreed soberly. "Greed rarely is. You got greedy, friend, and you got taken. You tried to barter the woman you profess to love for a few board feet of lumber and it backfired on you. You got nothing except humiliation. It's a classic case of the manipulator being manipulated. They made a movie about that kind of thing. They called it *The Sting*. In this case you is the stingee." I smiled into his contorted face, his inner turmoil revealed in the venomous eyes. He came to his feet in a surging rush, hands clenched, the wide shoulders hunched in a defensive posture, rangy body taut.

"Easy, Curly. You don't want to let your ire overload your ass. I've had a yen for your left kneecap ever since you came in. You can walk out or you can crawl. Your choice."

He stared down at me, breathing hard, at the .22 in my hand leveled at him, knee high.

"They tell you I had rat shot in this little gun? That's a fact. I've never pegged anybody in the knee, so I can't advise you. Maybe a lot of damage, maybe not so much. I'd sure like to know." Our eyes met, locked. My smile began to ache, to feel unnatural.

"All right, Curly," I said tiredly. "Get it on or get out. I'm fed up with this shit. I think you're lying and I hate liars like the pox."

He threw up his arms and I almost squeezed one off through pure reflex action. His breath gusted in a noisy hiss as he swung toward the door.

"Bullshit, Roman," he snarled. "You're all bluff. You ain't gonna shoot nobody who's looking at you."

Once again I almost shot him, this time out of pure damn meanness.

But I didn't, of course, and moments later I heard him vent his frustration on the Buick's engine, spewing gravel all the way across the lot, laying rubber among the pot-holes in the street. I listened to his hubbub recede, won-dering, wearily, why I always got the crazies.

* * *

I showered and shaved and stopped down the highway for another Waddy Special. That eased the gnawing feeling in my belly, but did little to dispel the vague sense of disorientation that comes with an almost sleepless night and intermittent spurts of adrenaline. At thirty-seven, my body demanded little of me: sustenance, shelter when needed, and a bit of pleasure now and then. But it liked its sleep and got a little cranky when I deprived it, for whatever reason. Foggy brains was its favorite way of making me pay.

I had some trouble finding Jacob Twill's back gate. For one thing, I was coming from a different direction and, secondly, I had lost the little derelict's map.

But I found it after a while, after a couple of wrong turns and a road that dead-ended in the biggest brush pile I'd ever seen. There were signs of clear-cut logging everywhere, entire hillsides stripped bare of lofty greenery, replanted seedlings waging an unsuccessful defense against erosion and the pillaging wind. Raw gullies where once there had been pine-scented forest floor, home of thousands of creatures. That one of nature's creations, supposedly the most intelligent, could wreak such havoc with impunity seemed grossly unfair.

I eased the Ramcharger to a halt in the turnout by the gate. I shut down the engine and got out, remembering General Ralston's caution about the road into the compound and little city cars. But this time I wasn't driving a little city car. I was riding a four-wheeled beast that sneered at rugged terrain the way a camel laughs at sand. Except for width, I could go anywhere a Jeep could go, more safely, and a hell of a lot faster.

But I soon discovered I wasn't going anywhere. Something new had been added. A shining new log chain and a heavy padlock that dangled down the gatepost like a punk rocker's medallion. Forged steel. Impervious to anything short of a sledgehammer and a cold chisel. Or the right combination.

I lit a cigarette and thought about it for a moment. How badly did I want to get in? I could cut the barbed wire fence easily enough, drive across the shallow ditch and onto Jacob Twill's land in a matter of minutes. The new chain and lock was nothing but puffery, an ostentatious display for the timid of heart. Twill knew that. A dog chain and a bicycle lock would have worked just as well, made the same statement. Posted signs could be ignored by averting the eyes; chains and locks were an entirely different matter. Obviously, since my last visit he had decided to discourage backdoor visitors.

Why? I wondered. Did he have something to hide? A guest, perhaps, or a moonshine still? Or both? Sandra Conrad, killer, running to her guru for sanctuary?

There was another way. I could walk in. I had no idea how far it was to the compound, but I seemed to remember hearing Twill's Jeep start up the afternoon of my first visit. That indicated a half-mile or less. But sound travels in a straight line. Roads don't. There could be a couple of miles up and down the sides of canyons, along switchbacks and ridges. The possibilities were discouraging, and anyhow, I didn't feel up to walking anywhere.

I glanced toward the hut, and that brought back General Ralston's remark about the "squawk box." Maybe they had a radio, a semipermanent installation for emergencies, or for the General to call in his tally of squirrels.

It was worth a look. Something to do while I made up my mind about my search for Sandra Conrad. I had no real belief that Jacob Twill was hiding her, believed even less that she had killed her husband and the Gomez woman.

I climbed the gate and trudged up to the pine hut. The

squawk box was a walkie-talkie wrapped in a plastic bag. Solid and professional looking. I keyed the button on the side and released it. A blare of static, a female voice.

"Yes."

I pressed the talk button. "I-uh, this is the east gate . . ." I hesitated. "No, I think it's the north gate."

"General, is that you? Will you quit clowning around? You were supposed to relieve Brewster at the creek a half hour ago. Where are you?"

"Not General, ma'am. My name is Dan Roman. I'm at the back gate, wherever that is. I'd like to talk to Jacob Twill, if you don't mind."

"Mr. Roman. This is Joline. I'm sorry, Jacob isn't here. Is there anything I can help you with?"

"Well, actually, I wanted to talk to you. I just figured I'd have to clear it with Twill before I came on his property."

"I'm sorry, Mr. Roman. We have just recently initiated a no-visitor rule. That's the reason for the new padlock on the gate."

"How about that? Well, far be it from me to break a rule. I don't suppose you would like to drive that little Jeep of yours on out here and talk to me?"

"Yes, of course. It'll take a few minutes. Will that be all right?"

"That's fine."

It took more than a few minutes, but I didn't mind. I hauled the folding lawn chair out of the hut and sat in the sun and dozed, lulled by inactivity, the wind teasing the majestic pines, sunshine that tickled my skin like a lover's breath. Pungent pine odor drifted by on the breeze, an occasional whiff of cedar, a weeping hardwood, and all around me rang the muted clamor of a million tiny lives.

I closed my eyes and sank into lassitude. This was my environment, where I felt secure, a kinship with the ages, the end product of countless minor miracles down through the centuries, thousands of people who had lived, struggled, and died that I might loaf lazily beneath a longleaf pine in Battle County, Texas, U.S.A. It was a poignant thought, awesome in scope, and just boring enough to put me to sleep.

21

IT WAS THE SUDDEN SILENCE THAT WOKE ME, THE CES-
sation of sound as she shut off the Jeep's motor. Reluctant
to be roused, I had cleverly incorporated the small vehicle's whining growl into my dream, a dream of long ago
aerial warfare. I had flown a Bell Huey in Vietnam, skimming the thick green jungle, the muddy paddies, and sudden silence meant only one thing—loss of power, loss of
lift, usually loss of life. It was a dream I had often: the
overwhelming *brickety-brack* of the rotor blades and then
sudden silence, a gut-swooping sensation of falling.

She sat in the open seat of the Jeep ten feet away, watching me with raised eyebrows, a smidgen of a smile.

"Sorry to be so long. The Jeep had a low tire. I had to
baby it down to the generator at the workshop."

"No problem," I said, automatically reaching for a cigarette. "I guess I dozed."

The smile widened. "Yes, I believe you did." She
scanned my face critically. "You look as if you could use
a little more dozing."

"I don't doubt it. Bad night. Motel beds, you know how
they are."

"No, I don't. I've never spent a night in a motel."

"Really? Then you've missed one of life's more mundane experiences."

She smiled politely. "It seems such a waste of money. I can sleep anywhere, curled up on a flat rock if need be."

"That must simplify things for you, living out here in nature's bosom, so to speak."

"Oh, we have quite good accommodations. Simple, but entirely adequate to our needs."

"The General said something about cabins."

She nodded and began turning back the cuffs on her lightweight flannel shirt. "Ten at the moment, but we're planning five more this summer, possibly more."

"This new rule about visitors. Is that hard-and-fast, no exceptions?"

She nodded solemnly, the dark eyes meeting mine solidly. "Yes, I'm afraid so. We voted on it in a meeting. The majority rules here, Mr. Roman, and most of us felt that visitors were creating more problems than we wanted to cope with."

"Like Sandra Conrad, for instance."

"Yes, it would include Sandy."

"You know that I'm looking for her?"

Her head bobbed, black tresses slipping across her shoulder. She flipped them back. "Yes." One slender brown hand stroked the thin fabric of her well-worn denims, ended up resting lightly on her knee.

"It occurred to me that she may have come back here, that whatever happened at her house in Midway City frightened her so much she couldn't stay and face the aftermath. Your sister once called Jacob Twill her guru. What better place could—"

"She didn't come back here, Mr. Roman. I can guarantee you that. Jacob Twill is not a guru. He is simply a man. Our leader. My—" She broke off, looking flustered for the first time since I'd met her. It was nice to know she wasn't all rawhide and whalebone after all. It was an unexpected advantage, and I pressed it.

"Your what, Joline?"

She shrugged, the color in her cheeks softening her face. "My man. Yes."

"You weren't really happy that Sandy came here, were you?"

"I liked Sandy. I made her a deerskin—"

"I know that. I saw it. But that doesn't answer my question. Jacob and Sandy were once lovers. I'm sure you knew that. It didn't matter to you? You didn't mind him being around an old lover?"

"You can't blame the cactus for its spines, Mr. Roman."

"Is that some old Indian axiom? I'm afraid you'll have to explain it to me."

"It doesn't matter. I don't own Jacob any more than he owns me. Jealousy is a sign of insecurity. I love Jacob and he knows it, and I feel just as secure in his love."

"No matter what happens, huh? It must be nice to be that sure of someone. I'm not even that sure of myself."

"That's a shame," she said, a caustic edge to her voice. "You look mature enough."

"Maturity? Isn't that a word swingers use a lot? If you're mature enough you can handle anything." I lit a cigarette and smiled at her, then switched abruptly to the subject I had come to talk about. "The night Sandy left, Wednesday night, I believe, I understand you dropped by sometime in the late afternoon to give her the deerskin blouse. I also understand that she and Jonas were going at it pretty heavy, fighting about the timber on Jonas's land."

She stared at me for a moment as if debating whether to answer. After a time she nodded, her face expressionless. "Yes. I left here not long after you did, after the rain stopped. I had put the finishing touches on Sandy's blouse, and I wanted to be sure she had it before she left for home. I assume Myna told you this, and if she did, she must have told you also that Jonas was drinking and that was unusual. He rarely drinks. Mostly, I think, because he can't seem to handle it. The one or two times I've seen him drink, he always drank too much and ended up passing out.''

"Do you remember what time you left?''

She wrinkled her brow, eyes squinted. "It must have been six o'clock or shortly thereafter. Perhaps six-thirty. I didn't stay long. It was too uncomfortable. Jonas was extremely angry with her for some reason, and he kept coming to the bedroom door and yelling something I couldn't quite understand.''

"Sandy was in the bedroom?''

"No, the adjoining bath. She had taken a bath and was washing her hair. She had the bedroom door closed, and Jonas would come by every once in a while and yell. Sandy would make a face and roll her eyes, but she didn't offer to tell me what it was all about. I didn't ask.''

"What was his condition when you left?''

She ducked her head and made a wincing gesture. "Pretty drunk, I guess. He was carrying a bottle around in his hand, and his speech sounded a little slurred.''

"You talked to him?''

"Yes. He followed me out to my Jeep. He wanted me to stop somewhere and call Myna. He wanted her to come home and help him reason with that . . . cold-hearted bitch.'' She paused. "Those are his words, not mine.''

"Did you call?''

"No. I drove to the hospital instead. I hadn't talked to Myna in a while and I . . . well, I thought it would be better to tell her in person what was happening.''

"Did she go home?''

"No. She couldn't. They were shorthanded or something. Anyway, she thought she should stay out of it. They were niece and uncle after all, and she was only an in-law."

"Sandy's in-law maybe, but she's his wife. I'd think she'd have been a little worried, as wild and erratic as he gets."

"I agree. At times Jonas is a bit . . . irrational. But if she was worried she didn't let on. She said Sandy knew how to handle him, that they were two of a kind."

"Two of a kind? I wonder what she meant by that?"

She sighed. "I haven't the slightest notion. I don't know either of them that well. But I do know Myna, and she tends to be a little . . . well, naive at times. She believes everything Jonas tells her, and waits on him hand and foot. It was the same with Curly Glazier: she bought his whole cockamamie act, hung on his every word. And he's one of the biggest b.s. artists East Texas has ever produced. She's my sister and I love her dearly, but I'll have to say she has terrible taste when it comes to men."

"Really?"

"Not that Jonas is not a nice man. It's just that he's so ugly, and lord, he's twenty-five years older than she is."

"Still, there is potential; possibilities."

Her eyebrows shot upward. "I'd like to know what, for heaven's sake."

"Two thousand acres of virgin timber, somewhere between eight and ten million dollars' worth."

Her upper lip curled scornfully. "You believe that's why she married Jonas? That goes to show how well you know Myna."

"Not well," I agreed, remembering her passionate declaration of love for her husband, her passion with me in her husband's bed a week or so later.

189

"She loves Jonas, if you can believe that, or thinks she does, which is the same thing, I suppose."

"And you find that hard to accept."

She smiled thinly. "I find it incredible."

"Why? A lot of women marry older men."

She waved a slender arm. "That's not the reason."

"Then what?"

"Because . . . because he's a Beechum." She wet her lips, the dark eyes suddenly chilled. "The Beechums have something—my grandfather would say they are poor in spirit."

"Translation?"

"I'm not sure I can. Oh, Jacob can explain it much better than I. He knows them well, all of the Beechums. I don't have the words like Jacob."

Or his bullshit either, I thought. Aloud I said, "Maybe they lack the ability to love. . . ."

Her face lit up like an exploding flare. "That's it! That's what Jacob said, only he put it a little differently. 'An emptiness of the heart' is the way he said it. But don't feel bad—Jacob is a poet. He has a way with words."

"I'll say," I said admiringly. "I'd never have been able to put it that eloquently. It must be exciting just listening to him talk."

She smiled wryly, eyes snapping. "You have a way with words yourself, Mr. Roman. I've noticed it before."

"You have to make do with what you've got. I'm not a fighter or a lover, and talking and running are all that's left. I never was much of a runner."

We were grinning at each other like two clowns in a slapstick routine. I knew why I was grinning, but I wasn't sure about her.

"You're being modest," she said finally. "You're a very prepossessing man. Myna, in particular, seems to think

so. I've never seen her act quite like she did at the cemetery."

"People handle death in different ways."

"Yes," she said, and let it drop. She looked up at the
sun. "I'm sorry if I appear inhospitable, Mr. Roman, but
I have very pressing duties waiting for me. Is there anything else you'd care to ask me?"

"Would I get the same answer a second time?"

Her lips quirked, but she canceled the smile before it
could blossom. "Yes, the very same. Sandy isn't here,
Mr. Roman, if that's what you mean."

"Then I apologize for interrupting your busy day and
thank you for your courtesy."

"You're very welcome," she said sweetly, slender fingers finding the ignition key, twisting. The Jeep's motor
growled, caught, shattered the silence. She waggled her
fingers and made a circle on the slope, crushing bluebon-
nets and saw briers alike.

Trailed by a plume of dust, she disappeared into the
forest of pine.

I folded the aluminum chair and put it back in the hut.
I rewrapped the walkie-talkie and stored it where I had
found it, then I ambled down the slope, climbed the fence,
and got into my truck. I lit another cigarette and felt the
weight of the last twenty-four hours settle on my shoulders
like a suit of rusty armor.

Futility and defeat, undifferentiated feelings of forebod-
ing. I was no closer to finding Sandra Conrad than I had
been the day I drove away from Macomber Beechum's
dilapidated old farmhouse.

And people were still lying to me. This time either Glazier or Joline. Somehow I preferred Joline's version of
why Myna had married Jonas, but maybe that was just the
romantic in me—what little there was left of him. It also

made me feel less a fool for deserting Myna's bed like a fundamentalist seized with sudden premonitions of hell.

I stared up the slope into the lingering pall of dust from Joline's passage and suddenly understood that I was quitting. Enough was enough. Nobody really gave a damn about Sandra Conrad, her welfare. Only her whereabouts as it related to them personally, to their fortune and future well-being. Furthermore, I was convinced I was chasing a dead woman. Her spoor had vanished too abruptly, too cleanly, as if she had walked into the night and been absorbed by the passing darkness.

And if she was dead, my job was ended. It was as simple as that. The game was back in Captain Homer Sellers's court, where it belonged, where it had always belonged. It wasn't my job to solve murders, to find murderers. Risky business, finding murderers—they generally resented it, did a lot of dumb irrational things like shooting at you.

Thoughts of quitting made me feel better immediately, the kind of feeling only martyrs released from the cross have a right to expect.

I started the Ramcharger and drove away from the gate, marveling at the peace and beauty of pine forests, the heady mixture of aromas, the invigorating spring day. I thought of home and hearth and a can of Coors, dozing in front of the tube, books, magazines, and the company of reasonable men and women who had no compulsion to lie beyond the petty demands of normal quotidian existence.

Thoughts of women brought me full circle, back to Myna Beechum of the intoxicating lips, seductive eyes, and pliant body, back to my incredibly neurotic behavior in her bed, which had left me with the paralyzing ache of a celibate monk.

Maybe I was finally growing up, acquiring adult self-control. I had given up carousing, hadn't I? Forgone tea and coffee because of the caffeine, scratched casual relationships because of herpes and the bitter soullessness of zipper intimacy. I had cut down on red meat; ate more fish, fowl, and fruit; denied myself ice cream, the chocolate-covered peanuts that I loved, soul food.

Restraint and self-control. That was where it was at in the eighties. The baby-boom generation doing its thing, keeping healthy, wholesome, and fit. It was boring as hell. They were boring as hell. I was rapidly becoming boring as hell.

I turned onto the winding county road. I lit a cigarette and tried to remember where I had seen the topless honkytonk featuring the neon lady with the incredibly sinuous body and impossible bosom.

But second thoughts made me reconsider. The parking lot had been filled with BMW's and Volvo's, which spelled Yuppies. Clear-eyed youngsters table-hopping around, eating grilled fish and drinking champagne by the glass, flossing their teeth while they talked about real-estate deals, stocks and bonds, and last year's vacations. That I didn't need.

A cowboy bar would be better, pool tables and sawdust on the floor, country western music and spittoons, heavy wooden furniture that would stand up under a free-for-all, wagon-wheel chandeliers, and boiled eggs in a widemouthed jar.

I needed a drink. Something was ending, and there would be no drumroll and applause, no speeches or plaques, no man-of-the-hour honorariums. I was quitting and quitters deserved no accolades.

But even us quitters had a God-given right to get drunk.

22

A HALF-MILE FROM THE STATE HIGHWAY I PASSED A BAT-
tered Ford pickup parked on the shoulder, hood in the air,
a Snoopy pennant aerial topper whipping defiantly in the
breeze. A hundred yards farther along I topped a rise and
spotted a familiar-looking figure trudging along the
roadbed. He turned as I came nearer and threw out an
arm, and the tentative identification became positive: General Ralston, all belly and beard, still as rumpled and unkempt as the first time I saw him at Jacob Twill's back
gate.

I eased to a stop beside him. He yanked open the door
and climbed in with amazing alacrity for a man of his
bulk. He thrust a hand across the seat, giving me a glimpse
of his yellowish grin.

"Dan Roman. Man, am I glad to see you. Beginning to
think I was gonna have to hoof it on into town. Two dang
cars already passed me up. Guess I look a little too ragtag
to suit 'em. How you doing?"

"Doing fine, General. What happened, your pickup go
bellyup on you?"

"Dang pile of junk. Yeah. Rotor busted. Happens every

so often. I generally carry a spare, but I forgot to pick one up last time. You been out to the camp?''

''I was heading that way when I came up against that new chain and lock on the gate. You folks getting antisocial all of a sudden?''

''Naw.'' He frowned and stroked his nose with two thick fingers. ''We just decided it was getting to be more trouble than it was worth letting folks come in and nose around. They ain't satisfied just seeing how us misfits live and all; they want to wander off into the woods, root around down on the creek—''

''You don't have anything to hide, do you?'' I looked at him and grinned.

His eyes glinted. ''Not a dang thing, but they's snakes and bluffs down on that creek and over on the river, and if somebody gets hurt first thing they'd want to do is sue. People getting so they love to sue somebody. Any little thing comes along, sue their ass. We ain't got no extra money to throw away on lawyers.'' He shifted to a more comfortable position. ''You really wanta come in sometime, just come to the gate and call and I'll come get you.''

''I don't know. I talked to Joline a while ago. She considers the visitor ban binding on everyone.''

He snorted. ''You wanta come in, by grab, I'll take you in. She's just got one vote like everyone else. Don't pay no attention to her.''

''No visitors at all in the compound right now?''

''Nope. None that I know of, and I'd know if there was. I'm working the mess hall this week, and they'd have to tell me if they wanted some extra food.''

''Not tending fence this week, huh?''

I saw his shaggy head swing toward me. ''That's working fence, not tending fence,'' he said patiently, as if explaining the obvious to a congenital defective.

''Oh.''

"Okay," he sighed, trying unsuccessfully to cross his legs in the small space. "I knowed I made a slip the other day, and I wasn't sure if you caught it. I guess you did. Okay, so we have a small still down on the creek. We make a few gallons—just for medicinal purposes and celebrations and stuff like that. If you turn us in you're a lot meaner'n I think you are."

"It's none of my business, General. Sandra Conrad is my business. I'd hate to think she was hiding back there and everybody was lying to me about it. I hate liars and I don't much care what happens to—"

"She ain't," he said earnestly, leaning forward to look in my face. "I'd swear that on a stack of bibles."

It was my turn to sigh. "No need for bibles, General. I'll take your word."

"You got it," he said, slapping a heavy thigh. "I ain't sure I'd come right out and tell you if she was, but I wouldn't lie to you about it neither."

I nodded, and we rode in silence for a while. I smoked another cigarette, and he exchanged a soggy blob of tobacco for a new cut off his plug. Traffic picked up perceptibly as we came into the outskirts of Irondale. We crossed a railroad track.

"You find that feller Jonas Beechum's place the other day?"

"No problem at all. Drove right to it."

"What'd you think of him?"

I hesitated, remembering the wild black eyes and the long-barreled gun in my face. "He seems a bit nervous at times, sort of impetuous."

He barked a short humorless laugh. "Ornery little cuss, is what I hear. I've knowed of him most all my life, but I never knowed him very well. Some say he's crazy as a rabid coon, then some say it's his way of getting people to leave him alone. Only thing I know is, I always stayed out of his way when he was drinking. Maybe he ain't crazy all the time, but when he's drinking, you want to steer clear. He's danged sure crazy then.''

"Does he drink a lot?"

"I can't say that for certain. I heard a few years back that he'd quit altogether, got religion or something, but if he did he's backslid 'cause I saw him not mor'n a week or so ago coming out of Lou Stearns Bottom Dollar liquor store with a couple of fifths of whiskey. He was already half-stewed, if I'm any kind of judge.''

"A week ago? Do you remember when exactly?"

He dug blunt fingers into the beard, massaged his chin. "Lessee . . . it was the day Cletus worked on the pump. I come in with him for some parts. He dropped me off for a beer at Lou's, and—say, that was the same day you came out to the camp. Cletus had just dropped me off when you showed up.''

"That would make it Wednesday, the same day Joline took the deerskin blouse to Sandy.''

His head bobbed. "Yeah, that's right.''

"Jacob seems to have a way with the ladies.''

His head swiveled toward me again. He was silent for a moment. "Yeah, that's a fact, I reckon.'' He grabbed the dash with both hands as I swerved to miss a pothole. "He's a ladykiller right enough, but I ain't so sure that's all honey and roses. We been close to bad trouble a couple of times because of it.''

"How's that?"

"Well, you know, one of the women shining up to Jake and her man not liking it much. He's our leader and all, and it's his land, but that don't mean—'' He broke off abruptly and pointed to a low, flat-roofed building made out of concrete blocks. "See that auto-parts store? If you'll just drop me off I'll pick me up a new rotor—''

"I can run you back out to your truck.''

"No need. I'll just stroll on down to Lou's and have me a couple of beers. Some of the boys always stop in there on their way home from the oil patches. I surely appreciate the ride, though."

"Don't mention it, General. Glad to help."

He wrung out my hand again and slid out of the truck. "You ever want to come in over at the camp, remember what I said. I'll see you get in."

"Thanks, I'll keep that in mind."

I watched him cross the street, big hands tugging at the jeans riding nonexistent hips beneath his pendulous belly, a faintly ludicrous figure, unkempt and unlovely, undoubtedly a walking disaster with an overworked heart and veins clogged with serum cholesterol.

But, presumably, he was doing what he wanted to do, living life on his own terms. How many people managed to do that? How many even tried?

I was a half-dozen miles north of Irondale, clipping along at a conservative sixty-five, when I remembered my determination to have a drink. Maybe more than one, since one was seldom enough. But getting drunk would mean another night in some seamy motel room, a long drive tomorrow with a cottony mouth and a bursting head.

I decided to wait, play my little Jack Daniel's game. Maybe I'd lose.

I didn't win, but I didn't lose either. Fate, as it has a way of doing, intervened in the guise of Homer Sellers. Three messages on the phone-answering machine, each one a little more heated, a little more bombastic and profane:

Where the hell you spend all your time? Out chasing pussy, I reckon. Look, give me a call when you come in—if you have the strength, that is.

Dammit, Dan. Where you been? I got better things to

do than sit here dialing your number and talking to your dumb machine. Call me, dammit! Now! I want to talk about the Conrad case.

Goddammit, Dan, are you avoiding me? Is this any way to treat a friend and the captain of your local police force? Wait'll the next time you want a ticket fixed, or some information. I'd better hear from you, boy. You're making me mad!

He hadn't bothered to put a time or date, and I had no idea when he had made the calls. And didn't much care. I was tired all the way to the bone, still thrumming with the vibration of synthetic tires on concrete pavement, lulled by the engine's relentless hum. I needed rest, not questions, sleep, not consultation on a case I was no longer involved in.

I turned off the telephone and patched together a meal of odds and ends, bologna and cheese and crackers, a shriveled drumstick left over from a barbecued chicken. Dry and unappetizing and tasteless; not bad washed down with beer.

I ate on a tray in the den, listening to Yuppie newscasters with bright eyes and patented smiles detailing the day's assortment of mayhem, mischief, and murder. A couple of bright spots: a new drug that showed promise in the treatment of AIDS, and a six-year-old girl found safe and sound after a two-day absence away from her home while hundreds of searchers scoured the countryside.

I was finishing up, looking forward to a final cigarette and ten hours' sleep when the doorbell chimes tapped out the first four notes of "Moonglow." At the same time a heavy fist hammered out shave-and-a-haircut on the door.

I pushed back the tray and sighed. I wouldn't have to bother returning Homer's calls after all.

23

I WASN'T FAST ENOUGH TO STOP THE SECOND ROUND OF notes, but I got the door open in time to catch him with an upraised fist.

He blinked and gave me a silly grin. "Beginning to think you was asleep or something."

"Good thinking, Homer. Were you going to pound on my bedroom window next?"

"Might have," he said complacently, and used the upraised hand to push open the door. "This ain't no time of day to be sleeping, son. God made the nights for that. I know you got a lot of other things to do at night, but us working folks got to have a little order in our lives." He thumped me on the shoulder and swept by me into the den, a rumbling laugh following him like the chugging cough of an overloaded semi.

The laugh turned to a groan as he caught sight of the still empty bar. "Jesus, you still into this teetotaler shit? Least you could do is have some pity on your—hey, looky here!" He chortled, and made a beeline for the bottle of Jack Daniel's on the kitchen table.

I stopped to pick up my tray, and by the time I reached the kitchen he was dumping amber liquid into a glass.

"Have a drink, Homer."

"Thanks, son, I do believe I will. Got any ice cubes?"

I opened the refrigerator and handed him a storage tray. He extracted two cubes with long spatulate fingers and delicately dropped them into his glass.

"Ain't the right way to do it," he grumbled. "Supposed to put the cubes in first."

"What earthly difference can it make?"

"I dunno," he said, and sipped. He smacked his lips and grinned at me. "That's just the way they always do it in the movies and on TV. There must be a logical reason." He took another drink. "Good stuff, but you know I really like scotch better."

"Sorry about that. I'll try to remember."

"Ain't you having one?"

"I just ate. It might spoil my dinner." I lit a cigarette and turned abruptly to the den. "Now, what is it that's so damned important it can't wait until tomorrow?" I dropped into the leather recliner and shoved back to elevate my feet.

He sat down on the other side of the fireplace, sighed heavily, and sampled his drink, eyeing me over the glass, a lank thatch of mud-colored hair curving above his right eye. I suddenly realized he had changed his hairstyle, if that was what it could be called. All of his adult years with a fifties pompadour, and all of a sudden he had gone modern. I wondered why. Female influence? Middle-aged vanity? I thought again of him and Mitsi together and couldn't keep back a smile.

"What're you grinning about?" he growled, and raked a hand self-consciously across his forehead.

"A joke I thought of," I said. "An Aggie joke."

"Just keep it to yourself." Although not a graduate, he

201

had attended Texas A & M long enough to be sensitive about it and to feel a smidgen of loyalty.

"What did you find out down in East Texas?" he went on, a trace of irritation still in his voice.

"How did you know I was in East Texas?"

He waved an imperious hand. "Don't matter how. I know. So, why don't you tell me about it."

"Deputy Hendricks," I said. "He must have called you. Nobody else would. . . ."

"Okay, it was Hendricks." He settled back in the chair and took out a cigar. "He said you thought you were pulling some fancy shit down there but that he was gonna keep his eye on you, and if you stepped out of line one inch he was gonna come down on you like a drop hammer."

"Yeah, that's him all right. He likes that phrase, drop hammer. Makes him sound tough, hard-bitten. Matter of fact, I think he's both."

"Okay. So tell me already."

I told him. From my conversation with Carrie at the bus stop to my Good Samaritan act with General Ralston out on the highway, omitting only the aborted love scene with Myna Beechum—he would not have understood and would probably never let me forget it, either.

I stopped once to get a beer and replenish his drink. He listened silently for the most part, asking a cop question now and again, his broad face impassive, receptive, the quick brain behind the hank of hair soaking up information the way a computer absorbs bytes.

When I finished, I went into the kitchen for another beer, fixed Homer another drink. He sat motionless in the chair, a hirsute Buddha, reflected light turning the thick bifocals into opaque disks, his broad even features stoic and introspective.

I lit a cigarette and reclaimed my seat. I rinsed my dry mouth with beer and thought of all the other times we had sat across from each other, exchanging ideas, conjecture, facts, and permutations. We had not solved all the homicides in our small world, but we had solved our share.

He stirred finally, drank half his Jack Daniel's, and put the glass on the hearth beside him.

"I'm beginning to think maybe you're right," he said.

"Right about what?" I was almost certain I knew.

"About Sandra Conrad being dead."

I nodded without speaking.

"Next question is, who killed her?"

"The same one, or ones, who killed her husband and the Gomez woman."

He picked up the glass and ran a thick curved thumb around the rim of the glass. "And who might that be, do you think?"

I grinned and shrugged and took a sip of beer. "You brought it up. You know as much as I do. You tell me, Homer."

He smiled faintly. "What was the caliber of the gun that old geezer carried?"

"Jonas? It was a .44. I told you that."

He nodded absently. "Yeah, I guess you did. Just wanted to be sure. Would it surprise you a lot to find out it was a .44 that killed Conrad?"

"Not enough to stun me, no."

"Then you figure it was him?"

"Not so fast. You telling me you found the bullet?"

He nodded solemnly. "That we did—Ted Baskin did, anyhow. Had to dig out a couple square yards of topsoil, but him and his men found it. Not hardly even damaged."

"Good ballistics, then?"

"When we get something to compare it with."

"Like a bullet fired from Jonas Beechum's gun?"

"I'd say that's the next step." He sighed and finished the drink.

"How do you propose to go about that?"

He took out a handkerchief and wiped the lens of his glasses, staring at me with bleary guileless blue eyes. "Figured you might be a big help there, seeing as how you know him and all. He'd probably—"

"Forget it, Homer. I quit this case once and let myself be sucked back in. Well, I've quit again, and this time it's permanent."

He gazed at me owlishly, wagging his head. "Never knowed you to be a quitter before, not when some poor devil got hisself murdered for no good reason."

"Conrad is not exactly some poor devil, and whoever killed him probably had a damn good reason. Besides, Homer, you're always reminding me that police business is none of mine."

"Yeah, that's so, but it's also a citizen's duty to assist a police officer—in fact, it's a damn law."

"Only in emergencies," I said. "Anyway, I have some problems with Jonas killing Sandy. If he was mad enough to kill her over the land, why did he let her come home on the bus, then end up following her up here and having to kill two other people? That doesn't make a lot of sense."

He grunted and replaced the glasses. He cupped the handkerchief around his nose and blew lustily, a gurgling liquid sound that made both of us wince. "He didn't do that, and you know it well as I do. If he killed her, he did it down there, probably right in his house, or maybe on the road to the bus. Out of cold anger, I'd think, or maybe drunken rage. Who knows? It don't matter much why, if he did it."

"Then who was the woman on the bus? The woman who wore the deerskin blouse?"

He shrugged. "Could be coincidence. Could have been somebody else. His wife, maybe."

"His wife was working at the hospital in Irondale all night that night."

He gave me a sharp glance at the lack of conviction in my voice. The shaggy eyebrows pumped up and down. "You know that for a fact? You checked it out?"

"No," I said tersely. "I didn't check it out."

"You liked her, huh?" He bared big teeth in a sardonic grin. "Don't worry, little buddy, I forget things now and then myself." He grunted and heaved his bulk out of the chair. "Well, we can find out about that little thing in short order. Where's your phone?" he asked unnecessarily, heading for the extension in the kitchen.

I lit another cigarette and finished my beer, listening to his gravel-coated voice going through the routine with the Irondale information operator, with the staff at the hospital, repeating his name and rank and badge number a half-dozen times before he reached someone with the authority to release the information he was seeking.

I listened halfheartedly, already sure of what he would discover. The simple answer to a simple question that had eluded me since the time I came to believe Sandra Conrad was dead. A routine follow-up check, something a rookie cop would have done automatically, something I ordinarily would have done without thinking about it twice.

So why hadn't I? The answer came smoking in behind the question: I wanted to believe her. I had been profoundly stirred by what I saw in the limitless depths of dark liquid eyes, seized by emotions so old they were almost new. On some deep, primordial level I had wanted Myna Beechum from the moment I first saw her—the instinctive desire to hold, protect, cherish. Or maybe only lust.

Homer came back and dropped heavily into the rocker-recliner. "She got a call around seven-fifteen, left at seven-thirty. The caller was a male. That's all they know, or all they're telling." He looked at me quizzically. "Seven-thirty. That enough time?"

I nodded slowly. "She could have made it. The girl Carrie said they had to hurry to catch the bus."

"So, whatta you think now?"

"I don't know, Homer."

"You wouldn't happen to have a picture we could show that girl Carrie?"

"No. Why would I have her picture?"

"I dunno, just thought you might. Ain't like you to screw up the details. Thought maybe she mighta blinded you a little."

"Go to hell, Homer. You know, sometimes you're hard to take."

"I know," he rumbled complacently. "Sometimes I make myself sick." He cocked his head to one side and smiled crookedly. "So? This change your mind about going with me?"

24

WE LEFT EARLY THE NEXT MORNING. DRIVING MY RAM-
charger. Homer hated driving almost as much as he hated
flying and walking, and, with my usual delicate cynicism,
I wanted to know if he had invited me along to be his
chauffeur and provide transportation.

He rumbled a laugh and thumped me on the shoulder.
"Hell, no, son. The city's gonna pay every cent of this
trip, and besides having your help in East Texas, I thought
you and me could have us a high old time talking about
hunting, wenching, football, or whatever else comes to
mind. You branded any cattle lately?"

And talk we did. Or mostly he talked and I listened,
and by the time we made the loop south of Dallas and
intersected with Interstate 45 South, the trip had taken on
an almost festive air, the somber thoughts that had kept
me awake half the night slowly receding to sulk in some
dark crevice of my mind.

We talked about Dallas, its sophisticated new look: a
skyline of angles, cylinders of glass and concrete and
metal, ultramodern and slick, big wheels and big deals
made behind thick walls and windows sealed for air-con-

ditioning, a city that died each day at five o'clock, was reborn again each morning at nine. Business-oriented, high-tech capital of the nation, it was rapidly becoming the New Hollywood in the moviemaking business with none of the Old Hollywood's glitz and glamour, none of its passion for life in the fast lane, none of its self-deceptions about movies and art. Product was the name of the game.

We waxed nostalgic, as they say, talking about old cases we had won, a number we had lost, about new forensic techniques, the new breed of cop with blow-dried hair and tailored uniforms who considered themselves as Yuppie as any of the three-piece-suiters who poured out of Dallas's skyscrapers at five o'clock. He told me about new things that had happened to old friends, some good, some bad, and I talked about a few of my cases that had ended happily. Some of it we had each heard before, but we listened politely and responded appropriately because it was all part of the ritual of male companionship.

We ate an early lunch at a cowboy bar between Irondale and Crater. Hamburgers and fries washed down with beer. A couple of boiled eggs for Homer. He paid the tab with a flourish and pocketed the receipt with a significant look in my direction.

"We shoulda had steak, by golly. I forgot the city was paying."

The old lady at the cash register leaned forward and winked. "Be glad you didn't. I'd as soon chew on an old cracked boot." She cackled and Homer guffawed. I smiled politely, no longer curious about the unchewable chunks of foreign matter I had found in my hamburger.

On our way again, Homer lit a plastic-tipped cigar and, with characteristic abruptness, brought the conversation to the reason for our long ride.

"I done some more thinking last night, Dan. From what Jonas told you, he knew Conrad was really running things at MCB. Maybe Sandra told him it was Conrad's idea to cut his timber. After he killed Sandra—for whatever reason—I guess it musta occurred to him that he hadn't solved anything, that Conrad would just go ahead with his plan—or at least pass it on to whoever took over. There he was with a dead niece on his hands and nothing changed, not really. I think that's why he went on up to Midway City, waited for Conrad to come back from the bus station—"

"How about the Gomez woman? Where does she fit in?"

He made an exasperated sound and puffed lustily on the cigar, blue eyes squinted behind the bifocals. I opened a window.

"Well, we talked about this before, but I think she was there from before he went to pick up his wife. Hell, we don't know for sure what her routine was. Maybe she stayed over once in a while for some reason. Lots of bedrooms in that house for her to use. Jonas woulda had a key, Sandra's key. Maybe he walked in on her and then realized he had to kill her too after she saw him. She coulda heard him in the house and got scared and hid in the closet." He leaned forward a little, looking at me. "And then when Jonas went in to hang up Sandra's clothes he found the girl hunkered there in the corner." He pounded a beefy thigh and hooted. "By God, there's our fit; it fits like a glove!"

I grinned at his exuberance and gave him a minute to enjoy it while I lit a cigarette. I added a ball of smoke to the growing cloud above our heads and cranked the window open a little more.

"I think you're partly right, Homer. Maybe the part about the Gomez woman. I think she was nothing more than a byproduct of the overall crime. In the wrong place at the wrong time. I don't believe Jonas went there to kill Conrad. I think he went there to cover up his own crime. That was the reason for the deerskin blouse, the moccasins, the clothes in the closet to make it look as if she had actually gone home, arrived there, removed the blouse, hung up her clothing, and then—only then—disappeared. Maybe he hoped they would blame Conrad for her disappearance. I don't know if Jonas is that devious, if he would have been capable of thinking it through that far under the circumstances. He knew Conrad would be at the bus station sometime around twelve or twelve-thirty—he may have watched from somewhere nearby until he left home. But then came the Gomez woman and everything went to hell. He had to wait for Conrad, kill him, dispose of his body to make it look as if he too had disappeared. Muddy up the water. It wasn't a great plan, but probably all he could think of in his state of panic."

"And his wife? What part did she play?"

I could feel his gaze on the side of my face. I flipped the cigarette butt out the window. "I don't know. None, I hope. She obviously caught the bus and rode it as far as Corsicana, maybe farther. Then she either caught another one back to the bus stop where she left her car, or she waited somewhere for him to pick her up."

He faced forward again. We rode in silence. I felt a ropy tendril of nausea coiling in my stomach, a hollow spot in my chest.

"Accessory after the fact, Dan," he said quietly. "That's the least I can see for her. Unless she can convince a jury that he duped her."

"Goddammit, Homer! We don't even know yet if Jonas is guilty, and already you've got his wife in a courtroom—"

He threw up a hand and cowered in the corner. "Jesus Christ. Don't get so hot. I was just exploring the possibilities. You know the law well's I do—well, almost as good.

You never was too sharp on the finer points, as I remember. You was just lucky you had me there to guide you."

I refused to look at him, refused to respond to his gentle raillery. He sighed and leaned forward again to look in my face.

"How long's it been since you done a little plowing, boy? You need to get married again. Ain't natural for a man to go without a woman as long as you do—"

"Shit, Homer! You've been a widower a lot longer than I have."

"Yeah," he said eagerly, obviously glad to have me talking again. "But I ain't got all them inhibitions like you do. I don't have to love a woman to get in the sack with her—hell, I don't even have to like her much. But you got all them restrictions, them limitations you put on yourself, on every damn woman you meet. Ain't no wonder nobody can measure up. Hell, son, you've got to take the world like it is, not what you think it is or would like it to be. There's all kind of women out there, and a goodly number of them are looking to pair off with a man. For a night, for a week, for a month—hell, forever. Christ, boy, they outnumber us three to one. And if you don't want one of them, there's always the hookers. I'll bet you don't know we got some of the slickest little hookers in the Metroplex right there in Midway City—"

"Homer. Shut up. Just shut the hell up."

He slumped back into his seat, grinning like a defective. He had accomplished his purpose—or so he thought—diverting me from my somber train of thought. I had no desire to disillusion him, so I joined his silence, a tightness growing in my chest as the miles of forest whipped by outside the truck.

A few minutes later we topped a rise and Crater was momentarily laid out before us like an ancient ruins, a jumble of decaying buildings, brick and stone and clapboard siding, multicolored roofs, graceless and unlovely, a grim reminder that all that was new and shining would some day be old.

It took an hour for the girl in the sheriff's substation in Crater to find Deputy Wally Hendricks and get him back to home base.

We cooled our heels in a gaily colored bar across the street called the What If. It was cool and dim inside, almost silent, no country music, no rock. Two working cowboys sat across from each other in a booth, and the vague shadowy outlines of four others hugged their slice of the curving bar like shipwrecked sailors abandoned at sea.

A muscular, orange-haired youth in leather overalls led us to a table next to a front window. He gave the table a courtesy swipe with a paper napkin and stood looking out the window, one hand on his hip, a bored expression on his narrow, handsome face.

Homer glanced at me, raised his eyebrows, and ordered a scotch rocks. I ordered a bottle of Coors. Homer watched the waiter waltz among the tables and looked back at me, one eyebrow cocked.

"This the kind of bar you hang out in a lot?"

"What's wrong with it? It's nice and peaceful."

He snorted. "You know what kind of place it is?"

"I kinda figured it out when I saw those cowboys over there holding hands."

"Cowboys my ass. Couple of namby-pambies trying to look macho."

"No, Homer, you're wrong. Look at their boots, their clothes, the dirty hats, that white band across their foreheads. They're working cowboys all right, but what does that have to do with their sexual proclivities?"

He shrugged. "Not anything, I guess—" He broke off as the boy approached with our drinks, leather-clad thighs

212

brushing together audibly, a petulant twist to cupid bow lips. "We're out of Coors, sir. I brought you Miller's. Is that satisfactory?"

"Sure," I said. "Beer's beer. It all tastes like bear piss, anyway." I was hoping for a chuckle, a smile, something to show that he could react to friendly interchange. But he nodded curtly and left, expression unchanged.

"Antisociable little cuss," Homer said. He took a sample of his scotch. "What I don't understand about gays is why they ain't scared out of their gourds what with herpes and AIDS—hey, I forgot to tell you. The Conrad woman had AIDS."

"AIDS?" I echoed inanely.

"Yeah, you remember. Doc Paris found out that Conrad had it and you suggested—"

"Yeah, I remember," I said, unwilling to admit I hadn't thought about it since our previous discussion. But Homer Sellers knew my faults as well as my few virtues, and he smiled knowingly.

"Forgot about it, huh? Well, don't feel bad. I forgot something once. Back in '69, I think it was—"

"Joline Coldwater said Sandy was sick. A 'sickness of the spirit' she said. Said she sensed it, some power inherited from her grandfather who was a shaman. I think that means medicine man. Maybe there's something to that voodoo stuff after all. I guess if you knew you were going to die, it might make your spirit sick." I thought of the paralyzing moment when I had glimpsed eternity through the bore of Jonas Beechum's gun and shuddered involuntarily. "Yeah, it damn sure can."

"Joline Coldwater. That's Beechum's sister-in-law, right?"

"That's right."

He emptied his glass, lowered it to the table, and touched my arm. "That our man?"

213

I turned and looked out the window. Across the street Wally Hendricks stood beside his patrol car stretching his lanky frame. He paused to light a cigarette, hitched at his gun belt, and went up the short flight of steps to his office.

I nodded and chugalugged the rest of my beer.

"Gunslinger, huh? He wouldn't get away with that shit on my police force. There's a regulation way to wear a sidearm and that ain't it. Cowboy stuff. Somebody'll make him eat that pistol one of these days." He scooted out of the booth and tugged at the split tail on his sport coat, hiked up his pants and, in a final act of grooming, ran thick fingers through his unruly hair. I followed him to the door.

"They'd have to get it away from him first. That might take some doing. Whatever you do, Homer, don't make any sudden moves toward his gun. He might forget you're a brother officer and blow off something you can't afford to lose."

He gave me a jaundiced look, an obscene grin. "At least I'd miss it."

25

DEPUTY WALLY HENDRICKS DROPPED THE PENCIL HE HAD been toying with. He picked up a pack of cigarettes from the desk and lit one, his gaze never leaving Homer's face. He had not interrupted once during the big man's dry, rough recital, had not moved anything except his slender nervous fingers, an occasional slide of lizardlike lids over bulging eyes. Now that Homer had finished, he appeared to move everything at once, reaching for his hat with one hand, cramming the cigarette pack into his shirt pocket with the other, shoving away from the desk with long sinewy legs.

"Okay, Captain Sellers. Sounds good to me. You two want to follow me, we'll hike on out to the Beechum place and pick up that gun."

Homer squirmed and glanced at me. "Uh, Deputy Hendricks, I, uh, don't you think we oughta go before a JP somewheres and get a warrant? Evidence won't be worth a damn without one."

Hendricks frowned. "I don't follow you there. We go out there nice and friendly like, ask Jonas to let us pick up his gun for a couple of hours. We shoot a couple test rounds and give him back his gun. You got your test rounds and Jonas gets his gun back. Everything works.''

''And what if it matches?'' Homer asked.

''If it matches, well, then we'll go back out there, pick up the gun, and arrest that skinny little runt's ass for you. But you won't know that for a day or two.''

''That's right,'' Homer said, having difficulty keeping irritation out of his voice. ''By then that gun may be resting in the bottom of some swamp out in the Thicket.''

Hendricks frowned again, plucked gently at the end of his nose, obviously unconvinced, just as obviously disgruntled at having his decision questioned.

''Illegal search and seizure,'' Homer said gently. ''We don't do that anymore.''

Hendricks gave him a sharp glance. ''I know the law.''

''I'd really prefer a warrant, if you don't mind. Makes things . . . tidy.''

''Well, hell,'' Hendricks said, slapping the hat on his head. ''You oughta made that clear in the beginning. I thought you just wanted to talk to him.''

''I do,'' Homer said. ''But I also want to keep that gun in custody until we make a ballistics check. It's up to you how we handle it. It's your turf and your system.''

''We'll get a warrant,'' Hendricks said firmly, as if the idea had been his from the beginning. ''I think we got mor'n enough for probable cause. Enough for J. T. Witherspoon anyhow. He'll sign anything that ain't against one of his relatives.''

He rummaged in his center drawer and came out with a printed form with snap-out perforations. He found a ballpoint pen and looked up with a wide grin. ''Lessee now, what're we gonna put on here besides that .44 revolver?''

Homer looked at me. ''What do you think about a look around the premises?''

216

DARK STREAKS AND EMPTY PLACES

I shook my head. "Without the ballistics linkup, I don't think you have enough to warrant a search of the premises. If he killed Sandy there, she certainly isn't going to be lying around and he's probably done all the cleaning up he's going to do. A good forensic tech team could find traces if they're there, but I think that's a little heavy at this point and I don't believe the JP will allow that much latitude with what we've got."

Hendricks spoke up: "Don't worry about the justice of the peace. I told you that. He'll sign whatever I put in front of him, take my word. While we're there, we might as well nose around a little. That little prick shot her with that cannon of his, there's bound to be some traces left. I'll just put down here that we want to search the premises for evidence of suspected homicide." He looked from Homer to me and back again, a combative light in slightly squinted eyes.

Homer looked at me, his expression still genial but tightening a little around the edges, an equally combative light glinting behind the bifocals.

"Sure," I said hastily. "Why not? Maybe Jonas will invite us in, save everybody a lot of trouble. He can be real hospitable when he wants to be."

"And damned inhospitable when he don't," Hendricks said, writing busily. "That's what I hear."

I nodded. I could jump up and clap my hands and testify to that.

Homer cleared his throat. "We don't know for sure that he shot her. There's lots of other ways to commit a homicide that don't leave nothing laying around but a body. I expect that'd be floating out in a swamp somewheres."

Hendricks looked up and grinned. "Not anymore. There's 'gators in these swamps. Woman her size would make about half a dozen good bites for a big ol' 'gator. Not to mention all the other little critters that like a juicy

217

bite of long pig now and again.'' He dropped the pen and shoved the form across the desk to Homer. "That look about right?"

The big man studied it impassively, slowly peeling the cellophane from a Texas-made cigar fitted with a plastic tip. His thick eyebrows lifted. "We're gonna search the barn, too?"

"Sure, why not?" Hendricks rose and resettled the hat on his head. "Might as well do it right, I always say. Maybe he carried her off down there and used a pitchfork on her. Don't know what to expect of a Beechum. They're devious people from what I hear.'' He glanced at me, his narrow face sobering. "You carrying that Smith and Wesson?"

"No. But it's in the truck."

"Leave it there," he said flatly. "I know you got a right to pack it, and it ain't noways likely, but if there's any shooting to be done, I'll handle it.'' His slender fingertips lightly stroked the butt of his gun.

"I'm sure you will," I said, and drew another quick searching look. "Man as fast as you," I went on, my voice carefully neutral, "doesn't have a reason to be worried about anybody. Even somebody as slick as Jonas Beechum."

His eyes lit up with interest. "He's slick, huh?"

"As goose shit in a greased chute," I said.

"Reckon we oughta be getting along," Homer said, and heaved to his feet. "Time's a'wasting." His tone was heavy and jocular, but I caught the note of warning. I ignored him, feeling a faint pulsing drumbeat of inexplicable anger.

"He drew on me that first time," I said. "I blinked and missed the whole thing."

"You don't say." Hendricks's pale face was slowly filling with color. "You saw me draw. Is he faster than that?"

218

"Where's this JP feller located?" Homer shuffled his feet and inched toward the door, trying to catch my eye.

"I didn't stopwatch either of you," I said, "but I'd say it was about even."

"Good," Hendricks said and snapped his fingers. "I wasn't half trying."

"Hey," Homer said, finally getting enough of our silly little game. "This ain't some sporting event we're going to. This is damned serious business. We ain't going out there to have a shoot-out with this feller. All we're gonna do is get his gun." He turned toward Hendricks. "Now, by God, *I'm* packing a gun. A .38 Police Special. And I'm gonna keep right on packing it whether you like it or not. You don't like it, then we'll tear up this silly-ass warrant of yours and get the sheriff himself out here."

"No need to get horsey," Hendricks said, a pained look crossing his face. "We was just talking." He straightened his hat again, hitched up his belt, and made for the door. He threw it open with a flourish and stomped out.

We followed him. Homer poked me in the ribs with an iron thumb. "What the hell you doing?" he hissed.

I moved out of his reach and gave him a foolish grin. "I don't have the faintest idea."

At the civic center, a decrepit jumble of weathered brick buildings, Hendricks informed me curtly I wouldn't be needed inside and that they'd only be a few minutes.

Homer stepped out of the Ramcharger, winked at me, and followed the swaggering deputy down the street. I made a U-turn and slid into a parking space at a small park across the street.

I lit a cigarette and got out of the truck, crossed the cracked and sinking sidewalk to the one park bench not occupied by the beleaguered old men and women who faced the street like a row of silhouette cutouts at a carnival shooting gallery. Looking lately dispossessed, by age, by life, they sat hunched and immobile.

That's what it all comes down to, I thought, watching an old couple who had to be in their eighties helping each other across the street. Infirm bodies and a groping mind. Vulnerability. Fear.

Behind me preschoolers yelped and screamed, ran crying to mommies knotted in small groups around the perimeter of the playground. Blue jeans and curlers, bandannas, chewing gum and cigarettes and deep intellectual discussions. One mommie read a book, another had found a sunny spot to sleep. Or pretend to sleep. I caught her stealing glances at three brawny youths digging a hole in the street for Texas Power and Light.

Small-town life. God bless it, it never changed.

The sun rushed busily through the budding trees, warmed my face. I dozed, lulled by thoughts of my own life in smalltown Texas, America, the rough spots smoothed by time, good times made richer by stealthy nostalgia and the invidious desire to go home again that infests us the moment we leave. But I had less to go home to than most. No family. Only a two-room cabin on four hundred acres of land my father had placed in trust for me long before he became a drunk and solved his whole damned life by lying down and freezing to death in the tail wind of a Texas norther.

26

THE MUTED BLAST OF A CAR HORN ROUSED ME. HOMER stood beside the Ramcharger, grinning, one beefy arm thrust through the window. He had lit a fresh cigar. It poked out from his broad face at a jaunty angle, gripped between big white teeth.

"You looked right at home up there with the old folks," he said as I reached him. "Little soon for that, ain't it?"

"They're quiet," I said, yawning. "And they mind their own business. That's more than I can say for most people. They know a lot about solitude and dozing."

He laughed and heaved his bulk into the pickup, slid across the seat. "Better get this thing moving—old Wally's all fired up and ready to go. He had to do some tall talking to get that warrant signed after all. The JP made him take out all that shit about the barn and searching the house. But we got what we wanted; we got the gun."

"We ain't got it yet," I said, mimicking his voice. "You know what they say about hatching chickens."

"We mighta done better without Wyatt Earp," Homer said, waggling his fingers at Hendricks as he zipped by us in his patrol car. "If we'd gone in there and asked him nice, he mighta given us the gun or fired a couple of slugs in a rain barrel or something. That's all we'd need. Why would he care if he ain't done anything?''

"I don't think you've got the picture, Homer. If we had asked for the loan of his wife, we may have had a chance. But not his gun. He's probably as bad as Hendricks in that respect."

"Hendricks?"

"Yeah, Wyatt Earp up there. He won't even let his wife touch his gun. He told me that himself."

"Bunch of damned idiots. These folks down here are a lot different than folks up in our part of East Texas."

"Not so different. We've just been away a long time. Small towns have limited horizons, damn few prospects. They tend to live in the past a lot. The present's a bummer, so they glorify the good old days. Hendricks seemed much prouder of his speed with a gun than being a cop."

"Ain't much pride in being a cop no more," Homer said gloomily. "Them bastards in city hall are always screaming about the budget, looking down our necks, second-guessing us every time we have to put a little hurt on some asshole freaked out on drugs or booze or—hey, you better pump it up a little, we're gonna lose him."

"I know the way," I said, slowing and swerving to miss a jagged hole big enough to swallow a Cowboy linebacker. "I'll catch him on the straightaway."

And catch him I did—a mile shy of the Beechum place, doing a hundred and five on the relatively smooth highway, grinning at Homer from time to time as he hunched his bulky shoulders under the belts and tried to shove a hole through the fire wall.

"Shit," he murmured when we spotted the silhouette of Hendricks's Plymouth, lights revolving, taillights winking as the cruiser began to decelerate. "Won't this thing go any faster'n this?"

"Don't fret, Homer. If we get a ticket, old Wally'll fix it."

He grinned and licked his lips, hawked something out of his throat, the cigar forgotten between white-knuckled fingers gripping his knees.

"Yeah, I was worried about that." He opened his window a crack. The thin wail of a siren rushed in on the wind. He shook his head. "Can you believe that dumbass is running his siren?"

"Likes to make a big entrance," I said, remembering his noisy arrival at the motel.

Homer snorted and punched his cigar stub through the window crack. "Cops in Dallas do that a lot. Gives the perps a chance to get away. Saves paperwork, and it's a lot less risky that way."

Up ahead Deputy Hendricks had turned into the Beechum driveway and parked at the outer reach of the sprawling live oak tree. I coasted to a stop behind him. We climbed out. Homer went through his grooming ritual, tugging at his clothing, raking thick fingers along the curve of mud-colored hair lying limply across his forehead.

The door on Hendricks's cruiser stood open, the lights still rotating, the motor chugging. Hendricks stood in front of his car and looked at the house some thirty feet away, hands on his hips, the white cowboy hat pushed back on his head.

Homer gave me a disgusted look over the top of the Ramcharger. He lumbered forward and reached inside the cruiser. He turned off the engine, the lights, stepped back and slammed the door.

Hendricks turned and looked at him, a scowl slowly spreading across his face.

"I guess you forgot," Homer said. "Hard on a vehicle, engine loping like that." He smiled innocently. "Not to mention the cost of gas nowadays. Besides, them damn lights make me nervous.''

Hendricks opened his mouth to reply, then closed it again as sounds came from the house, a closing screen door, boot heels on wooden boards, a muted cough.

Jonas Beechum stood near the edge of the porch, arms akimbo, wiry body stiffly erect, body language as easy to read as the poised alertness of a wary cat.

''Afternoon, gents.''

He left it at that, his voice as casual as a sigh, neutral.

Hendricks's head bobbed. ''Afternoon, Jonas. Real glad to catch you at home. We hate to bother you this way, but we'd like to have a word with you, if you don't mind.''

Jonas placed his left hand on a post, leaned outward, and spat into the yard. It could have been chewing tobacco or snuff, but to me it looked more like a gesture of contempt.

''Is this a friendly visit, Deputy? If it is, then you all come right on in here and we'll have us a glass of tea or a beer or something and talk about it.'' He stopped, spat again. ''If it ain't, then I reckon you've come about far enough.''

Hendricks changed position, shifting his feet apart, easing a pack of cigarettes out of his shirt pocket with his left hand, selecting one with his lips, lighting it without taking his eyes from the man on the porch. A slick little maneuver I had seen somewhere before—James Cagney in *White Heat*, Bogie in *The Painted Desert*—somewhere.

Hendricks's breath exploded in a gust of smoke. ''This here gentleman here is Captain Homer Sellers of the Midway City Police Department. Homicide. He's working your nephew's homicide—''

''Ain't my nephew,'' Jonas drawled. ''He just married my niece, is all.''

". . . up in Midway City," Hendricks went on. "He'd like to talk to you about that."

"Ain't nothing to talk about. I don't know nothing about it." He took a pace to his right, then changed his mind and returned to the post.

"Maybe we could have that beer you was talking about," Homer said jovially. "I hate to stand out here yelling like I'm calling in my dogs."

Hendricks stiffened and shot a baleful glance in Homer's direction.

Jonas laughed. He leaned against the post, his body relaxed. "You a hound-dog man?"

Score one for the big man, I thought.

"I been known to squat around a fire and bullshit a little."

Jonas laughed again and folded his short arms across his chest. "What do you run? Bluetick, redbone—"

"There's another thing to it," Wally Hendricks said thinly, flipping the cigarette in an arc across the yard. "We gotta pick up that gun you're wearing there, Jonas."

Beside me Homer muttered a curse as the little man moved away from the post, arms dropping to his side.

"What was that, Wally?"

"I said we have to pick up your gun, that there .44 you been telling everybody belonged to Whiskey Sam Coble." His voice rang full and rich now that he was back in charge of the conversation.

I stared at the side of Hendricks's taut flushed face and felt the stirrings of premonition. I took a step forward. Slowly. Carefully.

"Mr. Beechum. All we want are a couple of test rounds out of your gun—"

"The warrant says we pick it up and that's what we're gonna do. You stay out of this, Roman. You've got no say in this at all." Hendricks took a step away from me, his body movements fluid and graceful, almost indolent, a lazy smile tilting his mouth, pale eyes bright and intent.

"By God, I got a say, and I say we sit down and talk like civilized folks. This ain't no way to—"

"No!" Hendricks's left arm shot out, as rigid as a crowbar, his fist clenched. "You stay put, Captain. This is my county and I got a warrant to serve. It's gone past you and what you want. I'm the law here and this man is resisting me in the lawful pursuit of my duty. I've come for that gun there on his hip and I mean to have it. What's more, I'm arresting him for obstructing—"

"You know better than that, Wally." Beechum's voice was tinged with humor, full and deep-throated to rise above Hendricks's tirade. He moved backward until the porch overhang shaded his eyes from the sun. "You're on my land and you ain't been invited. A man's still got some rights in this country." He appeared to slouch, his wiry frame pliant and boneless, right hand poised, curved like a predator's claw.

I looked from him to Hendricks and back again, comprehension crashing down like the blaze of an August sun. I hung suspended, sounds and images of a thousand TV battles storming my mind—Marshal Dillon cleaning up Dodge, Doc Holliday at the O.K. Corral—shoot-outs, showdowns, death.

Behind me Homer cursed; I heard his feet grate on gravel.

"Jesus Christ!" I yelled, and leaped at Hendricks.

But I was two paces away and Homer caught me before I could make the second step, caught me and yanked me out of harm's way, out of the line of fire of the battle that was already going on, that had begun with the sound of my voice as if it had been a prearranged starting signal, two silver-tipped streamers of fire lancing at each other from thirty feet apart, unerringly and precisely together, the two sounds blending into one, one coughing roar that sent Wally Hendricks to the ground like a poleaxed steer, left Jonas Beechum groping blindly in empty air for something to prop up his falling body.

27

WALLY HENDRICKS HAD A SHATTERED THIGH BONE; JONAS Beechum was dead.

Homer called in on the cruiser's radio while I applied a tourniquet above Hendricks's wound. He was out cold, the thin face still wrinkled with the pain that had put him under. I thought seriously about waking him up, to let him enjoy it a little before the medics got there with morphine.

Judging from his babbling before he went under, the unholy light in his eyes, it had undoubtedly been the high point of his life, justification for countless hours before a mirror, a greased holster and a limber hand. His moment of truth and he had to sleep through it. A damned shame.

I poked around in the wound a little, picked out a few slivers of disenfranchised bone. At least he'd get a nice limp out of it, a badge of courage that should net him countless numbers of Saturday-night beers at the local bars, slaps on the back, and nicknames like Kid Lightning and Wally the Kid.

Homer came up behind me, cursing in a low monotonous voice. "Goddammit! What a hell of a goddamned stinking mess!" He wiped sweat and blew his nose, wrestled the cellophane from a new cigar. He walked over to the porch and looked down at Jonas, whirled and came back, his normally ruddy face pale.

"Well, I guess that ties it up with a pink ribbon."

I wiped my fingers on Hendricks's shirt and rose to my feet. "Ties what up?"

"The case. Me and you musta had it figured right down the line."

I shrugged. "I wouldn't be so sure. We don't know any more than we did. We won't until we get a reading on his gun."

He gave me a startled glance, then waved a heavy arm in a short half-circle. "If he wasn't guilty, what was this all about? Come on, Dan. A man don't draw down on three lawmen if he ain't guilty."

"One lawman. And this man just might. I'm not sure I know what this was all about, but I'm also not sure it had anything to do with Sandy's killing. He didn't draw on me and you. He drew on Hendricks. And I, for one, don't even know if he drew first. Do you?"

"Well, no, you were in my way—"

"It had to do with stiff-backed, misplaced pride, Homer, the obsessive need to try out a skill they've been perfecting a good part of their adult life. Hendricks more than Jonas, I think. He's in a violent profession, around guns all day long, constantly reminded that he's better at this one thing than almost every other man on earth. And no chance to find out, not for real. Drawing on cardboard cutouts and balloons is not the same thing as drawing on a man who can shoot back."

He stared at me, his face slowly growing slack with surprise. "You telling me you changed your mind, that Jonas didn't kill his niece—"

"I didn't say that. I was talking about this . . . this showdown between Hendricks and Jonas. I think the killings took a backseat to the real issue for them—which one was the fastest.''

''I dunno. Sounded pretty close to me. I only heard one shot.'' He puffed lustily on the cigar, the color back in his ruddy cheeks, features settled into their usual benign configuration. He lifted his head as the high thin sound of a siren wafted in on the wind.

''Here comes the cavalry.''

''Yeah,'' I said, and climbed into my pickup. He paid no attention until I punched the engine to life.

''Hey, where you going?''

''I'll be back in a couple of hours. Hitch a ride into town with one of the deputies. I'll pick you up at the What If?''

''Hey, dammit! Where the hell you going? They're gonna want to talk—''

''You're a captain, Homer. Pull rank.'' I eased the pickup backward. He lumbered alongside, holding on to the light bar.

''Dammit, Dan—''

''His wife, Homer. Someone has to tell her.''

''Oh,'' he said, and let go, stumbling to a halt. He thought about it for a few seconds, then came after me again, waving his arms, the cigar gripped between his teeth, dumping a spray of ashes down his shirt. He spit it out.

''Dan! Danny, dammit, wait a minute! She's a suspect! I need to talk to her—''

I gunned the truck, damping his bellow to an unintelligible roar, a heavy plume of fine white dust rising to stop him like a brick wall. He yanked out his handkerchief and covered his mouth and nose, and I didn't have to tax my imagination to visualize the uncomplimentary things he had to say. I tooted the horn and waved.

He bent over and scuttled along the driveway, looking like a kid searching for a rock to throw.

Seconds later I discovered that's exactly what he was doing. I was out of range by the time he found one, but he threw it anyway, then stood shaking his fist at me. I didn't mind. It was nice to know I wasn't the only one who flipped out and did something childish now and again.

Myna Beechum tripped lightly down the steps of the small hospital and came toward me, moving with the long smooth strides of someone used to walking. Crisp and clean looking in a white uniform, white shoes, and red-banded white cap, she slipped into the seat beside me with a faint rustling of starched fabric. Her heavy mass of black hair was swept upward from her slender neck, confined somewhere behind the skimpy hat, and pink, untinted lips curved faintly in an enigmatic smile.

"Sorry I was so long, Danny, but I had to find someone to cover my station." She sighed and settled primly in the seat. "We're shorthanded as usual." She gave me an apologetic look. "I only have fifteen minutes."

There was a touch of coquetry in her voice, a mischievous look in the dark flashing eyes, and it suddenly occurred to me that she may have made wrong assumptions from my urgent, cryptic call.

"No problem," I said, reaching across to help her close the pickup's door. I caught a whiff of roses, something else sharp and pungent I couldn't define. I straightened, and she settled herself again in the seat, hands clasped in her lap, feet together firmly on the floor, her expression lively and expectant.

I punched in the dash cigarette lighter, stalling, trying to remember why it had seemed so imperative for me to be the one to inform her of her husband's death. Now, in the cold reality of the moment, disconcerted by her phys-

ical presence, the warm glow in the passionate eyes, I
realized it had been a bad mistake, that my decision had
arisen more from an instinctive need to protect her than
to offer solace in her time of grief.

The thought jolted me. I had come here to warn her, to
help her find answers to the hard questions Homer would
ask. A small green worm of self-disgust began to squirm
in my mind. I ignored it and turned to face her. I reached
out and took one of her hands in mine, small and firm and
warm, curling instinctively around my palm.

"Listen to me. We don't have much time. I have something hard to tell you, but we can't spare the time for grief.
They may be coming even now, and you have to be pre-
pared, you have to have the right answers for Homer and
the sheriff—" I broke off at the look of utter wonderment
in her face, eyes round and swimming with perplexity, lips
parted in a half-smile of bewilderment, as if this was all
some recondite joke and she would grasp its meaning momentarily.

"Myna . . . listen, Jonas is dead."

We stared at each other in frozen silence; her eyes
moved across my face as if testing for sincerity, veracity.
Her lips came together, trembled, breathed: "No!"

"Yes." Her hand began to shake; I pressed it between
my own.

"Oh, my God!" She brought the other hand to her
mouth and moved against me. I put my arm around her
shoulder.

"I'm sorry," I said, watching her crumpling face, wondering in my eternal suspicion how deep and far the river
of grief would run. Neither deep nor far, if Curly Glazier
had spoken the truth.

She cried quietly, no wailing, no gnashing of teeth or
rending of garments. But she cried real tears, and I could

feel the tremors rushing through her body like small tidal waves of anguish.

I punched the dash lighter again and lit a cigarette. I let her grieve until I finished. Then I gripped her shoulders, turned her to face me, and wiped her eyes with my handkerchief.

"I'm sorry, we have no more time."

"Time . . . time for what?" She took the handkerchief out of my hand and wiped her cheeks. "I—I don't understand." She stared at me with brimming, red-rimmed eyes. "You haven't told . . . told me yet . . . how? Was it . . . was it his heart?"

"No," I said, and turned to look down the highway. It was taking too long. "No, he drew his gun on a deputy sheriff and—"

"A deputy? My God, whatever for?"

"We were there to ask him about Sandy," I said, turning back to watch her face once more. "I—they believe he may have killed her."

"What?" Her voice was a ragged whisper, the look of bewilderment back on her lovely face. "They're crazy! Jonas couldn't . . . wouldn't—"

"Maybe not," I said. "But right now that isn't the important thing. In a very few minutes a police captain from Midway City and maybe the sheriff of this county will be coming in here with some tough questions for you. You need to be thinking up some answers."

"Me? My God, why me?"

"Because you're his wife. It would be routine in any event, but in this case they're looking for an accessory." I winced inwardly as I realized I had changed completely to the impersonal pronoun they.

"An accessory? They think Jonas killed Sandy and I . . . I helped him?"

"We think," I said, looking straight ahead through the

233

bugspattered windshield, "that Jonas shot her because he was drunk and angry about the timber. A fit of rage. If that is the case, he had an accessory. Someone who wore Sandy's deerskin blouse on the bus, maybe not all the way to Dallas, but as far as Corsicana at least. That's the last time she was seen. A darkhaired woman with a bandanna across her head, someone about the same size as Sandy." I turned to look at her.

Her eyes were wide and round, one slim hand pressed to her mouth, the other one lying in her lap like a dead brown bird.

"And they—you think that woman was me?" She was silent for a moment. "I told you I was working that night— all night."

"Yes, you did, Myna. And you lied." I was facing forward again, wishing I was somewhere else, wishing I didn't have to hear whatever it was she was going to tell me, me or somebody else, wishing I could make her fit my first image of her, vibrant and warm, her eyes filled with the eternal compassion I needed in a woman.

Her hand clutched my arm. "I had some business, Danny. I did lie to you, but it had nothing to do with Sandy or Jonas or . . . anything." Her fingers bit into my wrist.

"All right."

"I'm telling you the truth this time."

"I believe you, Myna."

"No, you don't!" She jerked her hand away from my arm, a note of petulance in her voice. "You're just saying that."

"You don't have to convince me. I'm a bit player. The superstars will come galloping into view most any time now. You *will* have to convince them."

"Oh, God," she said, cupping her face in her right

hand, propping her elbow against the window frame. She looked small and weary and hurt. I wanted to hold her.

I lit another cigarette instead, and cleared my throat. "What we're not sure about is whether that woman left the bus at Corsicana and rode with Jonas to Midway City and participated in the murders, or whether she left the bus at Corsicana and made her way back to . . . to wherever she lived. Maybe by way of another bus, maybe some other way. Those are crucial questions that will have to be answered. The answers will determine the extent of her involvement and thus the subsequent charges levied against her." My voice sounded wooden, pompous, strained. It wasn't every day that I betrayed a friend.

"My God," she said again, her voice as hollow as an empty grave. She took her hand away from her face and looked at me. "Do you really believe that I—that I—"

"It doesn't matter what I believe. I told you—"

"Oh, yes it does!" she said passionately, her hands flashing out to cover one of mine on the steering wheel. "It matters, or you wouldn't be here."

"Okay. It matters to me. But it won't change anything. I'm not a cop; it's not my case. Even if it were, you'd have to tell me where you were that night; you'd have to prove it."

She bit her lower lip and dropped her gaze, her hands slowly relinquishing their grasp on mine. She sank back into the corner and averted her face, fingers steepled beneath her chin like a postulant before the cross.

"You remember what I told you, Danny? About Jonas and me? About sex . . . about no sex since . . . well, for several years?" Her voice was muted and oddly plaintive.

"I remember," I said, feeling my throat go dry, wanting her to stop, not wanting to hear what I knew she was going to say, whether it be falsehood or fact, understanding in the flare of a minor epiphany that now that she was

235

free I would probably stand in her line if it ran halfway around the block.

"You don't have to tell me. I said I *wasn't* a cop."

"I'm only human," she said, injecting a querulous note that set my teeth on edge. "I have needs . . . desires. Jonas was too . . . too old-fashioned to . . . to help me after he began to fail. He wouldn't do things . . . well, the other thing, so . . ." Her voice trailed off. She looked at me with a small defiant smile. "I'm only human."

"You said that."

She wet her lips. "I was with . . . with a man."

"Fine. Then you have no problem."

"Don't you want to know who?"

"No. You can tell that to Captain Sellers and the sher-iff."

"I'd rather tell you."

I shrugged. "It won't help. You'll still have to tell them."

"Curly Glazier," she said, leaning forward, her eyes fixed intently on my face, lips parted in a curiously child-like expression of malice—a woman scorned exacting ret-ribution. I wondered if they ever forgot.

I nodded, trying not to let my face reveal the turmoil inside.

"All night," she added almost breathlessly. "He'll tell you that."

"Okay. Then you have no problem."

"My God! My husband is dead and you say I have no problem."

I looked at her, feeling my lips move, not quite sure if I was smiling or not, an inexplicable need to inflict pain rushing through me like a small hot wind. I felt put-upon, indignant, betrayed. An absurd reaction, considering I had no claim on her whatsoever, but strong feelings require

236

expression, venting, and she was the focus of my emotion. And she was right there, handy.

"Ten million dollars. Perhaps that will help soften the blow."

"What?" Her eyes were big and round again, fingers at her lips.

"Two thousand acres of prime timber. Ten million may be a little high but—"

"No, no! I told you about the timber. Jonas doesn't have the right—"

"You told me he was worried, that he didn't know for sure."

"I know that! I told you that, but he found out—a letter and a copy of the land papers he received from Nelson Morrow, the head of MCB under Sandy."

"Then your little deal with Glazier and Jonas was all for nothing?"

"Deal? What deal?"

Everybody lies.

"The deal you made to marry Jonas instead of Glazier, with Jonas to die and you to inherit the land and Glazier to cut the timber—"

"Oh, my God! Danny! You can't believe that! I told you what happened the first time we met."

"Yes, you did," I said, staring into her stricken face, seeing truth, realizing with a sinking feeling of defeat that I had forgotten a basic tenet of human nature: people told lies for all sorts of reasons, not all of them having to do with greed or self-preservation. Busted egos needed to be salved, injured pride to be bolstered. I wasn't sure what motivated Curly Glazier, but if I ever met him again I meant to find out.

"I don't know where you got that idea, Danny, but I can guess. After all this time, he's never given up, never stopped hating Jonas, never stopped coming at me. I—I

237

finally gave in a . . . a few months ago . . . There was nobody else I could turn to. I—I needed . . . somebody. Maybe you can't understand that, but it's the truth. The rest of it isn't. Just like your idea about Jonas shooting Sandy. It isn't true either, Danny.''

"All right.'' I glanced at my watch. "You're five minutes over, Myna.''

I could feel her staring at me, a prickling on the side of my face. After a moment, she clicked open the door. "I'm going home, Danny. Will . . . will you be coming back?''

"No.''

She stepped out on the pavement. "Well . . . thank you, Danny.''

"You're welcome.''

"Good-bye.''

"Good-bye.''

I didn't look until she was at the entrance, and that was far too far to call her back, even if my pride would have allowed it.

28

I MADE MY STATEMENT IN HENDRICKS'S SMALL OFFICE. A pudgy sweating deputy picked out the words on an old Royal portable. Homer glowered in the background, interjecting a word now and then when he thought I was straying too far from the truth. When they got to why I had left after the shooting, I told them I had gone to the Irondale hospital to be checked for symptoms of shock, and added by way of explanation that it wasn't every day I witnessed a genuine showdown between two old-timey gunslingers.

Homer snorted, but said nothing. The fat deputy didn't even look up.

Later Homer informed me that we would have to spend the night. That redneck, pompous sheriff had commandeered Jonas's gun and would bring over a couple of samples the next morning. He went on to say he had rented us a room at the best motel in town, that he would buy me a steak dinner, and we would have a high old time drinking a few beers, cussing, and talking about women.

I laughed, told him to kiss off, went out and got into my pickup, and spent the next four and a half hours slouched behind the wheel, busting the speed limit wide open, riding the tail winds of eighteen-wheelers where I could, breaking my own trail where I couldn't.

I arrived home stoned on noise, the whining susurrus of a straining motor, the whistling wind, the blaring cacophony of sorry western music that was beginning to sound like rock and roll.

The bottle of Jack Daniel's was still on the kitchen table where Homer had left it. Three-quarters full.

It was enough. For openers.

Two days passed before I heard from Homer. A crisp, terse report, his heavy voice cool and curt.

"Reckoned you'd want to know. We got a match on Beechum's gun. It was used on Conrad, so it follows that it was used on the Gomez woman. Officially we're not closing the case yet, but it's finished. Sandy Conrad's murder is Sheriff Kincaid's problem, since she was killed down there."

"You know that for sure, huh? Well, I'm happy for you, old buddy. Everything neat and tidy."

"Works that way sometime. Your girlfriend, Beechum's wife, you remember her? She came out smelling like a rose—well, not a rose exactly, but she's off the hook. Seems she'd been catting around on the old man. Big strapping feller named Curly Glazier. Handsome dude, slick, smooth, has a way with the women, what I hear. Well, he owned up to it, said he'd been banging her for some time. Old man, young wife with hot pants—"

"Go to hell, Homer."

"Well, anyhow, she was with him all that night. Sheriff seemed inclined to believe Glazier, so who was I to argue? His case, his people, his decision. Right?"

"Right as always, Homer. Doesn't it get to be a drag?"

240

He chuckled, not a particularly friendly chuckle, and fell silent.

I seized the opportunity to light a cigarette and take a sip of Jack Daniel's.

"That it, Homer?" I said, after a time.

"Yeah." He hawked something out of his throat. "I'm waiting for you to apologize to me, boy."

"Hah!" I said, and hung up on him, laughing so hard I spilled my drink.

Mercy and Hope showed up the next day, looking voluptuous as always, rushing the season in gaily colored sundresses and sandals, tiny satin bows at slender throats, dressy white gloves I hadn't seen the like of since Jackie left the White House.

"You ladies sure do look fine," I said, watching them settle on my couch. "What can I get you to drink? I'm having Jack Daniel's rocks myself."

"No, thank you," they chorused, then looked at each other and winced.

"I'm Hope," Hope said. She got up and came over and looked closely at my face. "I do believe, Mr. Roman, that you are inebriated."

"No, ma'am, but I'm pretty close to being drunk. Are you real sure you don't want—"

"No, thank you," Mercy said primly, peeling the glove from her right hand. "We have been waiting for you to submit your bill, and since you haven't, we decided to stop by and get it. I'm sure you must need your money and you've certainly earned it."

"Have I? I was under the impression I had failed—miserably."

Hope leaned down and tapped my nose playfully. "Now, now, no self-pity, Mr. Roman. You did a marvelous job. Everything turned out just fine, although I must say we

241

were all distressed to learn what Uncle Jonas had done to Sandy and, of course, what happened to Uncle Jonas. But dark deeds sow bitter seeds and reap an ugly harvest.''

"Wow," I said. "You get that out of the Bible?''

"Don't mock," Hope said sharply. "All things come from Him.''

"I guess you got me there," I admitted, and saluted her with my drink.

"Poor Sandy," Mercy said, and peeled off the other glove. "Poor dear, she tried so hard.''

"Tried what?'' I asked, a little off balance.

Mercy made a vague graceful gesture. "Oh, you know, her love life, the company. The poor thing couldn't seem to make anything work. That shameful man she was married to, that beatnik she went to see every few months.''

"They call them dropouts now, dear," Hope said sweetly. "They called them beatniks in the fifties.''

"You mean Jacob Twill?''

"That's him," they chorused, then looked at each other and made faces again.

"We hate it when we do that," Hope said.

"She went to East Texas that often?''

"Oh, yes, every three or four months. And Peter stayed home and chased everything in skirts.''

"And designer jeans," Mercy added. She gave her sister a knowing look. "And not all of them wore panty hose.''

I digested that while I lit a cigarette. My whiskey-soaked brain might be working in low gear, but I knew a leading statement when I heard one.

"You mean he liked boys, too?''

They laughed together, a blending of lilting musical notes, decidedly harmonious, somehow a little chilling.

"Oh, yes, indeed," Mercy trilled. "Peter was a . . .

well, I can't think of the name, but it's like a nymphoma-
niac.''

"A satyr," I said.

"Yes, that's it, I believe. He even went so far as to try
us, didn't he, Hope?''

"Both at once?" I said, stifling a giggle at the mind
pictures that thought evoked.

"No, of course not," Hope said stiffly. "Even Peter
wasn't that gross.''

"He could be quite charming when he wanted to be,"
Mercy said. "How do you think he got around Sandy?''

"Poor Sandy," Hope said. "It was simply too much for
her. Just as it was for Father. Perhaps it would be for any
one person. Now that there are two of us, we can set
things right again. With the money from Jonas's timber we
can—''

"Two of you," I said inanely. "There have always been
two of you.''

"Yes, of course," Hope explained patiently in a tone
she might use to a particularly obtuse child. "There have
always been the two of us, but not in charge, you see.
Now we are in charge. We were never given anything important to do before. Sandy saw to that. She gave us money
and told us to have fun, to enjoy life. And all the time she
and her perverted husband were destroying our company,
our inheritance. But we had a friend in the company who
kept us informed. We knew all along what was going on,
what they were doing to us." Her voice rang with passion;
Mercy watched her, transfixed.

"Nelson Morrow," I said, catching the look that flashed
between them and realizing my stab in the dark had found
a vital spot. "MCB's executive VP. Is he moving up by
any chance?''

"No," Hope said sharply. "We are sharing the presi-

dency, Mercy and I. Nelson will remain where he is."
She flicked a glance at Mercy. "For the time being."

Mercy pursed her lips primly. "You know what they
say about new brooms cleaning out the deadwood."

"I believe you mixed your metaphors, but I think I get
the idea."

"But for the time being," Hope said hastily, "things
will remain as they are, and Nelson will retain his old
spot, of course." She frowned at Mercy as if she had just
revealed to me the secret formula for some revolutionary
new type of plywood.

"Not a bad spot to be, everything considered."

Mercy swept to her feet. "We must be going, Mr. Roman. If you will be so kind as to give us your bill—"

"Sorry, ladies, but I don't have it all figured out yet.
Shuttle flights, rental cars, three-martini lunches—you
know how it goes. But I will soon, and when I do you
ladies will be the first to see it."

Hope frowned, ugly wrinkles breaking across her forehead. "You will, of course, include everything in your
report? I mean everything you have learned about the . . .
the death of Jonas and Sandy and her husband."

"Yes, ma'am," I said, placing my glass carefully on
the end table, struggling erect, facing them with the best
smile I could muster. "You don't care about the Gomez
woman, huh?"

"Yes, of course," Hope snapped.

"I knew her quite well," Mercy said. "She was an
excellent cook. And not only the Mexican dishes."

"One other thing," Hope said. "I understand the police took Sandy's deerskin blouse. I would appreciate it if
you would get it back for us. She was *so* pleased with it.
I don't want it to end up on the back of some police officer's girlfriend."

"That's not likely," I said, staring blankly into her blue

eyes, a blip of thought skimming the surface of my mind like a flat stone skipping across a pond. I put out a hand to steady myself, grasped the edge of the mantel.

Mercy clucked. "You really should shave, Mr. Roman, and take a bath. How long have you been drunk?"

"All my life." I looked back at Hope. "How do you *know* she was pleased with it?"

"What?"

"Sandy's deerskin blouse. How do you know she was *so* pleased—"

"She told me, of course. When she called to ask us to pick her up at the bus station."

"Called *you*?"

She nodded vigorously, blonde tresses bouncing on rounded shoulders, a glint of humor in guileless eyes.

"But she called Peter."

"She tried to call Peter," Hope said. "Without success. So she called us instead."

"And did you?"

"Did we what?"

"Pick her up?"

They laughed together again, and exchanged commiserating glances. "Really, Mr. Roman, I don't believe you're thinking quite clearly. How on earth could we pick her up? She wasn't there, of course. Uncle Jonas saw to that." Mercy gave me an understanding smile.

"Yeah. That's right. How come you never mentioned this before."

"Nobody asked us," they said together, then stopped, and Hope continued without a pause. "And since she didn't show up, it didn't really matter, did it?"

I had to admit to the kernel of logic in that, and it explained why Conrad hadn't made sure his playmate departed the premises before his wife came home: he hadn't known she was coming. A thorny little question that had bothered me from the beginning. Such a simple answer. I smiled into their bright lovely faces and marveled at how well such things worked out sometimes.

"You're right, of course, it didn't really matter."

At the door, Mercy pressed my hand briefly and Hope waggled her fingers. I held onto the doorjamb and watched them float to their waiting Porsches, words and phrases like "an ugly harvest" and "perverted husband" and "panty hose" echoing in my head.

I closed the door and made my way back to the den, to the bar across the corner. I poured another drink, my final drink, and saluted my ravaged face in the back bar mirror.

Three days were enough. Celebration or wake. I wasn't sure what it had been.

Now it was time to sober up.

29

HOMER SELLERS REARED BACK IN HIS ANCIENT WOODEN swivel chair and laced his fingers across his ample stomach. He glared at me along the length of his nose. He had gone back to his contact lenses, and whatever effect his fierce scowl might have had was almost totally destroyed by teary, red-rimmed eyes and swollen lids, the look of a disgruntled bear recently awakened from hibernation.

I grinned at him and sat down in his one and only visitor's chair.

"How's tricks, Homer?"

He kept right on glaring, tiny beads of moisture glistening on his lower lashes.

I nodded and fished out a cigarette. "That's great. Things are fine with me, too." I paused to light the cigarette, then went on with my end of the conversation. "Getting any lately?"

I exhaled a cloud of smoke and shook my head ruefully. "Me neither. Things ain't like they was. Danged women have changed. Independent. Calling you on the phone, wanting to take you out to dinner, dancing, and what all. It's getting downright scary. Next thing we know—"

He came forward with a crash, big hands banging the scarred wooden desk. "Don't come in here running no number on me, boy! It ain't gonna be that easy this time. You ran out on me, goddammit! I had to *fly* home! You know how I hate to *fly*!"

"I'm sorry" I said contritely. "I guess I lost my head, seeing that killing right there in front of us like I did—"

"Bullshit!" he said, his tone already softening. "You seen gunfights before, you seen men killed before. Hell, you've killed men before. Don't kid me. It was that woman, wasn't it? I knowed that's where you went. I figured she told you about that Glazier feller and it sent you off in all directions like some lovesick schoolboy—"

"Don't push it, Homer. You don't know what you're talking about."

He smiled thinly and yanked a Kleenex out of a box on his desk. He stabbed at his eyes.

"Truth hurts, don't it?" His tone was almost kindly, the bleary eyes twinkling knowingly. "I still think you owe me an abject apology, leaving me in the lurch the way you did."

"I said I was sorry. That's as humble as it gets. You talked me into that damned trip in the first place."

"So you ran back up here and got drunk."

"That's right, I did. Stupendously drunk, gloriously drunk. And I enjoyed every damned minute of it."

"Yeah." He nodded sagely. "Does a feller good to do that once in a while. Long's he don't make a habit of it." He cocked his head to one side. "That Jonas feller, what little I seen of him, seemed to be a purty nice old guy. Too bad about what happened."

"He was a nice guy. Under different circumstances I think I might have liked him a lot. But I guess I met him too late. He was being pressured too much and from too many directions."

"Hendricks is gonna make it all right, they say, but that leg might be a little shy."

"He's damn lucky to be alive."

"That's a fact." He leaned forward and studied my face. "Something bothering you? You look—"

"What if we were wrong, Homer?"

He looked startled. "Wrong about what?"

"About Jonas—about everything. We based our conclusions on some pretty shaky circumstantial evidence."

"You're forgetting something, Dan. We didn't go down there to arrest Jonas Beechum. We went to check out his gun. Just a routine part of a murder investigation. We played it by the book, local law and all. It's not our fault them two gun-happy idiots decided to have a *High Noon* showdown. And the bullets do match the slug that killed Conrad. I see that as justification of our deductions and our actions. I hate that it happened the way it did, but I sure don't feel any guilt about it."

"Bully for you."

"That's what's bothering you, huh?" He heaved a heavy sigh. "Well, don't let it. We did what had to be done, and if it hadn't been for Hendricks . . ." He let it trail away, shaking his head in disgust.

I nodded and mashed out my cigarette. Homer was back to normal; I had mended my fences one more time.

"I had a visit from my clients," I said. "My ex-clients. They told me Sandra Conrad called them that day when she couldn't reach her husband. She asked them to pick her up at the bus depot."

He stared at me, a slow smile spreading across his face. "I'll be damned. That explains—"

"Why the Gomez woman was there. I know that, but doesn't it strike you as odd that they never mentioned it to me or to the investigating officers?"

"No, not so odd. They didn't think it was important

and nobody knew to ask. Anyhow, both them little dollies are a little odd, if you ask me.''

"They also wanted me to pick up Sandra's deerskin blouse. Can you release it?''

"Sure. Right now if you want it. If Ted Baskin is still in his office.'' He picked up the phone without waiting for an answer, dialed a four-digit number.

I sat back in my chair and lit a cigarette, only half-listening to his rumbling voice. From past experience I knew he was as relieved as I that this making-up meeting was over. It happened often of late, too often. He was my friend, but he was a cop first, and therein lay the root cause of our occasional head-on encounters. He did what was right because it was the law; I sometimes chose expediency because it was the way to get things done.

He hung up the phone and grunted with satisfaction. "Ted's on his way up. Usually can't find them guys at home. You're in luck.''

He took a cigar out of his vest pocket and began the ritual of lighting up, talking easily, carrying us past the awkward patch that follows reconciliation.

We were talking about turkey hunting, the two-week April season on gobblers, when Ted Baskin clumped into Homer's office. He carried the deerskin blouse in one hand, folded neatly inside a clear plastic bag. He dropped the bag in my lap and laid a three-by-five property release form on the edge of Homer's desk. I shook his extended hand as he spoke:

"How you doing, Dan? Sign right there and she's all yours. Nice piece of work. My old lady would love it.''

"Handmade,'' Homer said. "Lady lives out in the woods down in East Texas makes them. You didn't find anything, huh?''

Baskin shrugged. "Nothing but a little ring around the collar.''

I looked up from the form. "A little what?"

He flashed his ready grin. "You know the commercial, ring around the collar. A little skin oil, a little dirt, a little dried skin, traces of petrochemicals, salt—"

"But this thing is brand new."

"Pretty new, all right, but it'd been worn some. There were faint smudges on the cuff edges also—same thing as the collar, little more dust or dirt maybe." He frowned. "The petrochemicals probably came out of the air. That air down there is saturated with the stuff."

"How much wear would you say?"

"Jesus, Dan, that'd be impossible to say. Depend on where she wore it, if she was around dusty areas or not, if she sweat a lot maybe—impossible to say."

"How about eight to ten hours, five or so on a bus ride?"

He shook his head. "She'd have to be a dirty slob. Naw, I don't think so. There was too much there for any one-day accumulation." He took the package out of my hands and broke the seal. "Here, I'll show you what I mean."

He spread the blouse across Homer's desk, ran one freckled finger along the inside edge of the collar. "Here, see this dark line. Just like you get on your shirts. It's where it rubs the neck. Okay, we can see it better if we unfold the collar . . . like this." He lifted the flap of the collar and pressed it flat on the desk. The discoloration became immediately more discernible against the smooth fawn-colored fabric.

"Don't look like much," Baskin said, "but you scrape a little of that and put it under a scope and you'd be surprised at what you'd find. Mostly it's just dirt, though."

"What's the point," Homer said. "We know Jonas brought it up here with her other clothes. Hell, maybe he wore it." He picked up a pencil and bounced the eraser on his teeth, a bemused expression on his face.

"The point is," I said, "it's dirty and it shouldn't be." I refolded the blouse and stuffed it into the plastic bag. "Thanks, Ted."

Baskin nodded and picked up the property release form. "No sweat, Dan. Good to see you again." He lifted a hand at Homer, tapped me on the shoulder, and left the room.

Homer rapped out shave and a haircut on the edge of his desk, then tossed the pencil in a drawer. He got up and crossed to the single window in his office, stood looking down at the small Civic Center park, hands cocked on his hips, a semi-belligerent expression on his face.

"I don't like it any better'n you do, Dan, the way it turned out. But Jonas is dead, and I reckon he's the only one who knew exactly what happened. I don't think he had time to bury her, so she's probably in a canal somewhere—what's left of her—or a slough. Probably never know for sure, but things are very seldom cut-and-dried in this business. You know that well's I do. We only got what people tell us and what we can find for ourselves, and a lot of times that ain't much. So we make do with what we got, put it together the best way we can, and try to figure out the rest. This time we got Jonas's gun and two dead people, one missing and presumed dead. We got people telling us Jonas was a hotheaded, cantankerous old fool, and we saw some evidence of that. We got a motive—the timber on his land. We got opportunity. Nobody saw him from about six-thirty that night until the next morning when his wife found him passed out with a bottle in his hand." He moved back to his desk, sat down heavily, and sighed. "Not much to take to a district attorney, but that don't matter now with him dead."

I stood up and lit a cigarette. "You trying to convince yourself, Homer, or me?" I crossed to the door and stopped with my hand on the knob. "Answer me one question, Homer. How would you feel if Sandra Conrad should suddenly turn up—alive?''

He sopped moisture at the edges of his eyes with a Kleenex while he thought about it, the belligerent expression slowly forming again.

''I ain't answering no dumb questions like that, boy.''

''That's what I thought,'' I said, and let myself out the door.

30

I SPENT THE NEXT TWO DAYS THINKING ABOUT IT, SOBER
as a judge and hurting. I sat at the kitchen table with a
yellow legal pad and scribbled for hours, making notes,
sifting through the horrendous tide of verbiage, annotating
known lies in red, suspected lies in yellow, and the tiny
kernels of truth in black.

Hope called on the second day, imperiously demanding
my report and the deerskin blouse. I put her off with some
silly story about having a new strain of Asian itch that was
highly contagious and did its nasty work mainly in the
erogenous zones.

I slept little and ate a lot, drank copious amounts of
beer, and sucked on cigarettes like an antismoking machine. I paced the floor, jittery, nagged by the cutting edge
of doubt.

I sketched scenarios, peopled them with players, worked
out motivations and suspected aspirations—a round half-
dozen in all—and smashed them one by one against an
impenetrable wall of rationalization, common sense, and
logic.

Until there was only one.

And even then it wasn't a moment of cosmic revelation, of riddles solved, hypotheses cleared. It was a nebulous theory at best, bound together by tenuous threads and unknown factors I could only guess about, what-if's and maybe's, probably's and might's.

I slept on it and awoke the third morning confident and refreshed, burning with a righteous zeal, my thoughts crystallized around certainty rather than doubt, determination rather than indecisiveness.

It took time to set it up. Time, and Hendricks's pudgy replacement, whose name turned out to be Deputy Clarence Barr.

It took persuasion, a dangling carrot in front of Deputy Barr's turned-up nose, the siren song of fame, and on a more materialistic plane, almost certain promotion. It was too much for him to resist, which meant that he was young and human and only a little more gullible than most.

He called me late in the afternoon of that same day, drawled his report in liquid Texanese, abbreviated consonants and elongated vowels: "y'alls" and "heahs" and "thangs."

He seemed nervous at the end, and uncertain. So I took him over the plan again, soothed his fears, bolstered the fantasy, left him fired once more with an evangelical fervor for justice and the law, and his own shining future.

Shameful expediency. Sometimes it was all you had.

It was a few minutes after one when I pulled into Jonas Beechum's drive, parked the Ramcharger beside the Jeep, and got out to stretch the miles out of my legs, the kinks out of my back. There wasn't much I could do about my head, the keening highway noises, the pall of dread that had settled over me like a mourner's shroud.

I lit a cigarette and brushed at nonexistent dust, stretching the moment now that it had arrived, feeling infirm

suddenly, tired and vulnerable and uncertain—an old soldier at the end of a long campaign, the battle almost over,
still fearful of the war.

Behind me car tires grated on gravel, came to rest across
the end of the driveway. I paid no attention. It was only
Deputy Barr playing the game according to my rules. His
big entrance was yet to come. I reached inside the truck
and picked up the brown paper bag.

I crossed the tattered lawn, dry and dusty now, new
green shoots and dry curling blades from last year's clumps
of Johnson grass. Whatever else Jonas Beechum had or
hadn't been, he hadn't been much of a gardener.

Myna was waiting at the door, throwing back the screen
with a flourish and an unhappy smile, catching my hand
before I could object—as if I might want to—and drawing
me into the cool dim hallway that served as a foyer, dark
eyes shadowed with recent pain, larger than I remembered, set deeper beneath the fine arched brows.

"Danny. What on earth are you doing?"

I gave her a kindly smile. "Fulfilling my destiny,
child," I said, and patted her on the cheek.

"My God, you have everybody upset—"

"I know," I said sadly. "I'm all tore up myself." I
took her arm with my free hand. "Where are they?"

"In the kitchen, but—"

"Hush," I said, and ushered her down the hall to the
kitchen, a large breezy room with lots of windows and an
ancient stove, an old-fashioned wooden table, and
scratched and battered cabinets all across one wall. A
white enameled sink and matching refrigerator, both faded
and chipped. A straight chair in the corner, occupied.

Jacob Twill sat at the table with Joline Coldwater. General Ralston sat in the straight chair in the corner.

I stopped dead in my tracks. "General. What the hell
are you doing here?"

He pawed a hand through his beard and looked embarrassed. "Well, hidy, Dan. I guess I'm sorta what you could call their bodyguard." He gave me a yellow grin and fondled the breech of the .22 rifle lying across his almost nonexistent lap.

"I didn't ask him to come," Jacob Twill said, staring at me, disheveled and unfocused, his skin not as bronzed as it had been before, dark plum-colored pouches under his eyes.

Joline remained silent, dark eyes fixed somewhere on my face.

Myna sat down across from Joline, then bounced to her feet again. "We were just having some tea, Danny. Could I—"

I dropped my hand on her shoulder and shook my head. "No, thanks. Please keep your seat."

She sank back to her chair, picked up the glass of amber liquid in front of her, put it down again. "Danny, will you please—"

"I brought you something," I said, touching her shoulder again. "Just like my message said I would. And in case you're wondering, my messages were delivered by a deputy named Clarence Barr, and he's parked across your driveway right now." I looked at Ralston. "That was for you, General, just in case you decide I look like a squirrel or some other varmint that needs killing."

He grinned and threw up his hands. "Aw pshaw, you know better'n that. I was just joshing before about being a bodyguard. Hell, I got trouble enough just guarding my own. I come along 'cause I need some stuff from the store."

"As long as we understand each other," I said. I switched the sack to my left hand and palmed the .38 in one continuous motion. I held it out for him to see. "Besides, I can part your beard with this before you can get that rifle out from underneath your belly.''

"Hey," he said, and gave me a mocking grin. "That's scary."

I nodded and put the gun away. I opened the bag and took out the deerskin blouse. I leaned forward and dropped it in the center of the table.

"This is what I brought you ladies. One of you ladies. I brought it back where it belongs."

Myna reached out a tentative hand. "Why . . . why that's a deerskin blouse like . . ." Her voice trailed off. She jerked back her hand.

I looked at Joline. She was staring at the blouse, her face pale. She looked up and caught my gaze, her eyes flashing.

"That's Sandy's blouse," she snapped.

"That's what everybody thought," I said ruefully. "But danged if we didn't find out that it wasn't hers after all."

"Don't be ridiculous! I made that blouse myself. I gave it to her. I think I can recognize my own work."

"That's a fact," I said, and scrubbed my fingers through my hair. "Well, I guess you can't argue with the manufacturer—you're sure now that this is the blouse you brought over here the day she went home—well, the day she was supposed to—"

"Absolutely. I told you that before. I brought it over shortly after you left the back gate that day. I gave it to her and left right after that. Jonas and her were arguing and I felt uncomfortable listening—"

"Yeah, I remember now. That's what you told me, all right."

"What's this all about?" Jacob Twill rubbed his hands together briskly, as if they were cold. He looked haggard, the bronze skin almost sallow, dark rings under puffy listless eyes.

"It's about murder," I said. "Murder and an old man who died for no good reason."

Twill looked from me to Myna, to Joline, then back at me again. He shook his head. "I don't understand. Are you talking about Sandy, about Conrad? I thought that was all settled. Jonas—"

"Jonas didn't kill anyone. Not Sandy, not Conrad, and certainly not Gomez."

Twill did the traveling act with his eyes again, his face a ludicrous mixture of bewilderment and shock. "Then . . . who?"

"That's a good question," I said, launching headlong into my bluff, as cool as Amarillo Slim calling a ten-dollar pot. "Before I answer that, let's consider who had a reason. Besides Jonas, who stood to gain most by Sandy's death?"

Myna made a soft gasping sound; Joline glared at me angrily. Twill stared down at his hands coupled loosely on the table and, off to my left, General Ralston moved his heavy legs and had to lurch forward to catch the falling rifle.

Joline shoved her chair back from the table and stood up. "This is absurd! We all know Jonas killed Sandy—"

"Put it down, General," I said. "You're making me nervous." I held the .38 pointed at the floor, watching a foolish grin spread across the bearded face as he stared down at the gun in his hands, then flicked a glance at the one in mine.

"Whoooee," he said, and let it swing by the barrel from one clenched fist. "Fool thing ain't even loaded," he muttered.

"He's telling the truth," Twill said. "He only brought it to use Jonas's cleaning kit."

"Humor me," I said. "Put the goddamn thing on the cabinet!"

259

The big man lurched to his feet. "No need to get touchy," he said peevishly, laying the gun gently on the cracked Formica top and resuming his seat.

I looked at Joline. "Sit down." I put away the gun.

Her face tightened, lips thinned, a bloodless line circling her mouth and arching upward into olive cheeks, slender fingers curled into white-knuckled fists.

"Please," I added, and she sank silently into her seat, fulgent eyes still sparking fire.

"Thank you." I placed my hand on Myna's shoulder. "Is this your blouse?"

"No—I don't . . . no, it *must* be Sandy's."

"Then you still have yours? Somewhere here in the house?"

She nodded slowly. "Yes, I'm sure . . . yes, it would be in the bedroom closet."

I squeezed her shoulder and let my hand drop. "Would you get it, please?"

The sleek black head bobbed; she pushed away from the table, carefully placing her weeping glass of iced tea in the center of her napkin. She stood up and looked at me with stricken eyes. "I'll . . . I'll have to look."

"No, Myna," Joline said quietly, a note of anguish in her voice, and something else that sounded almost like relief. "You won't find it. This one is yours." She looked up at me and formed a sickly smile. "Is that what you wanted to know, you sonuvabitch?"

31

I NODDED AMIABLY. "THAT WAS IT," I SAID, RELIEF RUSH-
ing through me like an electric shock, leaving me a little
light-headed. I could have told her that until that moment
I had no real idea which of them had ridden the bus to
Corsicana, whose finger had pulled the triggers that had
killed three people. I could have told her all I had was a
hunch, a deerskin blouse with a dirty ring where it should
have been clean, and a deep instinctual certainty born of
past experience that a periodic drunkard such as Jonas
could not have performed with the impeccable precision
the murderer had exhibited on that long wet Wednesday
night. A man drunk is by nature careless, sloppy, imper-
fect. I had reason to know that to be a fact; I should have
realized it a long time before. Because I hadn't, Jonas
Beechum had died.

"This blouse," I went on mechanically, "was left in
Sandy's bedroom. It didn't belong to her. I assume she
was wearing hers when you shot her. So that leaves
Myna's."

"Mine?" Myna stood poised like a doe on the verge

261

of flight. "What do you—mine? It can't be mine! Mine's in—" She turned and ran out of the room.

Joline shook her head, her eyes turned downward. "I borrowed hers. I can see now it was a stupid thing to do."

"What?" Jacob Twill sat up straight. "What are you two talking about?"

"Not so stupid," I said. "You got the identification you wanted. The bus driver identified Sandy's picture after I mentioned the blouse to him. I think you just went a little too far, got a little too clever. Making the bus ride to Corsicana was a bit too much. You complicated it unnecessarily. That's the trouble with being an amateur." I smiled at her. "And that also means you had to have someone helping you, someone to pick you up at Corsicana, drive you to the Conrad house in Midway City."

"I rented a car," she said flatly, her eyes locking on mine.

"No," I said gently, wagging my head, catching sight of General Ralston inching cautiously to his feet and feeling a jolting shock.

Another wrong player; my money had been on Jacob Twill.

"Take it easy, General," I said. "Don't make me hurt you."

He made a whooshing sound, hanging crouched in a limbo of indecision, the huge arms akimbo like some great gangling bird forever rooted to the ground. "Man—" he began, but Joline stopped him with a calming wave.

"He had nothing to do with any of it. Believe me. All he did was drive my Jeep to Corsicana, then take the next bus back. I'll swear to that in court. He knew nothing."

Ralston dropped back into his chair, the seamed skin above his beard shiny with sweat. "She's telling you the truth, Mr. Roman. She said she was helping a pregnant friend home on the bus and asked if I'd take her Jeep up there 'cause she was gonna stay with her awhile. Man, I don't know nothing about no murders.''

I shrugged. "I'm not the one to convince of that."

"Convince of what?" Jacob Twill appeared dazed, glassy eyes shifting back and forth between me and Joline, his speech slurred, forehead beaded with a clinging film of perspiration, the edges of his finely chiseled mouth pulled backward in a grinning rictus from some inner turmoil or pain. Abruptly, without waiting for an answer, his head fell forward into his hands.

I looked at Joline. She was staring down at him, the taut lines blurred and softened in her face, the dark eyes warm and compassionate.

"What's wrong with him?"

She made a quiet sighing sound and brushed a tangled mat of hair back from his forehead.

"It's the radiation. And the drugs. It always affects him this way the day of the treatment." She looked up then, an enigmatic expression on her face.

I felt a creeping sensation of shock. "Cancer?"

She added a faint twisted smile to her baffling expression. "Sort of. Kaposi's sarcoma. Have you ever heard of that, Mr. Roman?"

I shook my head.

"I shouldn't wonder. It's a rare form of cancer, or tumor, of the blood-vessel walls." She paused, one hand gently stroking Twill's head. Her eyes lifted and found mine again, locked. "It's one of several rare illnesses peculiar to people who suffer from the world's newest Black Plague."

"No kidding?" I said inanely, unable to break away from her mesmerizing eyes, small black fires in fields of sterile white, blanched skin and lips that trembled perceptibly as she raked them with a lubricating tongue. Breath whistled through her teeth like the angry hiss of an adder.

263

"AIDS!" she spat.

I took an involuntary step backward, my throat suddenly constricted, dawning comprehension firing my veins with adrenaline, gripping my vitals with an icy hand.

"AIDS," I echoed, my voice dry and hoarse with wonder. "She had—Sandy had AIDS—" I broke off and swallowed, the sound clearly audible in the silent room. "And that's why—" I stopped again and looked at her for confirmation.

She shrugged, her face cold and distant, her hand still caught in the metronomic pattern across the top of Twill's bowed head.

"She was filthy with it. She knew it and she didn't care. She said the whole thing was silly, that she had had it for two years and nothing had happened to her. She laughed— my God, laughed—and said it was just propaganda by the drug companies to sell expensive new drugs. She said that Peter Conrad had had it longer than her and nothing had happened to him. She said it was just something the doctors used when they didn't know what was wrong."

I leaned against the sink and fumbled a cigarette out of my pack. "How long has he—"

"There's no telling, the doctor said. Incubation periods vary, and not everyone has a reaction to the disease. They're simply carriers. Like she was, like Peter Conrad was. There's no telling how many people he infected, how many people they, in turn, have infected. My God, it's a nightmare."

"I'm not going to die," Twill said, his voice thick and furry, querulous, a plaintive call for reassurance.

"No, darling," Joline murmured and bent to kiss the top of his head. "You'll be all right. The treatments will make you well again."

"Jesus, I'm sick," he moaned and made a retching sound.

"He needs to lie down." Joline slipped her hands under his arms and looked at the hulking figure in the corner. "Genny . . . please. Help me with him."

But General Ralston sat transfixed, his features frozen in horror, big hands clutching his knees, his ungainly body pointed forward like a runner in the blocks. He licked his lips and stared at Twill as if the moaning man was some mutant horror from the bowels of the earth. "By golly," he said hoarsely. "By golly—"

"I'll help you," I said, and between us we half-carried, half-dragged the rangy body to the living room, stretched him on the couch. He curled on his side, a handkerchief pressed against his mouth.

"What's wrong?" Myna stood in the doorway to the bedroom, looking disheveled, distraught. "I can't find the blouse," she said plaintively. "I've looked everywhere. . . ."

"Myna." Joline crossed the room and put her arms around her sister's slumped shoulders. "It's all right, honey. The one on the kitchen table is yours. I had to borrow it that night."

"That night? Then it's true . . . true what Danny said?" Her voice was a dry agonized whisper. She pulled out of Joline's arms and back against the doorjamb, one hand over her mouth, her eyes brimming. "Oh, my God, Joline. How could you?" She turned and looked at me, her face bleached of color. "Damn you!" she whispered and disappeared into the bedroom.

We stood looking at each other, listening to Twill's moans, the sound of Myna's sobs.

Joline smiled painfully, a look of resignation crossing her face, chased almost at once by a glimmer of tight-lipped humor. "What now, Mr. Roman? Leg irons and dungeons, or stoning on the square."

"That's not my job," I said, mimicking someone I had

265

once heard on a TV program, and doing a miserable job of it. "And, for what it's worth, I'm sorry."

She sighed and settled to a seat on the arm of the over-stuffed couch. "We all do what we have to do. All the times she came down here . . . and he went running to her . . . I told myself it didn't matter. I had him and that was what was important. He loved me, and that was what was important. I never let myself think about how much I . . . how much I hated her. And when this . . . this vile thing happened, when I realized that on top of everything else she had killed us—" She chopped it off, her voice breaking.

"Us?"

She took a deep shuddering breath and nodded, the meager smile returning. "I have it too. I found that out Wednesday morning. I had gone on Monday to my quarterly blood-donation appointment. On Wednesday morning they sent word for me to come back in again. The lady in charge came out—an old school friend of mine, by the way—and took me back into her office. She told me they couldn't accept my blood any longer. She told me that a new screening test showed the presence of . . . AIDS antibodies, I believe she said. At any rate, when I pressed her, she told me that was an indication that I had the AIDS virus in my body, and that it was active. And that's all she would tell me except that I should see a doctor. I had no clear idea what AIDS was, other than it was something like a venereal disease. I went directly from the blood bank to the library. There wasn't a lot of information, but there was enough." She stopped, breathing deeply again, her face vacant.

I lit a cigarette and waited. Behind me on the couch, Twill's moans had dwindled to heavy breathing. There were no sounds from either the kitchen or the bedroom.

"I knew, of course, that it had come from Jacob. There

266

had been no one else. Not for years, too many years. And after reading what I found in the library, I was filled with rage at him. I made the wrong assumption that he must have had sexual relations with a man. That appeared to be the consensus: it was a homosexual disease. I know now that isn't true, but I suppose that's why I didn't immediately think of Sandy. I knew he slept with her when she came down to visit. I had accepted that as being a part of my life with him. I had no choice. A part of him still loved her and I had to accept that or leave. It had been going on for a long time, three years, at least. So I have no idea when it was she . . . she infected him.''

"She was being treated," I said.

"I know. That's how I found out about her. Despite all her brave talk about AIDS being nothing to fear, she was taking an experimental drug called Isoprinosine that her doctor had to get from Mexico.''

"I think I've read about it.''

She nodded. "It was in one of the newspaper articles I read in the library. That's the only reason I remembered it later that evening when she asked me to get her cigarettes from her purse. We had walked down to the barn to get away from Jonas and she forgot to take them along. Actually, they weren't in her purse, they were in her Jacket pocket, but in looking for them I came across the bottle of Isoprinosine. The name seemed to leap out at me. I was stunned. I stood there looking at that bottle and all at once I felt a . . . a kind of overwhelming despair . . . a kind of numbing rage. What happened after that isn't too clear, no matter how much I think about it. I finally found the cigarettes in her jacket pocket in the living room, and I was on my way back when I heard Jonas snoring in the master bedroom. I walked to the door. I'm not sure why. The first thing I saw was his gun belt hanging on the doorknob.'' She shook her head and her black eyes narrowed. "I think I put the gun in my jeans, in the small of my back under my blouse. I know it was out of sight. The next thing I remember I was handing the cigarettes to Sandy and asking her point-blank if she had AIDS. I couldn't think of any devious way to do it. I just asked her."

"And she admitted it?"

"Yes. She admitted it. She said a lot of things. And then she laughed. Maybe if she hadn't laughed . . ." Her voice trailed off.

"Where is she?"

"I'm not sure. One of the swampy areas in the Thicket. I took Jonas's truck and drove and drove and . . . I remember there were alligators." She shuddered. "I was like a machine by then, moving, doing things, not thinking about what I was doing."

"And the trip to Midway City? How—"

She laughed, a small humorless sound. "A part of me was thinking, I guess. By the time I got back here I knew I would have to make it look like she had gone home as planned. I wanted her to disappear from Midway City and not here. And the only way I could think of to do that was take her clothes and the moccasins and the deerskin blouse to her house. But then I remembered she was wearing the blouse when I shot her. So I had to take Myna's. It was a couple of months old, but she had hardly used it and I thought no one would notice." She looked up at me and nodded her head. "You must have great powers of observation, Mr. Roman."

"No, I can't take the credit or the blame. Modern technology at work."

She shrugged bowed shoulders and picked at a ragged cuticle. "I was planning to drive to Midway City, put the clothes where they belonged, and drive back home again. I knew Peter Conrad would be gone around midnight to pick up Sandy at the bus . . . or that's what I thought. I took her to Riggin's store earlier to use the phone. She didn't bother to tell me that something had gone wrong. Evidently she couldn't reach him, because he was home in bed with the Mexican woman when I got there at midnight.''

''She called her twin sisters,'' I said.

''She didn't tell me that. I just assumed she had reached Peter. I used Sandy's key and walked in on them in Sandy's bed. They had fallen asleep, I suppose, but they woke up when I turned on the light, and . . .'' Her voice faded again, the serene facade slipping. She blinked her eyes rapidly. ''And . . . and you know what happened.''

''Why would Jonas tell me he took Sandy to the bus stop?''

''He thought he did. He never remembered anything when he was drunk, and I made sure by stopping at another Dairy Queen and buying a hamburger and a malt on my way back. I left the cup and napkin and part of the hamburger in his truck. That was enough to convince him, I guess. He never questioned it.''

''Why did you take Conrad to the well?''

She bit her lower lip and looked away. ''I had some idea about hiding his body. Sandy had taken us on a tour of the estate and she said the well was forty feet deep and about half-filled with water. I thought he would sink and . . . at least for a while. I thought if they didn't find him they might blame him for the . . . the Mexican woman and Sandy's disappearance. I don't know. I guess it wasn't very rational thinking.''

''Why did you make him walk? You did drive the Jeep?''

''I was afraid of him. Even with his hands tied I was afraid to have him in the Jeep with me. I chained him to the front bumper and made him walk ahead of me.'' She looked down at her hands. ''He . . . he didn't die well

. . . at all.'' Her face was threatening to dissolve again, tightly crimped lips and a quivering chin.

"Why did you change your mind and take the bus?" I wanted to back her up a little, ease her away from what must have been one of the worst moments of her life in the Conrad bedroom. Killing in a rage was one thing; killing in cold blood was quite another.

She sucked in an audible breath. "Genny. I saw his pickup at one of the tonks out on the highway. He was just getting out. I told him the story about the pregnant friend and asked him to drive my Jeep to Corsicana so I'd have something to drive while I was there. He didn't even question it. He just climbed into his truck and followed me to the bus stop. Then he got in my Jeep and took off for Corsicana. He really didn't know anything about anything. He was just being his usual obliging self."

She fell silent. I lit another cigarette.

"I feel terrible about the Mexican girl," she said after a while. "Peter Conrad deserved what he got. After all, he was the one who gave the AIDS to Sandy in the first place."

"Dark seeds," I said, "and ugly harvests."

"What?"

"Nothing. Some quotation or other." From out in front I heard the sound of a car horn, a polite tap, a succinct reminder that only so much time may be gambled on nebulous fame and elusive fortune. The real world of cops and jails and punishment awaited.

Joline smiled wryly. "Your stalwart minion is getting impatient, Mr. Roman." Her voice was harsh but there was no rancor.

I smiled back. "Yes. He's kept his bargain. I'll have to keep mine."

"Will you be going with us?"

"Only as far as my pickup. From there, I'm afraid you're on your own."

She came to her feet and crossed to stand over Jacob Twill. She reached down and felt his brow, smoothed back his hair.

"A month ago he got sick. We thought it was the flu, and maybe it was because sometimes that's the way it starts. It hung on and on and I made him go to a doctor. They wanted to put him in the hospital, but he wouldn't go. So then they began giving him treatments. The treatments are what's making him sick." She glanced up and smiled. "This was the first time Sandy came to visit and they didn't make love." The edges of the smile turned upward, became gently mocking. "I was so pleased. I thought perhaps it was over, but now I know that she understood what was happening to him and why. She never let on. I don't regret killing her, Mr. Roman." She spoke quietly, with firm conviction, but the brittle composure had begun to break away. Her eyes brimmed suddenly and the small square chin began to tremble.

She turned abruptly away from Twill and went into the kitchen. I heard Ralston's muted rumble, her soft reply.

I hesitated a moment, then followed her.

271

32

JOLINE SAT SLUMPED AT THE TABLE, HEAD IN HER HANDS. General Ralston stood behind her, one thick hand awkwardly stroking her hair, his broad face drained of color, empty of emotion.

I picked up the deerskin blouse and put it in the sack, hesitated again, then lifted the .22 rifle from the countertop.

"I'll leave this under the live oak, General. You can pick it up on your way home."

They ignored me; the big hand moved with clumsy gentleness across the sleek head.

I stepped to the door, stopped, old familiar feelings welling inside, a taste of bile in my throat.

"I'm sorry, Joline. I can't let this go the way you want it to go. I'll have to tell them the truth about Conrad and Gomez, the truth as I see it. Maybe I'm wrong; maybe you can convince them."

She spoke without looking up: "I don't know what you mean."

"I think you do," I said, stepping through the doorway into the living room. Twill hadn't moved. His eyes were closed, the handkerchief balled in his fist beneath his chin, long legs bent into a fetal curve.

I turned and looked toward the bedroom, listening to Myna Beechum's silence coming from within. I wanted to go to her, comfort her, somehow stand between her and the pain, the bad times that were sure to come.

Instead I crossed to the front door and went outside, remembering the scathing look in her eyes, the fleeting passage of horror across her lovely face.

Clearly she blamed me for the death of Jonas, the desolation in her life, and perhaps rightly so. Wrong conclusions had killed Jonas, that and his own unbending pride, willfulness, and the wild dark streak in his nature. But the conclusions had been mine, and I stood guilty as charged. My punishment would be regret and grinding guilt, and it would be a long time winding down.

It was clear also that she would need assistance. More than an egocentric buffoon like Curly Glazier could ever provide.

I lit a cigarette and crossed the yard toward Deputy Clarence Barr, pacing impatiently in front of his cruiser, short arms propped on well-padded hips.

The blast of the car horn had brought the dogs out of their houses. They milled restlessly at the fence, their barking strangely subdued. The two glossy bays watched my progress with bowed necks and tilted ears.

I detoured a few steps and leaned the .22 against the trunk of the live oak.

A pair of mourning doves rocketed out of the foliage above my head. Their furious passage startled a sunning squirrel. He scrambled up a branch, chattering his disapproval; a blue jay screamed raucously, and somewhere high above a cruising flock of crows added their derision to the cacophony.

Spring sounds. As normal as April mud. Loud and obtrusive, and diverting enough that I missed the clatter of the screen door—diverting enough that I almost missed the frightened yell of Deputy Clarence Barr.

I whirled in time to see the rotund deputy draw, a laborious procedure that involved both chubby hands, a twisting torso, and a look of pure terror on his face beneath the high-crowned hat; he died that way, suspended for a finite fragment of time beyond the slapping crack of the rifle, blankness replacing terror, a third eye in the middle of his forehead, the mushrooming bullet dissolving the back of his head in an exploding mist of red, sending the hat spinning across the hood of his car.

I beat Barr to the ground, drawing the .38 and almost losing it as I dove chest first into the yellow-green grass, rolled frantically for the protection of the live oak, hearing the ratcheting snap of the rifle's action and thinking almost abstractedly that I had forgotten one very important fact: Jonas Beechum had been a hunter. Hunters owned guns—rifles—without a doubt the very rifle that cracked again as I slammed painfully into the bole of the giant tree.

Dirt geysered in front of me, stinging my face with grit. I came to my knees beside the tree, pawing my streaming eyes, squeezing off a shot at the blurred figure crouched near the end of the porch, who was already jacking another round into the chamber, firing hastily from his hip, too hastily, the bullet ripping bark beside my head, caroming, whining into the brilliant morning sun, leaving the right side of my face numb from flying debris, filling my right eye with something wet and hazy red, something sticky and warm.

I fired again.

Hard on the heels of the concussive blast, I thought I heard a curse, or a cough, and Jacob Twill seemed to stagger, appeared to lean against the wall of the house, cranking yet another shell into the .30-30 held tight against his side, lips peeled back in determination, shoulder-length hair broken loose from its leather binding, flying free, shrouding his head like a mendicant's cowl.

We fired together.

I felt a blow to my side above the hip, an almost playful tug no worse than the urgent pull of a lover's hand.

Jacob Twill stood spread-eagle against the wall of the house, the gun gone, face hidden behind the spill of shining hair. As I watched, he slid slowly to a sitting position, hung there for an instant, hands scrabbling aimlessly at his bloody chest, then rolled onto his side, long legs curling toward his stomach, stopping, jerking, stopping again.

The dogs went crazy, and dark figures filled the doorway to the house, bursting onto the porch as Joline wrested herself out of the restraining hands of General Ralston, fell to her knees beside her prostrate lover. I heard a high wail that choked off abruptly into harsh racking sobs. I watched Myna come haltingly through the doorway, drop to her knees beside her sister.

General Ralston stood watching me, big brown eyes cowlike, shiny as polished stones. He shifted his feet and threw out a hand toward the huddled group at the end of the porch.

"Jake . . ." He cleared his throat harshly. "Jake . . . he wasn't a bad feller."

"He was a goddamned prince," I said, opening my shirt and inspecting the lover's tap that was beginning to burn like the fires of hell. A bloody, two-inch tear in the fatty tissue above my hip, it oozed bright red blood and added scope and dimension to the nausea already bubbling in my stomach, the sickness that had begun the moment I heard the first crack of the rifle, saw Deputy Clarence Barr die, and knew that once again I would have to kill or be killed.

I packed my folded handkerchief against the wound,

tugged my shirt as tight as it would go, cinched my belt another notch. I lit a much-needed cigarette and limped around to the end of the porch, my free hand pressed against the makeshift bandage.

Myna stood up, a look of shock in her eyes, lovely face stricken, hands clenched into white-knuckled fists at her sides.

"My God . . . he's dead." There was no accusation in her voice, but her eyes held mine with a mesmerizing force, a slowly dawning look of scorn, of condemnation. "Danny . . . you—you killed him!"

I stared at her blankly, unable to answer, my mind locked in a rigor of absurdity, resentment rising in me like a shout. Before I could collect my scattered wits, she whirled and dashed back inside the house. I watched her go and didn't try to call her back. Standing nearby, General Ralston clucked his tongue and shook his shaggy head. "She didn't see what happened, Mr. Roman."

I shrugged and turned back to Joline, quiet now, still on her knees beside the man she had tried to protect, one slender hand pressed against a pallid cheek, the other rearranging the long shining hair.

"I almost believed you," I said, and flipped the cigarette butt out across the yard.

"I killed Sandy," she said tonelessly, "just the way I said."

"I know that. But there were a couple of things wrong with the rest of your story. Conrad walked to the well, all right, but there were no car tracks at all. Twill walked him straight down the hill across the field. But, of course, you wouldn't have known that if he hadn't told you, and I guess he didn't. Also, the bus driver saw you talking to someone in Corsicana he took to be another woman in a deerskin blouse. He couldn't see you clearly, and from the

276

back, with his long hair, Twill might well pass for a woman.''

She didn't respond, didn't look up.

I lit another cigarette, felt my bandage slide on slippery blood as I returned my hand to it. I felt light-headed, a tiny buzzing in my ears.

"The Gomez woman and Conrad. I never really thought you could do that. It wouldn't be an easy thing to do. It would take—" I broke off, not entirely certain what it would take.

"He did it for me," she said softly. "Helping me. He came here looking for me when it got dark and I wasn't home. I already had Sandy in the truck. I—we . . . well, it all happened the way I said it did except that he went on to Midway City with the clothing and I drove my Jeep home from Corsicana."

"So you decided to take the rap for all of it?"

She looked up, finally, her features soft and blurred. "Why not? I started it by killing Sandy. All the rest of it sprang from that. He wasn't an evil man. He just got caught in something he couldn't handle, something he couldn't control." She sighed. "I didn't want him to die in jail. He had a horror of being confined."

I looked out toward the barn, the thick line of lofty pines beyond, evergreen and constant, waiting patiently for the rapacious hand of man, fire, the end of time, whichever came first.

"Yeah, well, I think Deputy Barr had a horror of dying, too." I turned and walked off, made my limping way toward my pickup, toward Deputy Barr's waiting cruiser at the end of the lane, Deputy Barr's waiting body.

Time for the law again, cold faces and hard eyes, guns and cuffs and endless questions; waiting. I wished there was some way I could skip it, get on with my life, such as it was.

But that was a foolish, fleeting notion, and I put in the call on the cruiser's radio, overwhelming their useless questions with a curt demand for assistance out at the Jonas Beechum place. I used Deputy Barr's name and turned off the radio when I finished.

Woozy and weary, I walked back down the lane to my pickup. I climbed inside and turned on the radio, running the dial for a golden oldie. But golden oldies are hard to find, and I settled for Marty Robbins and "El Paso," a cheerful tune about gunfights and lost love, about going back, and about dying.

I lit another cigarette and settled back to listen, looking occasionally toward the house.

Dammit! I still wanted to help her.

But first, she would have to ask.

ABOUT THE AUTHOR

Edward Mathis lives in Euless, Texas. His previous novel was FROM A HIGH PLACE, also published by Ballantine.

RICH
with Mystery...
William G. Tapply

Brady Coyne, a Boston attorney, makes his living doing trusts and estates for the Boston elite — but at the request of his wealthy clients he finds himself in one murder investigation after another.